# THE
# VANGUARD

# Dedication

Thank you to all my readers who stick with me through everything. Thanks to my editor for making this story and all my other ones as perfect as possible.

# Chapter One

Rathian, Prince of Launioc and Imperator of the Vanguard, stood staring out over the training yard at Bailius, his manor and the headquarters for the Vanguard. At that moment, the yard was empty. All of the men he'd brought back to the capital city were busy in other pursuits. He lifted his gaze to the horizon, beyond which lay the real battlefield in the disputed lands between Villious and Launioc. Rathian had left the rest of his ducenti there to support the regular army.

The prince snarled in disgust. His father had ordered Rathian back to the city to observe protocol and tradition. A silly and outdated law stated that at least one other member of the royal family, besides the king, needed to be present at all court functions and council meetings. Rathian's older brother had escaped the family bonds to travel to one of their allies for a royal visit. Rathian planned on beating his brother to a pulp when he returned.

Rathian hated the politics of the court. He didn't have the patience to deal with backstabbing nobles.

The straightforward life and death battles of war were more to his liking—at least then he knew who was trying to kill him.

After turning, he strolled over the guard walk to a set of stairs that led down to the main level of the guard house. The war with Villious had been going as well as could be expected before he'd been forced to leave. Rathian had been escorted back by his personal guard of fifty men. The rest he'd left under the command of his second, General Excelsie. He just hoped his friend would work with the commander of the regular army and not offend the other soldiers.

It was difficult for Excelsie not to act superior towards the men who ran the regular army. The men who fought in the famed ducenti were gods compared to the normal soldiers. Each member trained from the age of ten to be included in the two hundred soldiers who became part of the Vanguard. Another tradition, but one Rathian wasn't inclined to break.

The Vanguard served the purpose of keeping Launioc safe from invaders, but also from rebellion within the borders of the country itself. The men who made up the ten viginti were loyal to only one man and that was the Imperator. They took their orders from him, and not even the king could tell them what to do. Rathian had been the Imperator for three years and the weight of command caused his heart to ache at times.

The war his father had started with the Villious Queen was foolish. The disputed lands were there for a reason. They kept the people from sneaking into Launioc from the horrors existing in Villious. Ever since the current queen had ascended her throne ten years ago, fear and death grew in the northern country. Her subjects begged and pleaded for asylum in Launioc, but King Barkuc wouldn't allow any in. His father wanted the border lands so a fortress could be built and the only viable mountain pass sealed to the refuges. In his heart, Rathian wondered why there weren't more Launioc subjects trying to escape their country. Since the start of the war, conditions in Launioc had deteriorated.

A young page raced up to Rathian as he reached the last step. He waited until the youngster had caught his breath.

"A quainary is approaching, Your Highness."

"Thank you, Darius." He patted the boy on the shoulder as he went past, heading for the gates. He'd meet his men there.

Shock raced through him when the gates opened and Excelsie was the first man to ride through. Irritation quickly replaced his first reaction. He'd ordered Excelsie to stay at the front. Why would his friend abandon his post? The four Lancers accompanying the general rode in formation behind Excelsie. There was a sixth person, but Rathian couldn't see who it was because the soldiers were surrounding him.

Excelsie halted his horse in front of Rathian. "Imperator, General Excelsie reporting with a prisoner." The general saluted, right fist clasped across his chest over his heart.

Rathian returned the salute. His attention had been caught by Excelsie's statement. "A prisoner?"

"Yes, sir." Excelsie dismounted and handed his reins to a waiting groom. "He was taken by one of the regular army squadrons."

The four Lancers moved aside as Rathian and Excelsie approached the prisoner. Rathian bit back the gasp when he saw the wounds marring the man's body. A muffled groan reached his ears and the Villious raised his head. Their eyes met and all his breath left him. Dark brown eyes glazed with pain and anger stared back at him. He took a step without realising it, his hand held out. Another groan. Those fathomless eyes rolled back in the man's head and the prisoner fell off the horse.

Rathian reached the injured man before anyone else did, catching him before the damaged body could make contact with the ground. He had no thought for his clothes or the blood staining them. He gestured with his head for the other soldiers to follow him.

"Let one of the Lancers carry him, sir. You shouldn't get your clothes dirty." Excelsie stalked next to him.

Rathian knew he was upsetting his friend, but he didn't let it bother him. Something needed to be done before the Villious bled to death. The infirmary was just across from the gates. He headed for it and Darius scampered ahead to open the door.

"Medicus," Rathian demanded as he entered.

The senior healer waved him to an empty bed in the corner farthest from the door. "Lay him down there, Your Highness."

The Villious prisoner lay in the middle of the bed, head turned away and hands folded over his stomach. The physician started poking and rolling the man in different directions to get a good look at the injuries. The elderly man grumbled as he ran into Rathian who stood at the end of the bed.

"Go talk to the general, Your Highness. There's nothing you can do here and you're just in my way." The physician pointed to the exit.

"Yes." Excelsie touched his arm. "I must give you a report on the battles."

Rathian allowed his friend to lead the way out of the infirmary. In the doorway, he turned back to the doctor. "Let me know the moment he is awake."

"Yes, Your Highness." The doctor swung back, seemingly forgetting about the prince and the other men.

Rathian glared at Excelsie. "Tell me why you chose to ignore my orders and return to the capital?"

The general grimaced. "I must brief you on the course of the war."

Rathian glanced around, spotting the young page who never seemed to be far from him. "Darius, bring drinks and food to my study. Also, tell Cook to make something for the Lancers as well and then take them to the barracks."

"Yes, Your Highness." Darius dashed off.

Striding into the manor, Rathian knew he needed to be brought up-to-date on the progress of the army, but part of his mind stayed in the infirmary, wondering about the Villious prisoner.

# Chapter Two

*The next day*

Rathian frowned, staring at the Villious prisoner kneeling in the centre of the carcer. The prince hadn't been happy when he'd been informed that the physician had released the man to be put in the claustrum. With injuries so severe, the prisoner should have been kept in the infirmary for days. When confronted, the doctor had said there had been nothing he could have done to help the man heal. Several shallow wounds had already healed by the time the doctor had started treating his patient.

The Villious' breathing was slow and steady as if he were meditating. The claustrum guard had commented that there hadn't been any movement from him since he'd arrived in the carcer. The man's wounds had knitted together before their eyes.

"How did the regular army capture him?" Rathian fought the urge to go in and bathe the prisoner's dirt-encrusted skin.

"When the Villious army called retreat, this man was stabbed in the back and left on the battlefield. From what the captain of the squadron who found him told me, the prisoner fought with a trained viginti of men." Excelsie looked down at a small tablet, refreshing his memory.

Rathian shot his general a glance. "Like ours?"

"I don't know, sir. They were much like him in looks and height. They must have trained together because they fought as one."

"Yet they stabbed him and left him to die or be captured. Doesn't sound like anything our men would do."

"Maybe he's a troublemaker or a traitor. Maybe they thought his wounds were so great, he'd never survive." Excelsie didn't sound too worried or upset over the captive's betrayal by his fellow Villious.

A slight tension formed in the Villious' body. Movement returned as fingers were clenched into fists then opened.

"What is he thinking?" Rathian murmured to General Excelsie.

"Who knows?" Excelsie shrugged. "We have no way of reading his mind. He's a barbarian."

Rathian studied the warrior in the cell. He could understand why Excelsie would think that. The man's black hair tangled around his head like snakes, with beads and material entwined through the strands. He wore nothing but a brief loincloth that one of the prince's men had supplied him. Rathian couldn't tell what the man's face looked like since the hair hung over it, blocking his view. But the warrior's body was muscular and large, with broad shoulders narrowing to a trim waist. Rock-hard thighs and corded calves finished an impressive image.

"Do we have anyone who can speak his language?" With his gaze, the prince tracked the trail of blood trickling down the man's chest. It mingled with the light dusting of hair heading under the waistband of the loincloth.

His cock twitched and started to harden. It wasn't often he found himself aroused by one of the prisoners in his claustrum. He reached out to touch the bars separating him from the man. The cool smoothness chilled him and he shivered.

"I've asked the commanders to question the men. If no one is found, we'll branch out to the regular troops," Excelsie informed him as they moved away.

"Good. I never knew they healed like that." He thought about the massive wounds the warrior had endured.

"I don't think all of them can." Rathian rubbed his forehead. "When someone is found who can speak to him, alert me. I'd like to be here."

"Yes, Your Highness."

A damp chill brushed against the prince's cheek. He shuddered. "Also, make sure the captive has food, water and blankets. A bath if he wishes one." He held up a hand to stop Excelsie's protest. "They might be barbarians, but we aren't."

A slight snort was the only comment the general made. Rathian left, knowing his orders would be obeyed. Before he left the claustrum area, he turned to Excelsie. "I'll be dining at the court tonight. Though we're in the middle of a war, Father sees no reason to stop the parties for his nobles while good men die."

He usually hid his contempt and anger well—he'd have to watch his tongue. While he knew Excelsie and the ducenti were loyal to him, it wouldn't be wise to let them know how much he despised his father.

"I'll send someone to find you." Excelsie bowed.

Rathian made his way to his suite of rooms. He reeked of sweat and blood — Excelsie's report had kept him from changing after the general had arrived. Darius helped him out of his clothes and into the bathtub. Sinking into the steaming bathwater, he closed his eyes, allowing the heat to begin to soak his aches away. When he was finally clean, he gestured for the boy to dry him.

"Run and tell Pula to have my carriage brought around for me," he ordered, when he'd finished dressing.

"Yes, Your Highness." The page raced from the room.

The prince followed at a more leisurely pace. He made his way downstairs under the watchful eyes of his ancestors, whose portraits lined the walls of his home. The most recent addition to the gallery made him pause.

Prince Jelviut was Rathian's uncle and Imperator of the ducenti until three years ago, when he and thirty men were killed in a border skirmish. The prince stared up into the face of his uncle and felt a tug of sadness.

Jelviut had been more of a father to him than the king. Maybe it was because of the role they were given. Every second son of the ruling family commanded the Vanguard. It'd been the law for centuries. He missed Jelviut's gruff manner and his stern face that hid a soft heart. His gaze turned to the other man in the painting — Carius, his uncle's Custos.

Every Imperator had one. The Custos was the man closest to the Imperator. His lover and his bodyguard. The man who knew everything there was to know about the prince. Carius had been the opposite of his uncle. Quick to laugh and warm-hearted, Carius never let Rathian forget someone loved him. There was a hole in Rathian's soul caused by their deaths. In dark moments, he wondered if he'd ever find his own Custos and in even darker moments, he despaired that there wasn't anyone alive who could love him.

"Your Highness, your carriage is here," Darius reported from the entryway.

Rathian threw back his shoulders and set his face in a blank expression. It was going to be a long night.

\* \* \* \*

Stakel kept his head bowed as the enemy soldiers opened his carcer door. He studied them through the heavy fall of his hair.

There were three of them. One was armed with a sword, and it was that soldier who kept an eye on him. Stakel smiled to himself. A simple sword wouldn't stop him if he chose to attack. His speed and strength had been bought and unwillingly paid for by his soul. He didn't want to fight. He simply wanted to go home to the mountains.

The other two carried a tray of food and blankets. Setting them down close to him, one of them said something to him. He didn't move, deciding it was safer to stay still, since he didn't understand their language.

He waited for a few minutes after they'd left, making sure they weren't coming back. The smell of the food teased him, though he couldn't help but wonder if they'd poisoned it. He tore a small piece of bread from the loaf and dipped it into the stew. Chewing slowly, he tested the taste of it. No poison.

It wouldn't have mattered if it were tainted, though. Over the years, he'd built up an immunity to a majority of poisons. The Villious' priests were a vicious, vindictive lot if you crossed them. They spent more time punishing the Consorts than trying to gain favours in the gods' eyes.

He ate quickly, trying not to spill it. He didn't know when they'd feed him again. After he finished, he placed the tray by the door. Stakel stared down at the blankets for a moment. What was he supposed to do with those?

He glanced through the bars of his door and saw one of the other prisoners lying on top of one of them. The man had covered up with the other one. Stakel frowned, sitting down and wrapping it around his shoulders. The fabric was softer than anything he'd ever been given in the queen's army—even as a Consort, he'd been expected to sleep on the floor until called to her bed or to face more training from the priests.

The blankets and food would have been proof to Stakel's comrades that the Launioc's army was soft and ineffectual, but something was telling Stakel not to underestimate these men. They had driven the Queen's Consorts into retreat and the Consorts were the best of her army. The Launioc's unit was made up of two hundred men and they fought as if they could read each other's minds.

He shrugged. Maybe they could. The only knowledge he had of the unit the Villious called the Vanguard came from rumours. He'd reserve judgement until he knew more. He settled down to try to nap.

# Chapter Three

Rathian tossed and turned. He couldn't stop thinking about the Villious prisoner and what he'd end up doing with him. The prince's instincts screamed the man was important to him personally and to the ducenti as well, but he wasn't sure how to deal with him.

A swirling fog formed in the corner of the prince's bedroom. It crept closer to the bed and eased up to cover Rathian's restless body. As it settled over his head, he sighed and fell into a deep sleep.

\* \* \* \*

"Imperator, open your eyes."

*The voice rang through Rathian's head. He forced his eyelids open, staring at the imposing figure before him.*

*The being towered over the prince, standing at least seven feet tall, dressed in a loose red tunic and black pants. His fathomless dark eyes stared down at him. Shock exploded through Rathian and he dropped to his knees. Stretching out, he bowed until his forehead touched the floor.*

*"My God," he whispered.*

"Rise, Imperator. I have never made my followers bow before me." *Xasel, the High God of Launioc and patron of the ducenti, gestured for Rathian to stand.* "We have something important to discuss and I have little time in your dreams."

*"Why are you here?" He climbed to his feet. Looking around, he asked, "Where is here?"*

*A deep chuckle echoed around them.* "We are in the only place I could meet you. It's a holding place of sorts. A spot where mortal and immortal can talk."

*"Okay." He turned back to the god.* "Why would you want to talk to me?"

"I have always had the ducenti in my heart. While the others turn from me in favour of the new gods, the ducenti still pray to me. You and the two hundred men you lead are truly my children." *Xasel hesitated and Rathian wasn't sure he wanted to hear what was making the god pause.* "You've been troubled by the prisoner brought to you from Villious."

*"Yes. I can't decide what to do with him. I know some of my men, including Excelsie, see him as the enemy, pure and simple. There is no grey with them. Others will be more lenient and open to allowing him to change their minds." Rathian paced the small chamber.*

"How do you feel about him?" *Xasel seemed to be watching him closely.*

*"I'm not sure. I've only seen him twice since he arrived here." He shrugged. "I feel like he's going to bring change into the ducenti and my life."*

"Change is good. You have proven that by your own actions." *Xasel's form started to fade.* "Not even a god can control the realm of dreams."

*Rathian watched as the god's hand reached out and a single fingertip touched his forehead. Lightning ripped through his mind, blazing until he went blind.*

"Your love will ensure demons walk the world no more."

\* \* \* \*

Rathian shot up in his bed, pillows and furs flying. Darkness ruled the room. He blinked several times and began to see the faint outline of the curtains covering his windows. After rolling out of bed, he tugged on some clothes and headed out into the hallway. The guards posted at the side door of the manor acknowledged him, saluting as he passed by. He nodded, but didn't stop to chat like he tended to do on nights he couldn't sleep. This time, he had a destination in mind.

The heavy oak door creaked as he pushed it open. He stared down the aisle to the altar. The Temple of the High God was a simple structure made of granite and oak and the altar was carved from a single block of ivory marble. The master carver had worked without rest for thirty days to make it. The pillars making up the base of the altar were of four men. Time and age had weathered the faces, but the paint used to decorate the clothing never seemed to dull. Three of the men wore the black and red of the ducenti. The last man was dressed in the uniform of the Custos, the Imperator's lover.

Anyone who knew the legend of the founding of the ducenti recognised the men without needing to see their faces. They were the four who created the foundation for the ducenti, the most elite Launioc unit. Their hands rose above them and they supported a smooth basin. The basin was created out of white marble with swirls of purple throughout the stone. Etched deep into the marble with gold was a lion—the symbol of the Imperator. It represented the first Imperator. The basin was filled with oil and a single flame danced upon the surface. A flame that never went out, and couldn't be blown out. Every member of the ducenti knew the story. How the flame appeared the night the very first Imperator had died and continued to burn through the centuries. It would burn hotter and brighter on the day each new Imperator was named. Also, its glow blessed each Imperator and Custos who took their vows in front of it.

He made his way down the aisle and knelt before the altar. The flame pulsed once and settled back to the low gleam usually seen in the temple. Bowing his head, he closed his eyes and thanked the god in a silent prayer for visiting him. If his love for his country helped save it from its enemies, he would give everything he had to make it happen. If it allowed his men to live and not sacrifice their own lives, he'd give his up.

A gentle breeze traced over his cheek and he took the touch as an acceptance of his vow. He nodded, stood and went back to bed. His sleep was uninterrupted for the rest of the night.

\* \* \* \*

Stakel stared up at the stone ceiling of his prison cell. Night time had fallen and shadows bathed the walls. He shifted, uncomfortable lying on the blanket they had given him. Sitting up, he knelt in the middle of the room and closed his eyes. Meditation might help him achieve some rest.

He slowed his breathing down and calmed his heartbeat. When the priests first taught him how to go into a trance, he'd been frightened by the easing of control and he knew the priests would try to take his mind over if they got an opening. He hadn't been willing to give them the opportunity. He practiced his trance state when he was alone and found it strengthened his mind. Soon his barriers were so strong nothing except the most powerful of drugs could destroy them.

The walls around him blurred and he was surprised to realise he could see through one of them. A figure stood on the other side, gesturing to him to follow it. Stakel climbed to his feet and approached it. The being had a familiar feel to it, like he'd met it before. Besides, he doubted the priests' power could reach this deep into Launioc. He fell to his knees in front of the figure.

A warm weight rested on his head. *"You're an uneasy stranger in an odd land."*

*"I've always been a stranger, even in my own country. I've come to accept it as my fate."* His statement was matter-of-fact. He didn't want anyone's pity.

*"True, but I think you might be surprised about what awaits you in this unusual place. You might find what you were truly meant to become here."*

Stakel wasn't sure if he believed the creature, but he'd learnt not to argue with the spirits who visited him in his trances. Some exacted revenge in the most painful of ways. There were more than a few times he'd come out of meditation with scratches or bruises on his body.

*"It's all right if you don't believe me, son. You'll see soon enough what I mean."*

*"Who are you?"* He'd never dared ask any spirit such a personal question before.

*"Someone who has a keen interest in the future of Launioc and the ducenti's Imperator."*

It didn't really explain anything as far as Stakel was concerned, but he didn't ask again. He was getting drowsy. He hoped he could sleep when he lay down. He wasn't used to soft blankets or having a room to himself.

*"Rest now. Time has begun to spin and events are moving towards a time when demons return to hell."*

Stakel's vision dimmed and he sank to his side on the blanket. The spirit stood over him for a second, slowly disappearing.

# Chapter Four

Stakel rolled to his feet when the cell door opened. Three days had passed since they had locked him in the barred room. The Launiocs had continued to feed him and had even offered him water to clean the dirt off his body. He wished he could ask for enough to wash his hair. The grime in his hair was driving him crazy. The Consorts fought naked and rubbed dirt into their skin and hair to hide or disguise their scent. He loathed the practice—it made him feel like an animal.

He'd been trying to sleep on the blankets his captors had left for him. It was difficult, not only because Stakel had never slept on anything as soft as the woollen blankets, but he had been disturbed by dreams of his first years of education in the Queen's Temple. Being in a barred cell brought back the fear and anger he'd lived with during those training years.

Two of his guards pulled their swords when he stood up but relaxed when he made no attempt to attack them. The third soldier caught his attention. Surprise dashed through him at the man's words.

"Would you like to wash?"

"How do you know my language?" He wasn't sure if it was a trap or not. The Consorts had used this trick before to lull prisoners into believing the Villious weren't the enemy and then once the prisoners had told their secrets, the Consorts would fall on them like rabid dogs. He didn't want to risk the same treatment.

The soldier moved more into the light of the cell. Frowning, Stakel studied the man. There was something familiar about the man's round face, dominated by bright blue eyes and a turned-up nose. It gave the Launioc a little boy air. The perfect disguise for the enemy to use to their advantage.

"It is you." The soldier smiled slightly.

A strange voice spoke from the hallway. Stakel ignored the foreign words as he thought back to the first time he'd met a Launioc boy. He'd been young, only ten summers, when he had been taken from his mountain village and dragged to the Queen's Academy. He had been taught how to be a warrior and fight for the queen. Gods, he hated the Academy, but if he'd known what was in store for him only three years later, he would have done his level best to stay there.

They'd thrown him in a cell with another boy. The strange boy had spoken a language from the south. Eventually they'd learnt how to communicate. They'd become allies, but never friends. For Stakel had sworn he'd never get close to anyone. The other boy had sworn his people would come for him. Stakel had thought it was a nice dream. They'd lived together for three years, learning to fight. Then one night while out in the field near the southern borders, the strange Launioc boy had disappeared.

Stakel had been punished for the boy's escape, but he didn't mind. He'd hoped the boy had found his way home. Those three years were idyllic compared to what he'd endured next. He came back to the Launioc cell he stood in when the soldier turned to him.

*"You know him"*. A voice echoed through his mind.

"The Imperator would like for you to clean up. We'll provide some clothing and take you to His Highness."

Stakel nodded but waited until his guards gestured for him to follow. Clearing his throat, he wondered if he could bring himself to talk to someone. He rarely spoke to his fellow Consorts and they never paid much attention to him. He bore too many scars for his insolence towards the priests. It didn't pay to be seen as a friend or an associate of Stakel's.

"I wondered what happened to you all those years ago." He ignored the others around him to concentrate on the one he knew.

"I didn't think you would remember me. My uncle found me and took me back home. I tried to convince them to take you as well, but they wouldn't do it." The man's eyes held an apology.

"It doesn't matter." And it didn't. He didn't concern himself about things in the past. That path led to danger and anger. Neither of which he could take the time to deal with at the moment.

"I'm Martin."

"I'm called Stakel." It was the name the priests had given him before he had entered the Queen's Temple, after they had stolen everything else from him, even his life.

They entered a chamber where two large pools steamed in the chilly air. He stripped and climbed down into the first pool. He moaned as the warm water flowed around him. Martin settled close by. Stakel knew the Launioc didn't want to disturb his privacy, but he was used to not having any.

There were always guards around when the Consorts were allowed to leave their rooms. The priests feared they would try to escape. The guards were there to restrain them and take them for punishment from the High Priest. Spiked cuffs and collars. Steel-tipped whips. Those were the instruments of torture the Villious guards used to keep the Consorts in line.

He checked the areas where his wounds had been. There were a few sore spots. The rest had healed.

"Can all your kind heal so quickly?" Martin gestured to the fading scars.

"Only the Queen's Consorts can." He scrubbed clean.

Unlike most of the Consorts, he hated being dirty. It was one of the few things he'd learnt in childhood the priests weren't able to train out of him. Pulling out all the ribbons and beads, he tossed them to the side of the pool. He had to wash and rinse his hair twice to get rid of all the mud caked in it.

"Is there a comb I can use?"

Martin nodded and handed one to him. Stakel sighed as he ran the comb through the knots and tangles, straightening his hair out. He separated it into sections and braided it, reaching for a black piece of fabric to tie the end off.

He climbed out of the pool, dried off and tugged on the coarse cloth pants a young man had brought for him. He and the page were silent as they made their way through the dungeon. The stone corridors echoed with their footsteps. Martin walked beside him and they were surrounded by four other Launioc soldiers. He wondered if they were members of the Vanguard. They were dressed in uniforms consisting of tight black leather pants and red sleeveless tunics moulded to their chests. No possible way for enemies to hold onto them by their clothes. All of their hair was cut short to allow their helmets to fit more securely. The auburn-haired soldier leading the group kept glancing back towards Martin. Stakel got the feeling his interpreter was important to this man.

Stakel didn't bother keeping track of where they were going. As far as he was concerned, there would be no escape attempt. Whatever the Launioc did with him wouldn't be any worse than what he'd endured at the hands of the queen and her priests.

**\* \* \* \***

Rathian stayed seated as Sub-commander Antioc and his quainary escorted the Villious prisoner to him. General Excelsie stood at Rathian's right side, the spot tradition deemed only for the Custos. The prince didn't have time to move his friend before the men got to him. They stopped, clasped their hands to their chests and bowed. The prisoner remained upright.

The prince felt a jolt of lust spear through him when his eyes met the dark-brown gaze of the prisoner. Rathian remembered those eyes, but instead of pain and fear like he'd seen in them before, they held a calm light and a certain amount of arrogance. Rathian recognised that gaze, because he'd seen it in his own eyes while looking in the mirror. It was the expression of a man confident in his body and ability to protect himself.

The man's nostrils flared and his eyes widened. He must have felt something as well. The Villious was clean and his black hair was caught in a braid that reached the middle of his back. His dark skin gleamed a rich gold under the sunlight streaming in the audience room windows. It was marred only by scars crossing most of the man's body.

"Sub-commander, I assume you were able to find someone who can speak the prisoner's language," Rathian addressed the handsome young soldier.

"Yes, Imperator. One of the men in my quainary spent three years as a captive of the Villious." Antioc gestured for the soldier standing closest to the prisoner to come forward. "Martin."

The prince watched as Martin whispered something to the stranger then moved forwards to kneel before Rathian. Rathian saw the proprietary gleam in Antioc's eyes and realised this Lancer was the sub-commander's lover.

"Stand. I have no need for subservience. First, what is our guest's name?" He waved a hand, motioning for chairs to be brought for his men. Rathian paused then ordered, "General Excelsie, go and confer with my other commanders. Make sure they have all they need to be able to move out in three days."

"Yes, Imperator." Excelsie scowled as he stalked from the room.

Rathian knew his friend wasn't happy about being dismissed, but he also knew that Excelsie wouldn't be willing to listen to the prisoner with an open mind. He'd been friends with the general since Excelsie had come to live at the Royal Palace when they were children and he understood how judgmental and prejudiced his friend was.

"Antioc, you and Martin may sit. Let the Villious be seated as well. Send the other men to stand by the door." He played with the ring on his finger idly while the others rushed to do his bidding.

His head pounded, the pain threatening to split it open. Attending his father's court did that to him and he had only had a few hours' sleep before morning had come. It didn't matter that he wasn't at the front. During war, staying in bed until the afternoon wasn't an option for the Imperator. Rathian hated spending time at court. He and his men were meant to be out on the battlefield during war. Not back in the royal city, entertaining the king and nobles with their uncouth ways.

"His name is Stakel, Imperator." Martin pointed to a chair and said something to the stranger.

"Stakel." Rathian couldn't control the shiver running over his body, but he squashed the attempt his cock was making to react to the desire this man made him feel.

"Are you hungry or thirsty?" he asked Stakel directly.

Those dark eyes never strayed from Rathian's face, even while Martin translated. Stakel frowned then shook his head.

"Would you be willing to answer a few questions for us?"

His father had tried to get him to use force to coerce a confession out of prisoners, but Rathian refused to follow in his father's footsteps. Torturing someone until they talked didn't mean they told the truth when they broke.

"How do you heal so fast?" he asked — the question had been on his mind since the last time he'd seen the Villious.

Stakel listened to Martin before he spoke. Martin grimaced, asked another question then turned to the prince.

"Stakel says only the Queen's Consorts can heal like that. It has something to do with the rituals they go through when they become one," Martin explained.

"Consorts? He's one of the queen's lovers?" Rathian pressed his fingers hard against his throbbing head.

Martin turned back to Stakel. While the soldier spoke to the Villious, the prince couldn't help moving restlessly. Impatience set in.

"I wish we could talk to each other. It would make things go by so much faster," he murmured loud enough for Martin to hear.

"Imperator, Stakel says he has a way to learn our language, but he wants your permission to touch me."

Antioc protested. "No. He could be getting us to let our guard down. He could kill you."

Rathian held Stakel's gaze. The man's eyes met his. There was no shifting or twitching.

*"Trust him. He means you no harm."*

He wasn't sure if it was lust trying to convince him or if some other instinct was kicking in. He broke the stare off, looking over to Martin. "It's up to you, no matter what the sub-commander says."

Antioc started to speak. Rathian silenced him with a look. "Martin might be your lover, but he must make up his own mind about trusting this man."

Antioc frowned and looked away. Martin glanced between the prince, his lover and the prisoner. Rathian could tell it was a tough decision.

"Ask Stakel if we need a physician at hand." The prince wanted to make sure Martin had more information before the soldier made up his mind.

Stakel grimaced but shook his head to Martin's question. The prisoner spoke again.

"He says we'll both have mild head pains, almost as if we'd overindulged with wine. I trust him, Your Highness." The soldier reached out and touched Antioc's hand. "I don't believe he wants to hurt me."

"How do you know that for sure?" Antioc burst out.

"When I was eight winters old, I was captured by the Villious. I assumed they were going to indoctrinate me into their world. They threw me into a carcer with another boy. He was wild, constantly challenging our guards and trying to escape. I was given their language the same way I think Stakel is going to take ours. It wasn't pleasant, but it didn't incapacitate me. There were other things they did that were harder to recover from." Martin smiled ruefully. "Stakel was defiant. He'd hurt himself trying to escape. Our captors wouldn't treat his injuries, but somehow he always managed to heal without their help."

Martin reached out a cautious hand to run a finger along a jagged scar on Stakel's thigh. "My sword slipped and sliced his thigh all the way to the bone during one of the thousands of training sessions they had us do. I have never felt so guilty in my life. The look of relief and triumph on his face as he was slowly bleeding to death is burned in my memory. Stakel wanted to be free of that army so badly, he was happy to die."

"Obviously he didn't. He survived somehow," the prince interjected.

"It was magic."

Rathian frowned at the blond soldier. "Magic?"

"I don't know how else to explain it. The ground around him was saturated with his blood and I knew he was going to die. I held his hand and he smiled at me for the first time since we'd met. The trainers were screaming. They were so angry because I'd killed a potential warrior. As I watched and waited for the light to finally die in his eyes, an odd glow started to shine from his skin. I looked down and his muscles were knitting together before my very eyes. Within minutes, there was only this scar left. My uncle rescued me that night, so I never knew how his story ended." Martin stared at Stakel and shook his head. "I don't think anything good happened to him after that incident."

"Yet you trust him. Martin, many years have passed since you were prisoners together. You escaped them, but he didn't. How do you know he hasn't changed? Are you sure he doesn't believe in their world now? Why do you still trust him?" Antioc pleaded with his lover.

"After my uncle saved me and I came to live with the Vanguard, I've studied the Villious and their ways. I'm the closest thing to an expert we have. Everything I've learnt about what and who the Queen's Consorts are tells me Stakel could have killed all of us — the Imperator included — before any of us lifted a sword." Martin held out a hand to Stakel. As the prisoner took it, the soldier grew pale and grimaced.

Rathian could feel a pressure growing in his head. He gripped it and groaned. Stakel cast a quick glance at him and he wondered if he was supposed to feel the spell or transference or whatever it was Stakel did. Just as the pressure got to be too big, it burst like a bubble and the pain went away.

"Bring headache powder," Rathian ordered the page at the end of the room.

Martin moaned, grasping his own head in his hands. "It feels like someone stirred my brains up with a stick."

The prince watched as Antioc went to his knees next to his lover. "Are you all right?" Antioc demanded.

"He'll be fine. It's nothing a little rest won't take care of."

Everyone jumped as the harsh voice cut through the air. Their attention went to the Villious prisoner. A small frown marring Stakel's forehead was the only sign of his discomfort.

"What did you do to him?" Antioc jumped to his feet with his hand on his sword.

"It's an extraction spell. All of the Queen's Consorts learn this spell so we can interrogate prisoners faster." Stakel looked at Martin. "I've only taken knowledge of your language. Your memories and secrets are still yours. I wouldn't steal those."

"So there is a moral code." Rathian shifted, smiling at the page handing him a cup of wine.

Stakel shrugged. "It's my code. The Consorts take memories and secrets from people all the time. They see nothing wrong with it."

"But you are a Consort," the prince pointed out.

"Yes, but it doesn't mean I'm like them. No matter how many times they have punished me or all the rivers of my blood that have bathed the High Priest's chambers—they cannot make me use what they've forced on me against others." Stakel shrugged again. "This is why I ended up being stabbed and left for dead on the battlefield."

"A rebel." Rathian swallowed the last of his wine and turned his cup over to the page. "Antioc, take your amator to your rooms. I'll send some powder to you."

"Imperator, you shouldn't be left alone with the prisoner." Only Antioc's concern for his prince could override his worry about his lover.

"I think Stakel could have killed me before this, if he'd been so inclined. Go, Sub-commander. I'll be fine."

Antioc bowed, but as he helped Martin to his feet, he growled at Stakel. "If any harm comes to either of them, I'll hunt you down like a dog after a fox."

"Understandable, Sub-commander." Stakel didn't flinch or seem worried about the threat.

Rathian waited until Antioc and Martin left before he said anything else. He turned, glancing at Stakel. "Your name is Stakel?"

The man nodded. "It's not my true name. When I was brought to the Temple, they renamed me." A sad expression crossed over Stakel's face as he shifted on his chair. "I no longer remember my birth name."

Rathian stood then gestured for the prisoner to do the same. "Let's walk. My leg was injured in battle a few months ago. It's healed fine, but some days it likes to remind me of the wound."

Stakel nodded and joined him by the door. Two members of his decem stayed a few paces behind them as they moved down the hallway.

"As you might have gathered, I'm Prince Rathian, second son to the King of Launioc." He headed towards the garden door. He wanted to be outside. The morning air was crisp and he hoped it would drive away the lingering pain in his head.

"You're the Imperator of the Vanguard."

Stakel allowed him to enter the garden first and Rathian was pleased by the honour Stakel showed him. He laughed silently at himself. How did he know it was respect the Villious was showing him? Maybe Stakel allowed him to exit the room first in case there were assassins waiting to kill him. The prisoner could be ensuring Rathian caught the first blow.

"Yes. Do you know what the Vanguard is?" The prince strolled along the cobblestone path, trying to stretch his injured muscles.

"The queen's priests told us you were demons in human form. You couldn't be killed by mortal men and that is why the Consorts were sent against your squadrons." Stakel walked one step behind and to the right of him, as if the man was guarding his back. "I heard rumours as well, among the Villious camps, that your bonds go beyond brotherhood into the realm of beloved."

Rathian chuckled. "Those rumours are true, Stakel. The ducenti is an army made up of lovers. When each of my soldiers looks into the eyes of another man, he sees not only a brother-in-arms, but a person he could love like most men love women." He shrugged. "The Vanguard—as you call it—has been around since the first king was crowned. The Imperator has always been the second son."

Rathian's foot hit a root and he stumbled. Stakel grabbed his arm to help balance him. Lightning seemed to arc between them and they both gasped. The prince had the strongest urge to kiss the Villious. He shook his head and moved away, breaking the contact. The attraction he was feeling wasn't wise.

"Thank you. I'm still recovering and sometimes my leg gives out on me."

Stakel nodded.

"What is a Queen's Consort? Are you her lover?" Rathian pointed to a bench a few feet away.

# Chapter Five

Stakel followed the Launioc prince to a small wooden bench placed under an oak tree. His mind reeled from the surge of lust that shot through him when they'd touched. He'd never felt such desire for anyone, not even the queen.

The prince sat down, his left leg stretched out in front of him. Stakel saw Rathian grimace and rub his thigh.

"We are used as the queen's lovers but are more than that." Stakel tried to keep his mind on the conversation. He couldn't be distracted by the long, thick fingers of the prince.

"She allows her lovers to fight in battle?" Rathian shook his head. "I can't imagine my father allowing any of his mistresses loose with weapons. Of course, some of them are such harpies, I'd be afraid of dealing with them."

"We are used more like studs in a breeding programme than as actual lovers." Stakel shuddered at the memories chasing around his mind. "The

Consorts are also her bodyguards and the most feared unit in her army. The same as your Vanguard."

The prince chuckled. "Don't tell any of my men that. They'll be insulted. The Vanguard ducenti tends to believe we are far superior to even the regular Launioc infantry."

Stakel nodded. "Consorts believe they are superior to any other creature in the world aside from the queen."

Rathian shot him a glance. "Do you?"

"I don't consider myself a Consort, so it doesn't apply to me." Reaching out to touch the prince's leg, he hesitated. "I can ease the pain."

He noticed the prince's decem stiffen, waiting for a signal to stop him. Rathian's green eyes studied him. Stakel felt like the Launioc prince saw deep into his soul. He accepted the surge of attraction running through him at the musky scent drifting from the warm body of the man next to him. He'd never found men beautiful before, but this enemy ruler created illicit images in his mind.

Rathian nodded and his guards relaxed. Stakel laid his hands on the injured thigh, rubbing the tight muscles, and drawing on his own energy. Warmth pushed through his flesh into the prince's. Stakel closed his eyes and allowed his magic to tell him what was wrong with Rathian's injured leg.

The power took him deep into flesh and blood. He saw the wound in the muscles and realised the Launioc prince had taken an axe blow to the limb. Lucky for Rathian, the bone itself wasn't injured. Flesh and skin had healed nicely, leaving only a scar. The muscle needed to be rebuilt, so Stakel gave it a little boost of energy to regain its strength. Yet there was something else inside the blood of the prince. He frowned, wanting to root out the problem. Whatever it was wasn't a natural illness.

"Your Highness?"

A voice broke Stakel's concentration and brought him out of the healing fog he was in. He whispered the words of ending, easing his power from the prince. Settling back, he sighed.

Rathian stared at him with a shocked expression. "One more thing that makes the Queen's Consorts special?"

Stakel shook his head but didn't answer aloud. Healing made him tired. He was a natural healer, so any time he had to treat someone, he drew the energy from inside himself. As far as he knew, he was the only one of the Consorts who could heal others without using the spell.

"Your Highness," the speaker insisted.

They both looked to where a herald stood, shifting nervously on his feet.

"What is it, boy?" Rathian grimaced.

Stakel knew it wasn't an expression of pain. He wondered why the young man in purple clothes with white around the edges would bother the prince.

"Your father, His Majesty, King Barkuc, requests your presence at a council meeting, Your Highness." The herald bowed.

"I saw the man last night." Rathian stood, putting weight on his leg slowly, and a smile blossomed on his face.

Stakel was struck by how a smile made the stern-looking man beautiful.

"Thank you, friend. For the first time since I received the wound, I can stand without pain." He gestured to where another page stood just inside the garden door. "Get Sub-commander Antioc. Tell him I want Stakel treated as a guest, not a prisoner." The prince turned to him. "Would you prefer to be housed in the barracks or here in the royal house?"

Stakel would have preferred to have been allowed his freedom to return to his mountains, but he knew it wasn't an option. Not now and maybe never. Even if the Launiocs were inclined to set him free, he would be killed on sight by his own army. It was better to stay here and see what would come of his imprisonment.

"It would be better if I'm in the royal house, Imperator. I assume your men wouldn't like to be housed with me."

Rathian frowned but nodded. "You're right. They'll see you as a Villious, even if you don't see yourself as one." He turned back to the page. "Sub-commander Antioc is to make sure Stakel is housed in a room close to mine."

Stakel rose to his feet. "He won't be happy about that."

"It's possible, but I've lived this long by trusting my instincts and I don't think you're interested in killing me. You've had ample opportunity since we came out here. Something tells me you're going to be important to all of us before our time together is over."

"Your Highness," the herald persisted.

"My father lives to irritate me," Rathian snarled. "Go get my horse ready."

He waved a hand at one of his decem. "I'll be back and we can continue our conversation. If you need food or clothes, please let my page, Darius, know. He'll make sure you get anything you wish."

The prince bowed at him and stalked away, following the young herald. Stakel's eyes were drawn to the firm round globes of Rathian's ass, which flexed as the man walked away from him. Frowning, he wondered what it was about the younger man that drew his attention and made him wish the man would focus exclusively on him. The unusual combination of deep green eyes and white-gold hair intrigued Stakel. The Launioc prince had been dressed simply in black leather pants that laced up the sides and a white linen sleeveless tunic. Stakel felt his cock stir beneath his pants. He reached down to adjust himself as the prince turned back towards him.

The man's gaze burned into Stakel and his skin warmed. Even from the distance he stood, he could see the prince's nostrils flare and a faint pink flush rise on Rathian's cheeks. The prince had to be feeling some of the same lust Stakel did. Stakel started to turn away. In the Villious army and the Consorts, attraction between men was seen as an abomination against the gods.

*"You aren't in Villious anymore, child. Things are done differently. The very men you are surrounded by see love as something more than what your gods dictate."*

He furrowed his brow, trying to place the voice in his head. This was the second time that day he'd heard this voice. He hadn't heard it in a long time — since his initiation into the Consorts. Before that, it had always been there, talking to him when he'd found himself isolated in the Villious army.

*"Her priests blocked me from you. Here, you are emerging from the fog they put you under. In this place, you might have the chance to become what you were truly meant to be."*

A noise made him focus outside the conversation in his head. Sub-commander Antioc was Martin's lover, and not happy about what he'd done to the young soldier. He stared at the man, who appeared to be close to his age.

"The Imperator orders me to take you to the room next to his own. You are to have anything you want." Antioc's eyes narrowed. "What kind of spell have you cast over Prince Rathian?"

Shaking his head, Stakel maintained eye contact. He understood any type of backing down would be viewed as weakness. "No spell to confuse. I've only cast a spell of healing. Your prince's leg will begin to feel better soon. Do you have a healer here?"

Antioc glared. "Why? Do you need one?"

Stakel held his arms out from his body. "Do you see any wounds on me, young commander?"

Antioc's gaze skated over Stakel's body. He turned around so the man could see his back. A sharp intake of breath reminded him of the large hourglass brand seared into the skin at the base of his spine. He gritted his teeth as the memory of the pain from the brand washed through him. Cool fingers traced a light trail over the lines.

"What happened?" Antioc's voice was soft and hesitant, as if he didn't want to bring up bad memories for Stakel.

"All of the Queen's Consorts carry her mark on their bodies somewhere. We received it after the rituals were done and before we went to the queen's bed for the first time." His dislike for his queen dripped from the tone of his voice.

"It's barbaric that she brands you."

Stakel turned back around and Antioc's fingers trailed over his hip, ending up on his flat stomach. A shudder raced through both of them.

"You are marked as well." Stakel touched the dark blue slashes on Antioc's upper arm. "Does your ruler put them there to claim you?"

"No. First, none of us in the ducenti recognise King Barkuc as our true ruler. Prince Rathian, Imperator of the Vanguard, is our leader and the one we will die for. He would never do that to us." Antioc gestured towards Stakel's back. The soldier smiled sadly down at his arm. "These help me remember the amator I have lost in battle."

Stakel stroked his fingers over each slash. "Three of your lovers have been killed? Will there be one for Martin?"

"Only if I fail to protect him." Antioc stepped away, sweeping his arm in front of him. "Come, your room should be ready now. Would you care to join Martin and me for dinner tonight? I doubt the prince will be back until tomorrow morning at the earliest. The king doesn't see the need for our unit to leave as soon as we can replenish the supplies. He'll end up delaying our departure by days while he and the council debate the amount of grain we take with us."

"Your ruler sounds as foolish as the queen." Stakel stayed close to Antioc.

"Maybe all rulers are foolish because they aren't the ones who fight the wars. They merely declare a war started and the rest of us must die contesting it." Antioc chuckled. "It's an argument Martin and I have often enough. Please, we'd be honoured to have you join us."

Stakel studied the Launioc soldier. Was it a plan to get him alone and kill him? He knew some of the prince's men weren't happy about the way he'd been treated so far. At that moment, he wished he'd been given the ability to sense whether Antioc was sincere or not. He gave a mental shrug. Did it matter whether he died tonight or three days from now?

"Why would you invite me?" Stakel enquired. "An hour ago, you were willing to kill me. You even threatened me."

"True. Martin talked to me while I was making sure he was settled. He explained a few things to me. Also, for all that I might have misgivings about you, my prince doesn't. He says I am to treat you like a guest and I shall." Antioc gave him a slight smile. "We try not to disobey the Imperator."

"But you would if you thought he was in danger."

"Of course. His life is far more important than mine. Why allow him to die when I can protect him?" Antioc brushed Stakel's arm with a gentle caress. "Don't worry. I promise not to try and kill you while we eat."

"I'll come."

"Great. I'll send a page to escort you to our chambers. Prince Rathian allows his sub-commanders to stay in the royal house with him." Antioc stopped in front of ornately carved double doors. "The prince's suite is behind these doors. Yours is right next to his."

Stakel fought the urge to open the doors and dig through Rathian's possessions. The prince's deep green eyes spoke of secrets and passions that Stakel wanted to learn more about. He'd never been interested in finding anything out about his fellow Consorts.

# Chapter Six

"Stakel?"

Antioc had moved down the hall to where another set of doors stood. The Launioc opened one of the doors and gestured for him to enter. He stepped in and stopped dead in his tracks. There was no way this huge room was his. He shot Antioc a questioning glance.

"You always put prisoners in rooms like this?"

The auburn-haired soldier laughed, his hazel eyes lighting up. "Oh no. Usually prisoners are kept in the lower claustrum, but I don't think Prince Rathian considers you a prisoner anymore. Or at least you're not a threat in his eyes."

A serious expression took over Antioc's face. "Don't wander around without an escort, Stakel. I'm willing to give you the benefit of the doubt because Martin vouches for you, but there are those here who would kill you just for looking at them. It's mostly the regular army. We of the Vanguard ducenti obey our Imperator in all things and if he says you're not to be touched, we won't harm you."

"You have a lot of faith in your commander." Stakel strolled back across the ivory marble floor to stare out of the large windows overlooking the same beautiful garden he and Rathian had been in earlier.

"We are loyal to only one ruler and one god. Prince Rathian is both for us. We will give our lives obeying his orders. He leads from the front. In a battle, we always know where he will be. We need only look around to find where the battle rages the fiercest and he will be there." Antioc's voice held pride.

"You respect him." Stakel was surprised. His experience had always been that the soldiers hated their superior officers.

"We love him."

In that simple statement, Stakel understood the soul-deep difference between the Queen's Consorts and the Vanguard. The Consorts feared and hated the queen. They fought to escape her wrath. The men of the Vanguard saw Prince Rathian as one of them. Each man would die for their Imperator.

"You are an army of lovers?" He tested the mattress on the bed and knew he wouldn't be sleeping on it. Too soft after spending nights on stone floors.

"Yes."

He looked up to see Antioc leaning against the closed door. The neutral tone of the soldier's voice told Stakel that Antioc expected disdain or disgust from him.

"Your own people are fine with this arrangement?"

Antioc shrugged. "Have no idea really. No one will speak against the ducenti. I do think they see us as touched by the gods, which makes us fierce fighters and changes us in ways they'll never understand. It is much like religion and priests. Their ways are so mysterious that people tend to overlook some of the strange rituals they follow. Some of the ones who have left the unit have married and fathered children. Not all who are part of the ducenti love men to the exclusion of women." Antioc's grin was pure mischief. "Though I've never seen the attraction of women."

"Neither have I," Stakel muttered, moving to stand before the large woven tapestry hanging on the wall.

"As a Queen's Consort, aren't you supposed to fuck the queen?"

"Aye, her personal stud service." Stakel ran his hand over the brilliant fabric — the delicate silk strands caught on the rough calluses on his palm. He disengaged his hand and lifted the tapestry from the wall. A door was hidden behind it. "Where does this door lead?"

"Don't know. I've never been in this room." Antioc pushed himself from the door. "To be honest, I'm surprised the prince put you in here. It's not going to make General Excelsie happy."

"Are the general and your Imperator lovers?" He trailed his fingertips over the seam of the door.

"No, but the general tends to use this room while he's here."

Stakel turned, dismayed that he'd been distracted enough for Antioc to approach so close without him hearing the man. He stepped back and found his back pressed against cool wood. The younger Launioc soldier stood a few inches shorter than Stakel. Pushing up on his toes, Antioc brushed their lips together. Stakel gasped as heat filled his body, pooling in his groin.

Antioc must have taken Stakel's gasp as consent, for the soldier reached up, cradled Stakel's face in his hands and took his mouth without hesitation this time. Stakel had never been kissed like this before. His mouth was the enemy to be subdued and Antioc wasn't taking any prisoners.

Sharp teeth nibbled his bottom lip. Warm lips sucked on his tongue. The roof of his mouth got treated to teasing strokes of Antioc's tongue. Stakel flexed his hands, unsure of where to put them. Flat against the wall seemed the best place at the moment. Antioc's muscular body pinned him to the wall with gentle strength. Yet Stakel had the feeling that if he wanted to, he could get away from the Launioc soldier. He was nervous and it wasn't because he was worried about getting hurt, but because he didn't know what to do. His sexual encounters had never included gentleness or any possibility of protesting.

Antioc pulled away, chest heaving and hazel eyes hazy with passion. Stakel lifted a shaking hand to touch his swollen bottom lip. Antioc took Stakel's other hand from where it lay and pressed it to the bulge at Antioc's groin. He instinctively squeezed.

"*Wasis*," Antioc swore.

The Launioc gripped Stakel's hand and showed him how to stroke his cock in a rhythm Antioc liked.

Stakel studied the contorted expression on the soldier's face. It didn't look like the man was enjoying what Stakel was doing to him, but he had seen the Consorts make faces like that while they were fucking the queen. A flash of a shy smile crossed his face and he froze.

"What about Martin?"

Antioc moved a few inches away and frowned. "Martin won't mind."

"You aren't faithful to each other?" he asked. Shifting slightly, he tried to put space between them.

"In the ducenti, we each have our special amator. He is the man who shares our bed night after night.

Martin is the man I will die for. It is his face I will see every night before I sleep." Antioc smiled. "We play to strengthen our ties to each other. There are only two people I haven't played with since I became a soldier."

"Who are they?" Stakel eased farther away, dropping his hands away from the muscular body in front of him. He touched the edge of the door hidden behind the tapestry.

"General Excelsie and Prince Rathian." Antioc strolled back to lean on the bedpost. He seemed to understand that Stakel wasn't comfortable with pursuing their former course.

"Why don't they partake of what is freely offered?" Stakel grimaced. "At least, I'm assuming it is freely offered."

He could be wrong and the soldiers of the Vanguard could be forced, much like the Consorts, to pleasure their leaders.

"Oh trust me, if Prince Rathian were to crook his finger at me, I'd be in his bed, begging." Antioc's lips pulled into a leer. "And he has played with a few of the other men, but lately he has been too caught up in the war and fighting with his father that he hasn't invited any of us to his bed. Once he finds his Custos, they will be exclusive. The rest of the ducenti will be so disappointed, for a few minutes." The Launioc soldier laughed.

"Why doesn't anyone play with Excelsie?" He trailed his fingers over the outline of the door. There had to be some way to open it.

"He isn't one of us."

Stakel glanced over his shoulder at Antioc. "Not one of you? In what way?"

"Got sent here as a child as a goodwill gesture by his father." The younger man pushed away and headed

49

towards the hallway door. "I'll have Darius bring you some different clothes. Martin and I eat around moonrise. We'll come to escort you. Remember not to be found wandering the halls by yourself for now. Once the others get used to seeing you around, they won't bother you."

"Thank you."

He was grateful. Antioc could have continued being antagonistic, but the sub-commander had managed to overcome most of his distrust to try to make Stakel comfortable. Chuckling, he shook his head. It seemed making him comfortable meant fucking him in Antioc's mind. A shiver slid down Stakel's spine. He had felt lust for the young soldier, but knowing that Antioc was also in a relationship with Martin cooled any ardour he'd had for him.

Playing was a simple word for what they had done and it reminded Stakel too much of the orgies the queen and her Consorts engaged in. Those orgies had left him feeling dirty and more like an animal than a man. The priests would feed the men some sort of drug to force them to overcome any inhibitions they might have. He rested his forehead against the silk of the wall hanging as nausea made his stomach roil. He'd hated those times, the feeling of hard, hot hands touching him and not being able to say no. He'd loathed the mornings after, when he'd woken up without any memory of what had happened.

A soft click pulled him from his memories. Whatever spot his forehead hit must have unhooked the latch for the door. He tugged it open, shooting a look over his shoulder to make sure his bedroom door was shut. For some reason, he didn't want anyone to know he'd figured out how to open this. He pulled it ajar enough to fit his body through.

The door opened into a narrow corridor running parallel to the outside hallway and it led back towards Rathian's room. Stakel paused, wondering if he shouldn't just turn around and go lie down. The healing he'd done on the prince had taken a lot of energy from him, but curiosity teased his mind. What did the private apartments of the prince look like? Would they reveal Rathian's secret thoughts and dreams?

He frowned. He had no business invading the prince's dreams and hopes. Yet his feet took him down the corridor, not back into his own room. Looking back, he saw his footprints displayed in the dust on the floor. No one had been down this hallway in a while.

It was surprisingly easy to enter Rathian's room. The door wasn't locked or even shut tight. He stepped from behind the tapestry hanging over the entrance and gasped. It was beautiful.

The stone walls were covered with silk hangings. Birds, flowers, horses and trees were depicted in vibrant colours and with such skill it seemed as if they lived. One particular tapestry caught his eye and drew him towards it.

Reaching out, he traced the line of the flowing river created from the brightest blues and silvers. The water bisected a green clearing where yellow star flowers grew. He could almost feel the coolness of the water and smell the fragrant scent of the flowers. Golden-brown mountains rose in the distance. His heart ached. He longed to return home, to find his family and live the life that had been stolen from him.

*"A life you were never meant to live."*

He frowned, not wanting the voice to take his wishes away from him. A hope began to flicker in his heart. Maybe Rathian would let him go to the mountains. Maybe the Launioc prince would understand his need to be free.

*"Freedom comes in many forms and sometimes with the lightest of chains."*

Stakel shifted away from the tapestry, studying the rest of the room. A large bed rested against the far wall. Its huge four pillars, footboard and headboard were carved from the blackest stone. He went to investigate. Pillows were scattered over the furs and blankets on the mattress. He ran his hands over the brilliant jewel-toned squares created from lush fabrics of satin and velvet.

Sitting down, he relaxed against the dark bear and wolf skins, allowing the soft fur to caress his tense body. He'd never been allowed such luxuries in the Villious army. Not even the Consorts got to feel warmth or softness unless they were with the queen. He rubbed his cheek on the blankets and wrapped his arms around one of the pillows. He pulled it to his face and breathed in. A spicy scent filled his nostrils. His mind raced, trying to locate where he'd smelt it before. A distant memory from his youth flared up. Cognaki trees grew around his village up in the mountains. The villagers harvested the thick brown bark of the tree to sell as a spice. The musky, smoky scent served to remind him of all he'd lost.

Something cool trailed down over his cheek. He frowned, reaching up to touch his skin. Stakel pulled his fingers back and stared at them. The tips were wet. He licked one. Salt exploded on his tongue. What was going on? He glanced above him to see where the water was coming from. The mattress and furs cradled his aching muscles, causing him to moan. Warmth trickled through his body and soon his cheeks were awash with water.

No drips or leaks from above him. He couldn't figure out where the liquid was coming from. He followed the path up to the corner of his eye. Was he crying? It wasn't possible. He'd cried his last tears when he was ten. Two weeks after being taken from his village, he'd learnt tears did nothing except earn him more punishment. No matter what had happened to him since that dark moment in the night when he'd realised he would never be free again, no tears had escaped his eyes.

Stakel buried his face in the pillow he held and sobbed. The warmth and odd sense of safety that the Cognaki scent gave him helped to open a lock he'd kept sealed for years. No one would know he'd broken. He would rebuild those walls so he'd be strong enough to face everyone. His body shook from the strength of his sobs. The satin of the pillow beneath him darkened from his tears.

*"Let the tears wash your anger away. Let it clear your eyes so you can see what is right in front of you."*

Stakel ignored the voice and allowed exhaustion to drag him under. His last prayer was that he slept without nightmares.

# Chapter Seven

Rathian stalked down the hallway. He wanted to break something. Spending most of the day with his father often did that to him, plus he knew he'd have to suffer through another horrid night at court.

"Damn Travi for wanting to get married," he muttered.

His older brother, heir to the Launioc throne, was visiting Milina, trying to arrange a marriage to the oldest daughter of the Milinan king. With Travi gone, there was no one to keep Rathian from spending time with his father. He shoved his hand through his hair. Thank the gods that Travi was coming home in two days. Rathian didn't want to spend any more time with the king. He was reaching the limit of his patience.

Rathian waved off his decem as he opened the door to his suite. Unbuttoning his shirt, he shut out the rest of the world. He loved his room. His mother had decorated it for him in the colours and fabrics he loved. It was his one place where he could stop being a royal prince and the Imperator. He sighed. He had enough time to take a nap before he had to go back to the palace.

His shirt went flying as he stepped up to his bed. Gods, he looked forward to burying himself under his furs and catching some sleep. A sound came from the bed and he glanced up in surprise.

Black hair mixed with the furs and fanned over his pillows. His mouth dropped open when he recognised the body in his bed. How the hell had Stakel got into his room? He eased down onto the mattress, reaching out to run the soft locks through his fingers.

Stakel rolled onto his side, one hand landing on Rathian's thigh close to his groin. The prince sucked in a quick breath. He couldn't help wishing the Villious' hand had ended farther up. A close look at the older man's face made the tear tracks more obvious. Frowning, he rubbed a finger over a high cheekbone, wondering why Stakel had been crying.

The Villious grabbed his wrist and pinned him to the mattress. Rathian didn't fight. He lay still under the heavy weight of Stakel's body, trying to ignore how arousing their skin brushing against each other was.

Dark-brown eyes stared down at him and the vulnerable haze in them cleared as Stakel woke up. Rathian found himself fascinated by the visible re-building of the walls around Stakel's emotions. Once the walls were in place and those beautiful eyes went blank, Stakel climbed off him and stood next to the bed.

"Sorry to wake you." Rathian pushed up so he was leaning against the headboard.

"I shouldn't have fallen asleep here. Your men wouldn't be happy to find that I wasn't in my rooms." Stakel moved off towards the opposite wall.

"Probably not. How did you get in here?" He wasn't interested in letting Stakel go.

Stakel pulled aside a large tapestry to reveal a door. "I found a door in my room. It opened and I followed the corridor here."

Rathian frowned. "That's odd."

"I'm sorry. I shouldn't have come into your room." Stakel had said the words, but Rathian could tell the man hadn't meant them.

"I don't care about that. The corridor connects the suites of the Imperator and his Custos. It shouldn't open for anyone who isn't bonded to me." A yawn caught him off guard.

"Custos?" Stakel touched the door and it swung open.

"Like a second-in-command." Rathian climbed off the bed and started untying the laces of his pants. "I could kill my brother for taking off on me like this. Who the hell wants to get married anyway?"

He growled as the laces knotted. Tugging, he made them tighter and knew he'd have to call Darius to help him get undressed, even though usually he did it himself. Being alone was the best thing for him at the moment.

"Wasis," he swore, pulling on them in frustration. Finally, he dropped back onto the mattress and rested his elbows on his knees.

"May I help?"

A hesitant touch to his shoulder reminded him that Stakel was still in the room. He sighed and reached for the small dagger he kept under one of the pillows on his bed. Handing it to Stakel, he stood.

"You'll have to cut them off. I'm afraid the knots are too tight."

Stakel knelt before him and Rathian bit back a groan. Looking down, he saw the black hair gleaming and felt the heat of Stakel's breath on his groin. The image of Stakel's mouth wrapped around his cock flashed through his mind.

A knock sounded and absently he said, "Come in."

Stakel gripped the dagger and placed the blade underneath the first leather lace.

"What is going on here?"

The shout surprised both of them. Stakel sprang to his feet, placing his body between Rathian and Excelsie who rushed into the room, drawing his sword.

"Wait, Excelsie. There's nothing to worry about. Stakel is helping me cut the laces on my pants. I've managed to get them knotted up again." Rathian held up his hand to stop his friend while being secretly thrilled at the way Stakel shielded him.

The general glared at Stakel, but slid his sword back into its sheath. "He shouldn't be here, Your Highness."

Rathian placed his hand on the spot between Stakel's shoulder blades. The tension in the Villious' body eased with his touch. The prince memorised the well-formed back with broad shoulders narrowing down to a narrow waist. Shock raced through him when he saw the hourglass brand at the small of Stakel's back.

"It's all right, Excelsie. I'll be fine. You're dismissed." He didn't look up to watch his general leave. He was totally focused on the scars. "How did you get these?"

He traced the brand. Stakel gasped and shuddered. Rathian took a chance by stepping closer to the Villious. He remembered Stakel held the dagger in his hand and that the man could kill him with a simple stab to the artery in his leg, but Rathian didn't believe Stakel was interested in hurting him. Stakel's body shook as Rathian slipped a gentle arm around the slender waist, pulling Stakel back against him.

His chest met Stakel's back and both men moaned. The prince rested his free hand on Stakel's hip while spreading his other hand over the ripped stomach of the Villious. Stakel froze.

"If you want me to stop, just tell me," Rathian whispered into the ear closest to his lips. "There will be no force and no pain. Only pleasure if you wish it."

Stakel didn't say anything, so Rathian took his silence to mean the Villious was willing to let him continue. The prince didn't think Stakel was ready for him to touch him below the waist. He kept one hand where it lay on Stakel's hip. Overwhelming him wasn't the idea. For some reason, it was important that Stakel enjoyed everything Rathian did to him.

Slowly, he slid his palm up over Stakel's warm skin, enjoying the shivers causing tremors to rack the body in his arms. He stopped his hand in the middle of Stakel's chest, where he brushed one nipple with the tip of his finger and rubbed his thumb over the other. Rathian scraped his thumbnail over the flesh, causing it to harden.

Stakel jerked and Rathian held his hand still. "Are you all right?"

A brief nod had the prince pressing a kiss on Stakel's shoulder. He pinched the nub between thumb and finger, twisting slightly. Stakel hissed and arched his back. Rathian placed an open-mouthed kiss along the bared nape of the Villious' neck, licking his salty skin.

A knock sounded on the door and a hesitant voice called out, "Your Highness?"

Rathian sighed, wrapped both arms around Stakel's waist and rested his forehead on his warm back. "What is it, Darius?"

"General Excelsie said you needed help undressing. May I be of service?" The uneasy tone of the page's voice let Rathian know that the general had taken his temper out on the young boy.

"No, Darius. I'm fine. Come back and wake me in two hours. I need to return to court tonight." Rathian ran his hands over Stakel's stomach, hoping to soothe both of them with his touch.

"Yes, Your Highness." Darius' footsteps faded away.

Rathian chuckled softly. He eased back from Stakel, reaching down to adjust his aching cock. "The gods are conspiring against my seduction, friend."

Stakel turned and Rathian braced himself to deal with Stakel's anger. He met confused-looking brown eyes.

"Why?" Stakel's grip on the dagger was white-knuckled.

"Why seduction or why are the gods conspiring against it?" Rathian circled the on-guard Villious to sit on the bed.

Stakel moved out of reach and nodded.

Rathian scrubbed his hands over his face and rested his elbows on his knees. He stared at Stakel, studying the older man.

"Seduction is more fun than rape."

Stakel's eyebrows shot up and a blank look came over his face. He lifted the dagger into a defensive position. "I'll kill you first."

Rathian nodded. "I'm sure you would, but I don't rape men — or women for that matter. There's no need for you to worry." He reached out a hand to trail a finger over Stakel's fist. "I like you. As strange and crazy as that might sound, I don't think you're here to harm me. For the first time in a long time, I'm beginning to believe my gods are granting a few of my most fervent prayers."

No pulling away was a good sign. Stakel stared at him for a moment and Rathian had no idea what was going on behind those empty brown eyes. The Consort had regrouped and regained his composure. Stakel waved his other hand, gesturing for Rathian to stand up.

"We should get you out of these pants. It won't be comfortable to try and sleep in them."

The prince stood, holding his hands out to the side, allowing Stakel access to the laces on his pants. Stakel stayed an arm's length away, cutting through the leather strings without trouble. Rathian gave a soft moan of relief as the constriction around his erection eased.

Stakel shot him an amused glance before slicing the laces on the other side. With a gentle push, Stakel sent the prince sprawling onto the mattress, then set the knife on the small table next to the bed.

"The boots need to come off. Darius would probably have a fit if you got the furs and blankets dirty." Stakel tapped Rathian's left leg.

Rathian offered his foot and closed his eyes. Most of the time he'd get undressed on his own. As the Imperator, he fought battles alongside his men. He didn't have time or the inclination to make people wait on him, but his dealings with his father had worn him out and he welcomed the help.

His foot slid free with a firm tug on the boot. A thud announced the boot connecting with the floor. Without looking, he held out his other foot. Another tug and thud. Warm hands tapped his hips and he lifted them, giving Stakel the opportunity to pull his pants down. His hard cock slapped against his stomach and he groaned as the cool air caressed his body.

"Climb in bed, Your Highness."

Rathian opened his eyes to see Stakel standing beside the bed. The unguarded heat in that dark gaze stirred his groin. Stakel blinked and the lust disappeared. The prince rolled over onto his side, burying his face in one of the pillows.

"Sleep," Stakel ordered. "I'll go back to my room and be a nice little prisoner."

"Not a prisoner. I think you're going to be a friend," Rathian muttered as sleep started to overwhelm the need in his cock.

"Only time will tell, Imperator."

As he drifted to sleep, he felt the butterfly wing touch of a hand over his ass then heard a distant click. He looked over his shoulder and saw the tapestry that covered the hidden door swing in a breeze.

# Chapter Eight

Stakel stared out of his large bedroom window. He wore no clothing and didn't care if anyone saw him. He was accustomed to being naked. All of the Consorts were kept naked when they weren't fighting.

A few minutes earlier, he'd heard the prince leave for another night at court. The footsteps stopped in front of his door and Stakel had worried the prince would knock. He wasn't ready to meet the man face-to-face any time soon.

A shudder raced over his body and his cock stiffened. He grimaced. There was that reaction again and he fought the urge to stroke his shaft. Resting his forehead against the glass, he hoped the shock of the cool surface would douse his arousal. He glanced down and the flared head of his erection painted the glass with liquid. It didn't work. At this rate, he would need to bathe in ice water to ease the lust racing through him at the thought of Rathian.

Whirling around, he stalked to one of the chairs positioned next to the empty fireplace. He flopped down onto it and snarled. The scar on his thigh stood out. He traced it with his finger. Death had come close to claiming him and he'd been happy to go. His own body had turned on him and had healed the wound. Surviving an injury that would have killed anyone else had brought him to the priests' attention. After Martin had disappeared, Stakel had been taken to the Queen's Temple where he'd started receiving training in the duties of a Consort.

He buried his face in his hands and shuddered, but this time it was from disgust. Thirteen years old, forced to do things no child should. He didn't understand what the priests had wanted of him, but he had learnt to fear their touch more than the lash of the soldiers.

*"Brainwashing. When you got older, you wouldn't stand up to them, or so they'd thought. Those demon priests learnt that you were not broken. They learnt to fear you as much as you feared their touch."* The voice brimmed with pride. *"Why do you think your fellow Consorts abandoned you? The priests wanted to get rid of you."*

Stakel shook his head. "Why would they fear me? I was at their mercy. They punish with whips, chains, potions and pain. I learnt to do as I was told to avoid being called into the High Priest's chambers."

Bile burned in his throat as he thought of the cruel punishments meted out in that room. Screams leaking through cracks in the doors. Dark brown splashes decorating the grey stone walls. Memories of Consorts who had entered the room, but had never come out.

*"You bear their scars on your body, but not on your spirit. You've proven to those fiends you're stronger than they are. You bent but didn't break."*

Stakel wrapped his arms around his legs and rested his forehead on his knees. He'd been through the worst his world could offer. Anything that happened here in Launioc couldn't be as terrible as the seventeen years he'd spent in the Consorts. He took a breath and allowed his heartbeat to calm down. He needed to remember that ending up in a Launioc's bed wasn't a foregone conclusion. It wouldn't matter whose bed he ended up in the ducenti, he would go there without force and it would be his own choice.

The way both Antioc and Rathian had treated him told him there was a different view of sex here with these men. They enjoyed sex for sex's sake, for the pleasure it brought both partners. Their 'play' created a bond of brotherhood and love unequalled anywhere else in this country or the rest of the world, as far as Stakel could tell, but he wasn't sure he'd ever be able to join in because it brought back memories he wanted to forget.

"Sometimes it felt like with one more lash or one more touch, I'd lose my grasp on reality and fall into the abyss. So much darkness. So little hope."

The silence in his mind made him wonder where the voice had gone. A soft touch and the voice spoke again.

*"I wish I could have been there. I might have sheltered you from the worst of it. The demons' power is too great in their lair. I couldn't fight past it."*

Stakel laughed. "How can I blame you when I don't even know who or what you are? For all I know, you don't exist and are simply a part of my imagination I made up to ease my worries."

*"Eventually, all will come clear as to who I am and what that means to you."*

He shook his head. Great, the voice was an oracle. Just what he needed. A knock on his door pulled him away from his thoughts. He climbed to his feet.

"Come in," he called, making his way back to the window.

A boy of around sixteen summers peeked around the door. "Sub-commander Antioc told me to bring you some clothes and help you get ready. You're joining him and Lancer Martin for dinner?"

Stakel turned away slightly. "Please put the clothes on the bed. I can dress myself."

"Would you like to bathe, sir?" The boy slid into the room, his gaze skipping around the interior but never landing on Stakel.

"I'm allowed to bathe?" Surprise coloured the tone of his voice.

The page gave him a wide-eyed look. "Of course you are. In fact, you may bathe as much as you like. The prince wouldn't begrudge even a prisoner water to wash in."

"That's nice to know. I would love to take a bath." He saw an expression of shock cross the boy's expressive face.

"You would?" The page frowned. "I didn't think the Consorts bathed."

Stakel chuckled. "Rumours said all Launiocs were flesh-eating monsters seeking to take our lives and our land."

"Not true. You started the war." An indignant glare took shape on the page's face.

"That might be true," Stakel admitted. "Don't believe every rumour you hear, young one. Most of them have no resemblance to the truth. Now where is the bathing chamber?"

The boy bowed his head, acknowledging the wisdom of Stakel's words. "I'm Darius, sir. If you will follow me, I'll take you there. His Highness said I should take you to his private bath. The regular army would probably get upset at seeing you without a guard and out of the dungeon."

Stakel nodded. "Understandable." He held out his hands. "I'll carry my own clothes, though."

Darius started to hand them over. A blush washed over the boy's cheeks. "You'll want to get dressed, sir. While the soldiers of the Vanguard ducenti admire the male form, walking naked in the halls of the royal house tends to be frowned upon."

Stakel didn't argue. He slipped on the cloth trousers Martin had given him earlier. Once they were fastened around his hips, he took the clean clothes from Darius and gestured for the page to lead the way.

* * * *

"Sir, if you don't get out, I think you'll turn into a fish and also, Sub-commander Antioc will come to find you."

Stakel jerked as Darius' touch brought him out of his doze. When the young man tried to scrub his back, he took the cloth from the page and shook his head.

"I'm used to taking care of myself, son. Run and tell Antioc that I'll be there soon. Return for me in ten minutes."

Darius blinked at him and he realised the page wasn't used to prisoners giving him orders. Maybe Stakel was acting more like an honoured guest than a captured enemy, but he'd take advantage of everything they gave him until Rathian clarified his orders. He ran the cloth over his body, testing the areas where his wounds had been. The spots weren't even sore anymore. The nap he'd taken had healed him completely.

He slid under the warm water, allowing the liquid to support his body. Closing his eyes, he could feel his muscles relax. Just as he started to break the surface of the water, hands grabbed his shoulders and forced him back under. He struggled, trying to wiggle free, but his attacker's grip remained solid.

His chest burned as the breath in his lungs started to run out. Stakel fought the urge to gasp, knowing the water would flood his body. He tugged and scratched at the fingers digging into his skin. Opening his eyes, he looked up through the water, searching to see if he could see the face of his assailant. The wavy image told him nothing and his vision started to darken as his breath ran out.

*No.*

He shook his head, clearing his mind and eyes. A surge of strength raced through Stakel and he shook loose of one hand. Twisting, he drove his hand down on to the man's other wrist. A yelp muffled by the liquid teased his ears, but the grip stayed tight. He pushed off the floor of the bathing pool, breaking the surface of the water enough to gasp a fresh breath. As the clean air filled his lungs, a blinding pain entered his head and his mind went blank.

# Chapter Nine

"Wasis."

Stakel frowned. Who was swearing so loudly? He moaned, reaching for his head.

A cool hand grasped his and kept him from touching the throbbing area at his temple.

"At least he's awake."

Light fingers traced over his cheek and he forced his heavy eyelids to open. Antioc and Martin knelt on each side of him with Darius hovering over their shoulders. Concern showed on their faces. He swore he saw tears in the young page's eyes.

"I'm fine." He tried to sit up.

Antioc pressed a hand to his chest. "I think you should lie there for a moment. We have a physician coming to check you out."

Stakel wanted to shake his head, but he figured it would fall off his shoulders if he did. "I don't need a healer. I'll be fine. Just need to get dressed and go back to my room."

Darius moved to his other side, knelt down and touched his hand. "I'm sorry."

He frowned up at the boy. "Why? You didn't do this to me."

Antioc glanced at Martin then back at him. "How do you know that?"

"No offence to Darius. I'm sure all young Launioc soldiers are quite capable, but to keep a grown man twice his size under the water for as long as I was and then hit me in the head would take a stronger man than he." Stakel tapped Darius' hand. "It wasn't your fault."

"I left you alone and I was ordered not to because something like this could happen." The page looked very upset.

"You couldn't know anyone would disobey the Imperator's direct order, boy." Antioc agreed with Stakel. "You did the right thing by coming to get us when you found Stakel."

Martin squeezed Darius' shoulder. "Not to mention you pulled Stakel out of the water before you got us. Prince Rathian will be proud of you."

"Help me sit up?" Stakel asked Antioc.

The sub-commander slid his arm behind Stakel's back and supported him as he eased into a sitting position. His vision blurred and his head spun. He took a deep breath, calming his pulse and allowing everything to adjust to the new angle. The sharp pain at his right temple eased a little, forcing him to focus on the stinging at his shoulders.

"What the hell happened?"

General Excelsie stalked into the bathing chamber, followed by the Vanguard's physician.

Antioc and Martin sprang to their feet, saluting their superior officer. Stakel grimaced when the physician pushed Darius out of the way and tried to make Stakel lie back down.

"I'm fine, Healer. There's nothing you can do for me."

"I'll make that decision, Villious." The elderly soldier medicus glared at him.

"Actually, I'll make the decision," Stakel said as he surged to his feet, holding out a hand to the page. "Pick up my clothes for me, Darius, and come with me to my room. I think I'll take your help with getting dressed."

"I don't think you should be wandering around the hallways without a guard." Excelsie moved to block the way out.

"Will you be escorting me, General?" Stakel gave the general an incredulous look. "I would think that you are too important a person to waste your time with an inconsequential prisoner."

Excelsie sneered. "His Highness has given the order that you are to be treated as a guest, not a prisoner. I wonder what type of spell you cast over him to make him believe you're harmless."

"He doesn't think I'm harmless. Prince Rathian knows I'm not interested in killing him, or anyone else for that matter. All I want is my freedom. I'll do whatever I have to do to get it." Stakel faced the general without fear.

Stakel could tell Excelsie didn't like him. In fact, the general probably believed he was a demon, like the legends stated. He studied the taller, older man. Excelsie's dark eyes were sunken and gleamed with animosity towards Stakel. Yet he would never back down from this man. If the priests had taught him one thing, it was to stand his ground no matter how much rage he would face. His blood had painted the walls in the High Priest's chamber because of his stubborn inability to show fear.

He lifted his chin and took Darius' hand without looking away from Excelsie. A sweaty palm connected with his. He closed his hand and walked forward, forcing Excelsie to either challenge him or yield.

"Prince Rathian gave Queen's Consort Stakel honoured guest status, General," Martin reminded the older man. "I'm sure he wouldn't be happy to hear that his orders were disregarded."

"Gods were smiling on you tonight, Villious. Someday they might not be." The threats were whispered as he and the page walked past.

Stakel knew Darius had heard the threat by the boy's sharp intake of breath. He squeezed the hand in his grip, telling Darius not to react. It was possible that Excelsie would take his anger out on the page and Stakel wouldn't allow that to happen.

The general hissed and pushed past them to stalk down the hallway. Looking at Martin, Excelsie growled, "I'll make sure the Imperator is informed of the attack."

Martin and Antioc caught up to them. Martin frowned, staring after Excelsie. The blond turned to ask Stakel, "Who attacked you?"

"Didn't see him. I'd slipped under the water to rinse off, and when I tried to come back up for air, hands held me under. I managed to break free and was surfacing. That's when I got hit on the head. Never saw anything to use as a clue."

Darius gestured to the door, indicating it was Stakel's room. Martin and Antioc joined them, watching in silence while Darius helped him dress. He ran his hand over the soft linen tunic. The dark green fabric caressed his skin. He'd never felt anything like it before. Any clothing he'd had in the Consorts was rough and he'd always been happier without the clothing on. Which was what the queen and her priests had wanted.

"Dinner will be waiting for us in our suite," Antioc reminded him.

Stakel smiled at the other men. He'd got lost in the sensations surrounding him. Reaching out, he cupped the smooth skin of Darius' face. A shy grin crossed the page's lips. Without thinking, he leant forward and brushed a kiss over the boy's cheek.

"Thank you."

Darius nodded and turned away, gathering dirty clothes and straightening the room. Antioc chuckled, grabbed Stakel's arm then dragged him from the room.

"Poor kid is going to have a crush on you," Antioc commented.

"I'd never do anything. He's not old enough." Shock raced through Stakel.

"Where have you been living? Do you really think Darius and the other pages haven't been fooling around with each other?" Martin shook his head. "The ducenti don't involve themselves with the pages until they are old enough to be inducted into the units."

Antioc stroked a finger over Martin's cheek. "That's how I spotted Martin. I waited until he took the oath and then I seduced him into my bed. It wasn't easy, though."

"I wasn't about to make it easy on you. As much as I wanted you, I knew I had to make it a challenge or you'd fuck me once and move on to someone else. From the first moment I saw you, I'd planned on being with you for a long time." Martin nuzzled into Antioc's hand.

Stakel watched the lovers with deep interest. He'd never seen anything like the gentleness with which these two men touched each other. Soft fingers trailing over a chin. Lips meeting in a whisper of a kiss. Antioc pushed Martin back against the wall. They had perhaps forgotten about Stakel being there. Martin's head fell back as Antioc kissed his neck. Passion-glazed eyes met Stakel's and the young soldier gasped.

"Antioc, love, we can't do this here." Martin tugged on Antioc's auburn curls, easing his lover away from him.

"Please don't stop on my account." Stakel's cock was hard and he wanted to explore the tingling his body had been feeling since the two men had started.

Antioc groaned but moved to stand beside Stakel. The sub-commander's gaze skated over the bulge at Stakel's groin. Slapping the Villious on the shoulder, Antioc winked.

"Wait until after dinner. I think we might be able to give you more of a show." Antioc held out his hand to Martin. "Let's get to our rooms and eat. I want you well-fed before I take you."

Martin took Antioc's hand and pulled him down the hall, eagerness showing in every step. Stakel followed, unsure about the excitement rising in him. The rest of the night looked to be very informative.

# Chapter Ten

Stakel leant back against the cushions, his hands resting on his stomach. Groaning, he pushed the plate away. He smiled at the page cleaning up the remains of their dinner. A whimper caught his ear and he turned his attention to the couple across the floor from him.

Martin and Antioc were wrapped around each other, their lips locked together. Both men were naked, having stripped before dinner. Stakel admired their dark skin gleaming in the firelight. Martin arched as Antioc's hand trailed down the younger man's spine to caress the small of Martin's back. Stakel shifted to sit closer to the couple. A shot of desire ran through him when Martin moaned.

"Would you like to touch?"

Stakel looked up to see Antioc staring at him. Before he could say anything, Martin leaned over and pressed his lips to Stakel's. Shock held him immobile for a moment, but a quick swipe of Martin's tongue over his bottom lip encouraged him to open to the blond Lancer. He reached out, touching Martin's shoulder, sliding his hand over the man's warm skin. Their tongues duelled, stroking and teasing.

Martin gasped and Stakel pulled away, glancing over Martin's shoulder to see Antioc's fingers playing along the crease of Martin's ass. Settling back, he let Antioc draw Martin onto the sub-commander's lap. He tapped his friend's nose and winked.

"I'll watch this time."

Antioc's knowing gaze met his and it was obvious the auburn-haired soldier understood Stakel's reluctance to join in. The sub-commander rolled Martin over to rest on the cushions between them. Antioc tasted Martin's throat with little nibbles as his hands slid down over Martin's stomach, cupping his erection.

Martin groaned, his eyes closing as Antioc flicked his nipple with his tongue. Stakel's cock hardened. His eyes widened while Antioc made his way down to where Martin's cock rested in Antioc's fist. Antioc knelt between Martin's spread thighs and licked his way up the length of Martin's cock.

Stakel sighed along with Martin. He focused on Antioc's tongue as it swirled over the flared purple head of Martin's shaft. Stakel wondered what the clear liquid forming drops at the slit tasted like. Antioc seemed to be enjoying it.

"Wasis," Martin whimpered and Antioc swallowed Martin's entire length.

Antioc's hands gripped Martin's hips and encouraged his lover to move. Amazement filled Stakel as the blond soldier began to fuck Antioc's mouth. Martin threaded his hands through Antioc's curls, holding the man still while Martin controlled the thrusts. Stakel reached out and stroked a finger over Antioc's hollowed cheeks.

"Here." Martin took Stakel's hand and touched the tip of Stakel's finger to Antioc's mouth.

The sub-commander sucked Stakel in and he was able to feel the tight suction created by Antioc on Martin's cock. Stakel bit his lip, swallowing the moan wanting to get free. His gaze was riveted on the joining point where Antioc met the blond nest at the base of Martin's shaft. He looked up at Martin.

"He's the best cocksucker I've met in the ducenti. He loves it." Martin managed a harsh chuckle. "Gonna spill, love."

Antioc hummed and Martin jerked. Lean hips lifted off the cushions. Antioc buried his nose into Martin's groin. Martin's eyes rolled back and his hips jerked. The most intense expression of pleasure Stakel had ever seen crossed the younger man's face. Antioc's throat worked until Martin stopped thrusting.

The sub-commander rocked back on his heels, licking and cleaning Martin's softened cock. He grinned up at the Villious and winked. "Now comes the really fun part."

Shooting up to his feet, he pressed a hard quick kiss on Stakel's lips, swiping his tongue into Stakel's mouth. A salty bitterness coated Antioc's tongue. Stakel chased after it, trying to get more of it, but Antioc pulled away.

"That's what Martin tastes like." Antioc leered at the blond soldier. "My favourite taste in the world."

Martin laughed softly. He waved a lazy hand towards the nightstand next to their bed. "Get the oil. We'll show Stakel that sex doesn't always mean pain."

Stakel frowned. Somewhere in the back of his mind, he'd always known that what he'd experienced at the hands of the priests and the queen wasn't the truest expression of love, or even sex for that matter. It was for that reason that he was willing to watch and learn. Maybe with the right man, he'd be willing to try.

Martin's hand covered one of Stakel's and squeezed. "Don't worry. When you and the Imperator come together, it'll be perfect."

"How do you know he wants me?" He wasn't sure why he didn't immediately protest the assumption of his attraction to Rathian.

"We've seen how he looks at you." Antioc joined them on the cushions. "He's never looked at anyone like that."

Martin placed a finger under Stakel's chin and lifted until their eyes met. "Trust us. Rathian wants you and if it hadn't been for his duty to the king, you would probably already be sharing his bed. He can be persuasive when he wants to be."

Antioc slapped Martin's hip. "Hands and knees, love."

Martin shook his head, never breaking the connection between him and Stakel. "I think I should be on my back for this, Antioc. Something tells me if you mount me that way, we might bring back some bad memories for our friend."

Stakel shrugged. Any memories he had of the orgies the Consorts and the queen engaged in were covered by a drug-induced fog. He had glimpses of positions and feelings, but nothing concrete. Those images only haunted him in his dreams.

"Fine with me. I like it better this way. I can see your face." Antioc leant down and kissed Martin.

Stakel eased away, putting a little distance between him and the couple. Martin kissed Antioc back, his hands trailing down Antioc's sides before dropping to wrap around Martin's knees. The blond spread his legs up and out, creating a cradle for Antioc to settle into. Antioc's fingers dipped into a small earthen jar he'd set next to them on the floor.

The sub-commander eased to his left, giving Stakel an unobstructed view of Martin's most private opening. Antioc's thumb rubbed over the little rose-like pucker and Martin moaned. Those lean hips tilted up as Antioc slid one finger all the way in.

Stakel's eyes widened. One finger became two and Martin started to beg.

"More, lover. Please, give me all of you." Martin's hips rocked as the blond impaled his ass on Antioc's fingers.

Three fingers slid in and Stakel saw a grimace almost like pain cross Martin's face. Then Antioc twisted his hand. Martin shook and his blue eyes glazed over with passion.

"Right there." Antioc winked at Stakel.

Somehow, Stakel didn't feel uncomfortable watching the intimate episode that was going on in front of him. Martin and Antioc wanted him to see what it was like to make love to someone instead of just having sex, or being forced into it.

"Antioc, going to spend if you keep that up," Martin warned.

"No, you won't. I want to feel you come on my cock. Wait one moment, love."

Antioc pulled his fingers out of Martin and reached for the jar again. Pouring a palm's worth of oil out, he coated his long cock and placed its head at Martin's opening. "Push," he ordered.

Martin bore down and Antioc thrust in. Stakel wasn't sure how it would all work, but within seconds, Antioc was buried balls deep into Martin's ass. All three men groaned. As Antioc started moving and Martin rocked with him, Stakel had the impression he was watching the ultimate expression of love between men. One making his body vulnerable to another and trusting that his lover wouldn't hurt him, but only bring him pleasure.

"Ah." Martin's back arched.

"Come, Martin. Come now." Antioc slid a hand between their bodies and stroked Martin's hard cock.

"Wasis," Martin shouted as white ropes of cum shot from his cock.

Stakel pumped his own cock, spreading the clear liquid dripping from the head over the entire shaft to ease his way.

"Gods," Antioc grunted, burying his cock deep into Martin and jerking. His head fell back and a frown of passion formed on his face. One. Two. Three thrusts and Antioc came.

Before Stakel could say anything, two hands joined his on his shaft. His balls tightened and his climax exploded through his body. Wet heat coated his hand, stomach and thighs. He fell back on the cushions, staring into the satisfied and happy gaze of Antioc and Martin. He'd never had a climax brought on by his own hand and for his own pleasure.

"Thank you," he said to the men who had shown him the joy of sharing his body with another person.

"You're welcome." Martin smiled.

Antioc rolled off and got to his feet. He padded over to grab a cloth and dip it in a bowl of water on the dresser. He cleaned all of them off before tossing the cloth towards the dresser. He lay down to one side of Martin and wrapped his arms around the blond. Martin snuggled back close to Antioc and held his arms out to Stakel.

"We have time for a nap before we have to return you to your room." Martin waited until Stakel moved over to him, before throwing an arm around the Villious' waist. "Besides, Prince Rathian won't be back from court for several hours yet."

Stakel shivered at the thought of touching the prince like Martin and Antioc had touched each other. His cock twitched and he decided the shiver wasn't from fear.

# Chapter Eleven

Rathian stood outside Sub-commander Antioc's room with his arm extended to knock on the door. When the sleepy-eyed page, Darius, had told him that Stakel had joined Antioc and Martin for dinner, Rathian had been surprised. Antioc seemed the least likely of his men to accept Stakel, but maybe Martin had more influence on Antioc than Rathian had thought. He also knew that Martin and Antioc liked to engage in trios and jealousy shot through him at the thought of Stakel joining in.

Before he could knock on the door, it opened and Stakel slipped out. The Villious' dark-brown eyes widened as he turned and saw Rathian standing there. Instead of backing away from him, like Rathian expected, Stakel reached up, cradled the back of Rathian's head in his hand and kissed the prince.

Shock held Rathian still until Stakel's tongue caressed his and he jerked. He crushed Stakel tight to his chest and plunged his tongue into the Villious' mouth. He traced down Stakel's scarred back and cupped his firm ass. Squeezing, he enjoyed the resilient skin under his fingers.

"Why are you naked?" He slid his thigh between Stakel's legs to give Stakel something to rub against.

"Umm…" Stakel's eyes glazed and Rathian could tell he was having trouble thinking.

"Were you going to wander the halls without clothes?" He wasn't sure why he kept asking when it didn't really matter. He should be dragging this willing man to his room and having his way with him.

Stakel nibbled along the line of Rathian's jaw, rubbing his cock along Rathian's thigh, and the prince moaned.

"Never mind," Rathian muttered, pushing Stakel back into the door. It was late enough there wouldn't be anyone around to notice them.

He encouraged his lover to move, rocking their hips together. A harsh groan tore from his throat as Stakel's long, hard erection brushed over his. Rathian kept one hand on Stakel's ass while managing to fit his other hand between them and grasp Stakel's shaft. The liquid seeping from Stakel's slit helped eased Rathian's strokes up and down. With each up stroke, he twisted his wrist, dragging his rough palm over the blunt head of Stakel's cock.

"Oh," Stakel murmured, hips pumping, driving his cock through the tunnel created by Rathian's hand.

The prince kept his grip while flicking Stakel's hard nipple with his tongue. Stakel's rhythm started to fall apart and the Villious' thrusts became rapid. Rathian clenched his fist tighter and drove Stakel towards the edge.

He teased Stakel's hole with his other hand, knowing that his lover was distracted by the impending climax. Rubbing his finger over the puckered opening, he sucked Stakel's nipple, enjoying Stakel's surprised gasp as he pressed just the tip of his finger in. Stakel stilled and Rathian pulled back to gauge Stakel's reaction. Stakel's eyes were closed and a frown creased his forehead.

"Is this all right?" Rathian asked, somehow coordinating a pump of his fist and a push of his finger.

The Villious didn't open his eyes, just bit his bottom lip and nodded. Stakel tilted his hips, taking more of Rathian in.

"Rathian."

The prince decided he liked his name said with such passion. He knew Stakel was close to spilling his seed, so he impaled Stakel with his finger, thrusting all the way in and hitting that spot inside.

"Gods."

Stakel's head went back, hitting the door with a thud, and his cock swelled. Wet heat spilled over Rathian's hand. The prince kept fucking Stakel with his finger while milking all the seed he could from the cock. Stakel relaxed against him with a sigh as Stakel's climax left him. Rathian eased out of the passage that seemed reluctant to let him go. He began to wipe his cum-covered hand on his tunic when Stakel stopped him.

The drowsy brown eyes studied the seed on his hand and his muscled stomach. Stakel's hand cupped Rathian's aching cock and Rathian groaned.

"Do you want to fuck me?" Stakel's question surprised the prince.

"I'd love to fuck that tight ass of yours, but not here. Our first time should be on a bed covered in furs and silks. We should have oil, not spit and cum." Rathian's heart had spoken those words. His head and his cock said it didn't matter. All they wanted was for him to be deep in Stakel's ass.

A soft smile graced Stakel's face and Rathian made a vow to do whatever he needed to keep that look on his lover. Stakel leant forward and pressed a gentle kiss on Rathian's lips.

"Next time you can seduce me. You can have candles, wine and a bed. Tonight, I just want you with nothing between us." The Consort untied the laces of Rathian's pants. "I always told myself that the things the Consorts, the queen and the priests did weren't love. It was about power, control and pain. I made sure to repeat those thoughts even while the drugs took hold and I lost myself among the fog. The scars on the outside of my skin have healed. Help me heal the wounds on my soul."

Rathian wasn't strong enough to turn down that plea and the feel of Stakel's rough hand stroking his cock. He scooped some of the still-wet cum off Stakel's stomach then reached around to press two fingers into Stakel's hole. The Consort's eyes widened and a silent moan issued from those lush lips. Rathian waited until Stakel shifted, indicating he was ready for the prince to move.

He took Stakel's lips, easing his tongue in and mimicking the movements of his fingers. Soon Stakel was joining in, sucking on Rathian's tongue and pushing his hips back to help the prince stretch him. Stakel didn't flinch when he introduced the third finger. A few pumps and Rathian knew he wouldn't be able to wait any longer. Just getting his lover ready brought him to the brink of his own climax.

"Will you take my cock into your mouth and get it wet for me?" He wasn't sure how Stakel would react to that.

The Villious dropped to his knees and sucked Rathian's cock.

"Wasis." Rathian stared down, feeling the flared head of his cock bump the back of Stakel's throat. "Get it good and wet." His voice was harsh.

Stakel's head bobbed. Rathian wrapped his hand around the base of his cock to ensure he didn't come. Shivers racked his body and a tingling pooled at the base of his spine.

Rathian tugged on Stakel's dark curls. "That's good. I'll come if you do anymore. Stand up, turn and face the door. It'll be easier this way."

Stakel nodded, turned and braced himself against the door. Rathian had a fleeting thought to being thankful no one was wandering the halls that night. He stroked four fingers out of Stakel's ass while lining his cock head up with Stakel's opening.

He placed his hand over the hourglass brand on Stakel's back. "I'm going to take you all the way. Afterwards, as soon as you're comfortable, let me know and I'll start moving. I'm not going to last."

Stakel's head dropped forward in a movement Rathian took to mean 'yes'. In one smooth steady stroke, Rathian buried himself in Stakel's tight ass. His balls hit the back of Stakel's thighs and both men groaned. The prince held Stakel's hips and forced his body to stay still, even though the urge to move almost overwhelmed him.

"Are you ready, Stakel?" He leant forward to drop a kiss on Stakel's shoulder, driving his shaft deeper.

Stakel grunted and his inner muscles clenched around Rathian. "Move."

He didn't need to be given the order twice. His climax blossomed through him and after only three thrusts he poured his seed into Stakel's inner passage.

"Stakel," he murmured, unable to think or breathe as he reamed his lover's ass.

Stakel massaged his cock, milking every last drop of seed from Rathian. When the last drop emptied from him, the prince collapsed on top of Stakel, his arms wrapped around Stakel's lean waist. Their breathing calmed together and Rathian's cock softened. He slid out of Stakel's warm channel.

Rathian eased away, barely managing to get his tunic off to clean them up. He turned Stakel around and embraced him. He pressed short kisses over the man's face, ending with a long kiss on the lush mouth that had tempted him for days.

"Thank you," he whispered against those lips.

Stakel blinked at him. "You're welcome. I think I'd like that bed now."

Rathian chuckled and slipped his arm around Stakel's waist, leading the sleepy man back towards his suite. They stumbled down the hallways but made it back to Rathian's room without running into anyone.

Rathian washed them both and tucked Stakel under the covers beside him. Stakel snuggled close.

Rathian asked, "Were you coming back to your room when we met outside of Antioc's?"

Stakel's words were so low Rathian had to lean in close to hear them. "Knew you were outside. Came to see you."

Rathian frowned. He hadn't knocked or made his presence known in any way. "How did you know?"

A gentle snuffle was his only answer. He chuckled softly, making a note to ask Stakel about it later.

# Chapter Twelve

Stakel shifted, his body protesting the noise intruding on his sleep. Quiet laughter danced in his ears. He rolled over onto his side and opened his eyes. Frowning, he studied the tapestry hanging on the wall in front of him. It didn't look like his room.

Another laugh drew his attention. Pushing up on his elbows, he glanced around the room. Rathian sat at a large desk and Darius stood next to him. Both men were studying something resting on the desk in front of them.

Curiosity got the best of him and he slid out of the bed, then padded over to see what they were looking at. Darius looked up as Stakel's shadow fell over them. Rathian smiled at the page's gasp.

"Stakel, my friend, we must do something about your tendency to wander around naked." Rathian reached out, stroking a finger over the top of Stakel's thigh. "I don't mind, but it's very distracting for my men."

A shiver twitched through him at the rough touch of Rathian's skin. "Sorry. I need some more clothes, I guess."

The prince measured him with his eyes. "We should be the same size. Darius, can you bring Stakel one of my shirts and pairs of pants?"

"Yes, Your Highness." Darius gave Stakel a shy smile.

"I see you've managed to win over my page." Rathian gestured to the chair on the other side of the desk.

Stakel shrugged. "He's a good boy. When he's old enough to take the Vanguard's oath, he'll be a welcome addition." He smiled at Darius as the page brought him a set of clothes. Darius held up the shirt and Stakel didn't argue as he helped him get dressed.

"Your bruises have disappeared," Darius remarked, running light fingers over Stakel's shoulders.

"I heal quickly, which is why I didn't need the healer last night."

"What happened last night that you would need a physician?" Rathian's voice was calm, but Darius winced.

Stakel squeezed the young man's hand. "I had a little accident in the bathing chambers and Darius was kind enough to help me. He worried my bruises would need to be looked at, but I convinced him I'd be fine." Leaving his shirt unbuttoned, Stakel fastened his pants and sat down in the chair. "Darius, is it possible to get some food this morning?"

"Yes, sir. I'll bring a tray for both you and His Highness." Darius bowed, relief shining in his eyes.

"What sort of accident?" Rathian's eyes narrowed and Stakel could tell the prince would dig until he learnt the truth.

A sigh eased out of Stakel's throat. He didn't see the point in describing the attack to Rathian. It was over and done with. He hadn't died, which was what his attacker had wanted, so the man had failed.

"Someone doesn't like me. I don't know who because I never saw his face." Stakel held his hand as Rathian rose to his feet, fury flushing his face. "It's over with, Rathian. There's no point in punishing anyone."

"I gave an order and someone disobeyed. That is punishable by death, Stakel. I can't allow my authority to be disregarded like that." Rathian stalked towards the door.

"So you'll punish all for the actions of one?" Stakel wasn't familiar with that sort of sweeping discipline.

Rathian turned back to look at him. "The ducenti works because I am the ultimate authority. They obey me, Stakel. When one flaunts me and breaks my commands, he endangers all his brothers. My men understand that they are responsible for their brothers' actions and so will be punished when even one of them breaks the rules." Rathian jerked the door open. "Darius, call for Excelsie and tell the commanders to assemble the men in the courtyard."

"Wasis," Stakel muttered, following the prince. This wasn't how to win friends in the Vanguard. Hatred would certainly set in after this morning

After issuing the order, Rathian bathed, shaved and dressed in the purple and white of the Launioc royal house. Rathian's burning gaze traced over Stakel's body. "We need to get you boots."

The calmness that the words implied was a lie. Stakel could tell anger had settled over Rathian like a cloak. The barely controlled fury held Rathian's back straight and made his gestures crisp.

Darius returned. "The men are assembling as ordered, Your Highness."

Rathian stalked from the room, pointing at Stakel and Darius as he left. "You two, come with me."

Reluctance dogged Stakel's every step. He understood why Rathian had to do this, but he didn't want to watch. He was an enemy soldier, yet they were going to be punished because of him.

Darius touched his arm. "I'm sorry," the page whispered, keeping an eye on the prince.

"For what?" Stakel kept his voice low.

"For asking about the bruises. I didn't realise no one had informed the Imperator." Darius' cheeks were pale. "I've never seen him so angry."

"I'm sure someone would have told him before long," he tried to reassure the boy. "It seems a good thing for you that you were the one who said something."

General Excelsie met them at the bottom of the staircase. "Sir, what is this about?"

Stakel met the general's disgusted gaze.

"*Such irrational hatred towards you,*" the voice pointed out.

"*Not irrational when you consider the fact that I'm the enemy.*" He answered silently, not wanting to speak in front of the general.

"*Maybe, but I would keep an eye on him.*"

Stakel didn't reply.

"I've been informed about an incident that happened while I was at court last night." Rathian's words were fierce.

Excelsie blinked and the prince growled. A single step brought them nose-to-nose. "You knew about the attack and you failed to alert me."

Excelsie's words were halted before he could do anything other than open his mouth.

Rathian waved an imperious stroke of his hand. "Stand with the men. Your punishment will be forthcoming."

Excelsie saluted and bowed before turning to march to the courtyard.

"He won't be sending me gifts any time soon," Stakel muttered.

Darius stifled a giggle while buttoning up Stakel's shirt. "Some of them believe you're no more than a barbarian. An uncouth mountain man. You must present an appearance to make His Highness proud."

He wasn't sure why his appearance would make Rathian proud, but he let the page fuss with his clothes. His own gaze never wavered from the tense figure of the prince. Rathian stood, staring up at a shield hanging above the door leading out of the manor.

*"He prays."*

*"Prays? For what?"*

*"Guidance. Courage to do what he must. Strength to control his anger."* A hint of laughter tinged the voice. *"Patience."*

*"Patience? Why?"*

*"That's something you'll find out later, I'm sure."*

"It's time." Rathian straightened his shoulders and gripped his sword.

Stakel met his green eyes and nodded. This was Rathian's world and by some twist of fate, he'd become a part of it.

He and Darius walked ten paces behind Rathian, who made a stunning image. The prince was dressed in a fitted white tunic with tight purple sleeves. His black leather pants were moulded to every muscle in his lower body. Stakel had to look away, his lust threatening to make itself known in an inappropriate way.

They stood on the front steps overlooking the courtyard where fifty-five men stood. Fifty of the men were the ones Rathian had brought back to the capital city when the prince had been recalled. The other five were the quainary who had brought Stakel from the front lines.

Stakel looked over the soldiers. He didn't see any emotion on their faces — even Excelsie had managed to conceal his hatred. The men stood, dressed in red and black, waiting for their commander's words.

"Yesterday, before I left, I issued a royal order stating that Stakel, a Villious resident and former Queen's Consort, should be treated as an honoured guest. He was to be given the same respect you would give one of your commanders." The breeze caught Rathian's voice and carried it out over the yard.

"I was assured by General Excelsie that he would inform my men about my order. I'm not interested in knowing whether he did or not." Rathian shot Excelsie a glare. "What I am interested in knowing is why I wasn't informed about the blatant disregard of my orders."

Puzzled frowns appeared on the men's faces. Stakel noted their confusion. *"So the attack was the work of one man."*

*"There's more than one snake in this bunch."*

Stakel didn't doubt that.

"Why did I learn about the attack on my guest from my page?" Rathian gestured to Darius. "A boy who hasn't even taken our oath yet."

Stakel spotted Antioc and Martin standing side by side to his left. He wondered if they would blame him for their punishment.

"Aside from the harm inflicted on my guest and the disrespect shown to him, how dare you disobey a direct order?" Rathian's words cut like knives into his men—Stakel could see them react. If words could wound, the Vanguard would be bleeding now.

"This attack is a daring disregard of my authority. My word is law. When you took the oath to join the ducenti, you vowed to obey me in all things. Someone has broken their oath and because he has, you all are responsible for his violating our code."

Stakel shivered. The blazing heat of Rathian's fury had cooled into icy disappointment.

"When I became Imperator, I vowed not to command with sword and whip. Forcing you to obey me by making you fear me was cruel and barbaric. I believed we were better than the regular army." Rathian paced from one side of the steps to the other. "I guess I was wrong. So if violence and blood is the only way to get you to obey me, then that is what we will have."

Rathian turned to Darius. "Page, go to my arms instructors. Ask them to come and bring the whips."

"Yes, Your Highness." Darius bowed and raced away.

Stakel bit his tongue. He had to stay quiet. It wasn't any of his business how Rathian disciplined his men.

"Sub-commanders and General Excelsie, you will take the punishment for your men. As commanders, you are responsible for the men in your units. Remember each of you is your brother's keeper. The actions of one are the actions of all."

The arms instructors came and the sub-commanders stripped off their tunics.

"Twenty lashes for the sub-commanders, Arms Master. Forty for General Excelsie." Rathian stared down at his second-in-command. "Your punishment is worse because of your wilful disregard of my authority."

When Antioc stepped forward to join the other men, Stakel moved towards the prince. He wouldn't let Antioc take a whipping for something Stakel knew he didn't do. Darius grabbed his arm. Glaring down at him, Stakel tugged at the hand holding him.

"You must not interfere." Darius shook his head.

"He didn't do anything wrong." Stakel trembled.

"Most of them didn't." Darius' gaze skittered to Excelsie and back to Stakel. "But the prince has spoken and Antioc must obey him. The only law we live by is the law of the Imperator. Our obedience to him is absolute—or it should be. Disobedience leads to discontentment. If the men are unhappy or distrustful of their commanders, then mutiny brews."

The first swing of the whip whistled through the air and struck flesh. Stakel flinched, his skin burning like he was the one who had received the blow. He turned so he wouldn't have to look.

"I don't want to be here. I don't want to watch." His throat started to close up. Breathing became hard.

"I know." A rough hand took the place of Darius' smaller one.

He glanced up enough to see Rathian was standing next to him. The prince didn't look at him, his gaze focused on the men being punished in front of him. Rathian's grip got tighter with each stroke of the whip. Stakel realised that even though Rathian had ordered the whipping, he regretted doing it.

"This was not supposed to happen. I was never going to punish my men using whips, watering this ground with their blood. Centuries ago, the Imperator ruled with love, not fear. I wanted to go back to those traditions, but someone has chosen to defy me."

Stakel could barely make out Rathian's voice over the hiss of the whip. He didn't whimper as the pain in his arm got worse.

"Some practices are hard to break. Your men know you love them. They will see how much this hurts you. I think they will love you more for ordering this because if you didn't, they would see you as weak." Stakel gritted his teeth.

After that, they suffered in silence as the five sub-commanders and General Excelsie endured their punishments. The only one to cry out was Excelsie, at the last stroke across his striped back.

Rathian stepped forward. "Take them to their rooms. Send for the medicus. He'll treat their backs. Remember, each one of you is responsible for every other man in the ducenti. The punishment will be worse next time I am disobeyed."

Darius tugged on Stakel's arm, waking him from the trance he'd fallen into, and led him back into the manor. Rathian caught up with them just before they got to the stairs.

"I'll have Darius find you when the medicus is finished with Antioc. Your healing power will help him more than any medicine our healers can give him."

Stakel stared into the prince's eyes, seeing sadness and pain swirling in their depths. He longed to help heal Rathian's heart, but he knew the man wanted to be alone to deal with what he saw as the failure of his dreams. Without thought or care, he leant forward and kissed Rathian, putting all the affectation he felt for the prince in it.

He pulled away. "If Antioc will see me, I'll go to him. Sit in the sunshine in your garden. Accept what you had to do today. Don't let it eat at you. There is one of your men who hides great hatred in his heart. We'll find him and destroy him."

Rathian nodded and Stakel watched him wander out of the main hall towards a door that must have led to the garden. Two guards followed him. When the prince disappeared, Stakel looked down at Darius.

"I'm going to need your help, Darius. Gather some herbs to make tonics and lotions. If we have enough, we can send them to all of the men who were whipped today." He grimaced. "Even Excelsie. They will help heal them faster."

"Give me a list, sir, and I'll see what I can find."

He told the page what he wished for and the boy raced off to find the ingredients. Stakel made his way to his room, constructing the recipes and formulas in his mind for the healing potions.

# Chapter Thirteen

Stakel stopped, reluctant to knock on Antioc's door. For the first time he could remember, he was worried someone might be angry with him. It was a strange feeling since he'd never cared before. His fellow Consorts had loathed him and the feeling had been mutual.

"What are you waiting for?" Darius grumbled from where he stood beside Stakel. "This tray isn't getting lighter."

Stakel glared down at the page. "How do you know they'll even let me in? I'm the reason Antioc received his whipping in the first place."

Darius rolled his eyes and sighed. The boy kicked the door twice. "You're feeling guilty for something that wasn't your fault at all. Odd, because you don't strike me as a martyr."

Martin opened the door. A bright smile erupted on his troubled face.

"Who is it?" Antioc's strained voice spoke of pain.

"Stakel and Darius." Martin stepped back, waving them in. "Come in. What did you bring us?"

"Food." Darius set the tray down on the table by the window.

"I came to heal you, Antioc. You shouldn't have been disciplined. You didn't do anything." Stakel went to the bed where the soldier lay on his stomach.

The curtains had been opened to allow the afternoon sun in. He closed his eyes, blocking the wounds from his sight.

"Can you really heal Antioc's back?" Martin brushed past him to sit beside Antioc.

*"You've seen worse,"* the voice reminded him.

*"I know, but it's never been someone I liked before this."*

*"So you've said. Could it be you're learning what having a friend is like?"*

Stakel wasn't sure if that was the issue or not. He just knew that he didn't like seeing Antioc hurt.

"Sir, can you heal the sub-commander?" Darius poked him.

"Yes, I can. The other men have received tonics and lotions I've infused with healing properties. You get it straight from me." He went around the bed to sit opposite Martin.

He placed his right hand on the nape of Antioc's neck, his little finger touching the first lash mark. "Usually it works best for me to place my hand directly on the wound. Yours are such that as long as I'm touching one, they'll all heal."

"What would you like us to do?" Martin asked in a low murmur.

"Do you have a god you pray to?" Stakel wasn't sure about Launioc gods.

"The ducenti have always asked for guidance from Xasel, our High God. He's the father of the new gods and has fallen out of favour with our temples now," Antioc informed Stakel. "The men of the ducenti know the miracles the High God performed and we'll always worship him."

"Pray to Xasel then and hope he'll answer."

Stakel closed his eyes, steadied his breathing and imagined the wounds marring Antioc's back. He sank deep into Antioc's body, finding the paths through which his blood travelled. He knitted those together. With pulses of energy, he encouraged the growth of new muscle and the mending of the sliced skin.

He didn't loosen his control on the healing until he was sure he'd found and treated every injury. When he felt the last one close, he opened his eyes and allowed the energy to slip away. Antioc's back was marked with several faint pink lines. Stakel ran a finger over one and Antioc shivered.

"Your back will still be sore, but that'll disappear over the next few days." He stood and his knees buckled.

Darius was there to lend support as he made his way to a low couch close to the bed. Stakel settled down with a sigh. He'd need to rest soon.

A knock sounded and then Rathian came in. Martin and Darius saluted. Antioc struggled to sit up.

"Stay still, Sub-commander," Rathian ordered.

Stakel met the prince's gaze and saw more peace than pain in them. He gestured to the cushion beside him. "I'd show you some form of respect, but I'm afraid I'm too tired to do so."

"Too tired?" Rathian joined him on the couch. "Why? I see you've healed Antioc. Were his wounds so bad you had to use all your energy?"

He knew the thought upset the prince. He patted Rathian's hand. "No. I made medicines and sent them to the others. Any type of magic like that draws energy from me."

"Here's some wine and food, sir." Darius handed him a plate before setting his wine glass beside him. "Would you like something, Your Highness?"

Rathian shook his head and the page served the others. Stakel knew the prince hadn't eaten at all since they'd missed breakfast. He broke off some crust from his bread and held it up to Rathian.

"You have to eat. With us, you may show weakness, but in front of the others, you have to stay strong."

Rathian nibbled on the bread in Stakel's hands, then used his tongue to clean the crumbs from Stakel's fingers. A moan threatened to slip out. His cock filled as desire flooded him. He was thankful for clothes. Rathian winked and sat back.

"Who was supposed to inform me about the attack on Stakel?" The prince's gaze swept between Martin and Antioc.

Both men dropped their eyes. An obvious reluctance stiffened their bodies.

"General Excelsie, sir," Antioc finally answered Rathian's question.

The prince frowned, accepting another bite of food from Stakel.

"Maybe it slipped his mind," Stakel suggested.

"Maybe, but Excelsie isn't known for forgetting things."

"He could have been on his way to tell you when you found out this morning."

*"Why are you working so hard to erase the doubt from his mind?"*

*"He's hurt that his friend would undermine him in such a way."* Stakel gave a mental shrug. *"I don't like it when he hurts."*

*"One night together and already you want to ease his pain. Maybe you don't need my help after all."*

"He should have been waiting for me when I returned home last night." Rathian shifted closer. "I stopped by my room before I came to find you. There wasn't even a note."

"We should have made sure someone was waiting for you." Antioc scowled.

"No. Your commander told you he would take care of it. You trusted him and he let you down." Rathian rested his hand on Stakel's thigh. "I'll deal with him. He seems to deserve more punishment than just a whipping."

Stakel leaned over and curled into Rathian's side. The warmth of the prince's body combined with his deep voice lulled Stakel into a light doze.

After a few minutes, Rathian moved and Stakel sat back up. His lover stood, holding out a hand to him. "Come on. I'll take you back to my room and you can rest."

"Thank you." He allowed the prince to pull him to his feet.

Martin and Antioc were getting dressed. Darius was gone.

Antioc walked over, looking at Rathian like he wanted permission for something. The prince nodded and Antioc gave Stakel a hug.

"Thank you for healing me. I don't blame you, Stakel. I blame the man who attacked you and the men who let it happen." Antioc smiled.

He accepted the hug then surprised himself by kissing the sub-commander's cheek. "You're welcome."

As they went out into the hallway, Rathian wrapped his arm around Stakel's waist, allowing him to use his body as a crutch. They made it to the prince's room and he let Rathian undress him. After climbing under the covers, he lay down with a sigh. Tension and exhaustion eased from his body.

"You were upset with me for ordering the whippings." It was a statement, not a question. "Why?"

Stakel rolled over onto his side, facing Rathian who sat in a chair next to the bed. "The priests whip the Consorts. I've seen too much of it."

"But…" Rathian's protest died when Stakel held up his hand.

"I understand why you did it, Rathian. You did it to discipline and achieve order. The priests do it to create fear and for their own pleasure." He shuddered. "They feed off the pain and blood."

Stakel's wrists burned as he remembered the hours he had hung from chains between the black pillars in the Senior Priest's chamber. He saw the dark streams of his blood flowing into the bowl under his feet.

"I'm sorry."

The prince's soft apology and gentle touch drew Stakel back. Rathian joined him in bed. He stroked his hand over Rathian's lightly furred chest, pausing to feel his heartbeat.

"There is no reason for you to apologise. You didn't wield the whips. You didn't draw my blood." Stakel curled his body up against Rathian's. "I can see the difference."

"Was it really bad?" Rathian trailed a hand down Stakel's back.

"You've never been whipped, have you?" Stakel closed his eyes, breathing in Rathian's scent.

"Not to the extent I imagine you have. I've been punished for things. I don't bear the scars from it. Maybe ten lashes, but nothing that would damage me." The prince's warm breath caressed Stakel's ear.

"Seeing Antioc's wounds brought back memories." He pressed his lips to one of Rathian's pectoral muscles.

"What kind?" The question was soft and Stakel knew Rathian wasn't sure about asking him.

"You see my ability to heal as magic and a miracle. For me, it is the gateway to hell." He pulled away and climbed out of bed. Naked, he wandered over to the window. Silver moonlight bathed the trees and plants. He placed his hand on the cool glass.

"The moment I entered the Queen's Temple, I became the rector's favourite play thing. He'd spend hours torturing me. In the rector's chamber, there are two black pillars. I never figured out what type of stone they are. Probably nothing created in this world."

He saw Rathian sit up and rest against the headboard. The faint light pouring through the window shaded his lover's face. A shiver raced over his skin. The shadows gave the prince a forbidden cast to his features.

"Torture you? Why would they do that? What kind of priests do they pretend to be?" A frown marred Rathian's forehead.

"They don't worship any god I've heard of. When I call them demons, I'm telling the truth. The priests come from some level of hell unknown to man." He shrugged. "I don't know why the others were tortured, except to inspire fear and dominance over them. I was a toy for the rector to use to hone his skills."

"Hone his skills?"

Stakel closed his eyes, seeing the leering smirk of the rector dancing in the dark. Whenever the demon had looked at Stakel, he had always felt like the creature had been trying to decide whether to eat him or just suck the soul out of him. He'd seen the results of both events and had done his level best to not let that happen to him. Unfortunately — or fortunately — his healing ability had saved him from that fate.

"He used me as a test subject. I've had strips of skin sliced off. I've been flayed alive. Almost all of my blood has been drained from my body. The healing power you see as magic has been a blessed curse for me. No matter what he did to me, I couldn't die. Some force outside of me would drag me back from the abyss. An abyss I was eager to jump into and lose myself in."

He was caught up in the past. Strong arms wrapped around his waist, pulling him tight against a warm chest. The cold that had been invading him from remembering disappeared at the prince's touch. Soft lips brushed his cheek.

"I can't imagine the world you come from, Stakel. It seems so different from mine." Rathian's words flowed over his ear.

"Your men would die for you out of love, not fear. The Consorts and the regular Villious army fight because they aren't afraid of dying. They're afraid of what else is in store if they lose."

He turned in Rathian's arms and pressed their mouths together. He didn't want to talk about the priests or the Consorts. He feared talking about them might draw their attention and he didn't want to risk the prince. One of the prince's hands slid up to cradle the back of his head. The other grasped his ass and pushed their groins together.

"We can find better things to do than discuss my pathetic past," Stakel whispered. He thanked the gods they were both naked as he sank to his knees in front of Rathian. He glanced up and met the prince's gaze.

"The last time you were kneeling like that, it was all I could do not to beg for your mouth on me," Rathian confessed.

Stakel grinned. "You don't have to beg now."

Leaning forward, he sucked just the crown of the prince's cock into his mouth. He swirled his tongue around the flared head, tasting the salty bitterness of Rathian. The prince rested one of his hands on Stakel's shoulder and entangled the other in his hair. Stakel didn't mind the tightness of his grip, knowing it was a simple urge to touch him, not control or force him.

He applied suction but didn't take any more of Rathian's shaft in. He slid his right hand over his lover's thigh to cup the prince's balls. His lover's hips jerked each time he pressed the tip of his tongue into the slit of the cock's head. Rathian moaned when Stakel teased the soft skin behind his balls.

"Are you going to torture me or suck me?" Rathian tugged gently on Stakel's curls.

Backing off and allowing his cock to pop from his mouth, Stakel winked up at the prince. "Torturing sounds good if I can get you to make those types of noises."

Rathian growled and a loud groan cut through the air as Stakel took his cock deep enough in his mouth that the head bumped the back of Stakel's throat.

"Wasis," Rathian cried.

Stakel swallowed around the prince's shaft, massaging it with his throat muscles. He brushed his teeth lightly over the velvet skin as he pulled back a few inches, hoping to give a little pain with the pleasure. Rathian jumped then pushed back in.

Humming his approval, Stakel relaxed his throat again and squeezed Rathian's balls, letting him know it was all right to move. Rathian started thrusting, stroking in and out of Stakel's mouth like he was taking Stakel's ass. Stakel moved his hands up to grip Rathian's hips while Rathian cradled the back of Stakel's head, holding him steady.

The prince's cock throbbed and lengthened. Stakel knew his lover was close to the edge. Reaching around, he slid his fingers along Rathian's crease and caressed the puckered opening to his body. Rathian shivered and thrust deep into Stakel's mouth, his seed exploding from his cock. Stakel drank it down like the finest Milinan wine.

He licked, cleaning Rathian's cock as it softened. After it slid out of his mouth, he placed a quick kiss on its head. His knees protested being on the cold stone floor and he started to climb to his feet. Rathian reached down, cupped his elbow and helped him up.

"Thank you, amator," Rathian whispered, pressing their lips together.

Stakel opened, welcoming the prince's tongue into his mouth. Rathian grasped Stakel's cock in his hand and pumped. He moaned, fucking Rathian's rough hand fast. All the sucking had made him hard and he knew it wouldn't be long before he exploded. Two more pumps. The last one ended with a swipe of the palm over his weeping head and a twist at the base of his shaft.

"Rathian," he whimpered, spilling his own seed over his lover's hand and on their stomachs.

Rathian held him until his climax ended, and they supported each other as they made their way back to the prince's bed. Rathian cleaned them up before they climbed under the blankets. Stakel rolled onto his side with Rathian cuddling close behind him, his arm wrapped around Stakel's waist.

A gentle kiss brushed over the nape of Stakel's neck and Rathian chuckled.

"We'll actually do this in my bed next time."

# Chapter Fourteen

Stakel woke up when warm lips brushed his. He opened his eyes to see Rathian leaning over him with a smile.

"I always wanted to wake someone up with a kiss," the prince teased, bending down to give Stakel another kiss.

"Bit of a dreamer, aren't you?" Stakel slid his hands along the short cut hair on the back of Rathian's head, pulling the man down for a real kiss. No teasing.

"No interruptions this time." Rathian's breath mingled with Stakel's. "Everyone should still be in bed."

"Good. No pages or generals to bother us."

Rathian crushed their mouths together. There was something addictive in the prince's taste that drove Stakel to want more. They teased and played with each other. Their tongues tangled in a sweet slow thrust and counter thrust. He trailed his fingers down Rathian's back, caressing each bump of the man's spine. Rathian moaned, arching his back and grinding his groin against Stakel's.

Stakel managed to brace his feet on the mattress and, lifting his hips, gave the prince something hard to rub on. Their cocks aligned and they stroked slow to start with. He leaned his head back on the pillow, encouraging Rathian to move down to his chest.

"Yes…" he hissed as the prince's mouth latched onto his nipple.

Keeping one hand behind Rathian's head and one on the prince's ass, Stakel stopping Rathian from stopping or pulling away. Teeth bit his flesh, tugging and pinching. His lover was making his nerve endings burn and his body ache. Pleasure pooled at the base of his spine and his dick leaked, making the movement of their cocks together easier. They rocked faster and harder.

"Soon," Stakel grunted.

He wrapped his leg around Rathian's thigh, urging the prince on. Rathian bit down hard and Stakel climaxed, spilling his seed all over their stomachs and chests. Rathian slowed slightly, undulating in gentle strokes. When Stakel stopped coming, he ran his fingers through Rathian's sweat-drenched hair.

"Take me," he ordered the prince.

"I'll get the oil." Rathian started to reach across the bed towards a small table.

"No. Don't worry about that." He grabbed Rathian's hand and sucked his fingers into his mouth. He got them good and wet.

Letting go, he hooked his hands behind his knees and spread his thighs, offering his ass to Rathian. "Don't take too long."

The prince's long fingers pressed into his inner passage, pushing deep. Three fingers were soon stroking in and out. He bore down and within seconds he was ready for more.

"Now," he told his lover.

Rathian spat in his hand and coated his dick. Stakel closed his eyes, exhaling as Rathian eased the flared head of his cock into Stakel's opening. His lover buried himself inside Stakel, nailing Stakel's spot and making him cry out.

"Ah!" was the only sound he could get out, because Rathian started riding him hard. Rough hands gripped his ass, lifting him up so he could feel him as far inside as he could possibly get. He moved the opposite way to Rathian's thrusts, feeling his second climax build.

"More," he begged.

Rathian dropped his hips and braced his hands on the mattress beside Stakel's shoulders. Stakel wrapped his legs around Rathian's waist. Rathian drove into him with grunts. Sweat dripped off his lover's skin to bead on his chest and roll off. One last deep stroke and Rathian stilled, flooding Stakel's channel with warm seed. The wash of heat filled him, pushing him over the edge into his second climax.

"Gods," he sighed.

When they stopped moving, Rathian collapsed on him. He encircled Rathian's body with his arms. They lay, entwined, until their breathing evened out. Rathian slid out and stood before strolling over to the bathing chamber. Stakel turned his head to watch his lover clean off. He gave Rathian a smile as the prince came back to wash him off.

He yawned and stretched, enjoying the muted tiredness in his muscles. "It's not time to get up." He patted the mattress next to him. "Join me in bed."

Rathian climbed back under the blankets and snuggled closer to him. Stakel's eyelids grew heavy and he went to sleep with Rathian's body keeping him warm.

* * * *

Later that afternoon, Rathian and Stakel wandered through the hallway of the manor and down the grand staircase. The prince pointed out the portraits of his ancestors.

"When you look at the portraits, the man in the front is the Imperator of the ducenti. Tradition demands we always wear the purple and white of Launioc royalty when we go into battle." Rathian smiled up at the painting of his uncle.

"Who are the men in the back?" Stakel gestured to one farther down the wall.

Rathian moved over to stand beside his lover and see which commander he had pointed at.

"That is Sillinga, my great-great-great-great-grandfather, or as we say here, my fourth grandfather. The man behind him is Lonte, his Custos." Rathian always enjoyed remembering the stories he'd heard about Sillinga and Lonte.

"His Custos?" Stakel eased behind Rathian as they made their way down the rest of the steps, seemingly to guard the prince's back.

"Yes." Rathian grabbed Stakel's hand, leading him out into the garden.

They sat on a blanket under a Cognaki tree. Stakel leaned his back against the trunk and Rathian rested his head on Stakel's lap.

"I told you before, the Custos is the Imperator's true second-in-command. He's so much more, though. The Custos is a bodyguard and a lover. The truest friend and the person the Imperator expects to be totally honest with him." Rathian closed his eyes, loving the feeling of Stakel's hand running over his hair.

"Is the Custos the reason the Imperator doesn't play around with his men?" Stakel's question was soft.

"Once they pair up, the leader of the ducenti has no reason to look for love or sex from anyone else. In many ways, the Custos is the other half of the Imperator." Rathian chuckled. "Take Sillinga. He was horrible at war. Didn't understand strategy or battle tactics. Sillinga was a terrible soldier, but he was great at creating peace."

"Creating peace?" Stakel rubbed his thumb over Rathian's lips.

"Aye. Sillinga was best known for his treaties. When the wars or skirmishes were over, he would get the best concessions from the vanquished, but in ways that wouldn't embarrass the other side."

Rathian licked Stakel's thumb and the tang of salt teased his tongue.

"If he couldn't fight, how did he win any of his battles?" Stakel's voice became husky.

"Sillinga's secret weapon was Lonte. His Custos was one of the most brilliant military minds in Launioc history. He never lost a battle. His trouble was he had no diplomacy. Lonte hated dealing with nobles and royals because he loathed the intrigue and lies. Sillinga had to do some fancy talking to stop several wars from breaking out because of Lonte."

Rathian pressed his cheek against the hard bulge at Stakel's groin. He smiled at Stakel's moan.

"The Imperator and the Custos complement each other. Where one is weak, the other one is strong. That is one of the gifts of the ducenti."

Rathian was done talking about his ancestors. He placed an open-mouthed kiss on Stakel's leather-covered erection. The Villious tensed. Rathian looked up to see Stakel frowning down at him.

"What's wrong?"

"We shouldn't do this out here." Stakel waved a hand to encompass the garden.

"Says the man who enjoyed having sex with me in the hallway," he teased.

"No one was around. Anyone can see us out here." Stakel's cheeks flushed.

"No one will mind. My men will be thrilled to see that we're enjoying each other's company." He sat up, cupped Stakel's face in his hands and pressed a kiss to his lips.

Stakel moaned and slid his arms around Rathian's waist. Maybe that was the key, Rathian thought. Don't give him time to talk.

Stakel's mind went blank. With Rathian's lips devouring his, he couldn't think of a reason why he should protest. Rathian nibbled on his top lip and then stroked inside his mouth with his tongue.

"Please," he moaned.

"With pleasure," Rathian replied before taking the kiss deeper.

In seconds, Stakel found himself lying on his back with Rathian pressing between his legs. He spread his thighs, offering his body to his lover. They rocked their hips together, creating marvellous sensations that enveloped him.

"Your Highness." A loud, nervous cough sounded from the other side of the garden.

"If we ignore him, I'm sure he'll go away," Rathian whispered in Stakel's ear as he ground his groin against Stakel's.

Stakel couldn't manage anything more than a nod. A tingling at the base of his spine warned him that his climax was near. He slid his hands down and cupped Rathian's ass, encouraging the man to rub faster.

"Your Highness."

The voice sounded closer and got louder. Stakel could hear the impatience and insistence in the tone. Rathian groaned and rolled to the side.

"Gods blessed, boy. The Villious better bloody well be attacking the manor or I'll strangle you for interrupting," Rathian growled.

Stakel rested his hand on Rathian's arm. "Calm down. He's only doing his job, love." Stakel turned to glance up at the herald dressed in purple and white. "Looks like your father wants you again."

"Yes, sir. The king wishes you to attend tonight's ball. Your brother has returned from Milina and his engagement to the Milinan princess is to be announced tonight." The herald's eyes were averted from the men.

"Great news for Travi and for us." Rathian leapt to his feet and reached down to help Stakel stand.

"Why?" Stakel matched Rathian's determined strides, heading back into the manor.

"Travi actually loves this girl and has been trying to get her father to agree to a match for two years now. I'm glad to see it worked out." Rathian sent Stakel a wink. "In two days' time, you and I will be heading back to the front lines. I won't need to be around anymore since Travi can take my place."

"Two days' time? Won't you need more than that to get the men ready?" Stakel was surprised. It took the Queen's Army weeks to get ready to move out.

"No. If Excelsie has been doing his job, we could conceivably move out right now, but I want to spend some time with my brother. I haven't seen him in months and he's the only one of my family I like." Rathian dashed up the stairs while Stakel trailed behind.

Stakel frowned. In all the memories he still had of his mountain village, the most vivid one was of him and his younger brother fishing in a chilly stream. It had been early spring, so ice had lined the edges of the bank. The cold hadn't bothered them. They had spent all winter shut up in their cottage and then it had been time to run and play.

Stakel stopped and closed his eyes. He felt the weak spring sun on his skin and heard his brother Bale's high-pitched laughter. A sharp stab of loneliness tore through his gut. He was building a place for himself here in Launioc and in the arms of the Imperator, but he was an outsider to their ways. He longed to look upon his brother's face, to stare into eyes that were so like his own. He wondered if he would ever return to his home.

*"Someday you'll go back."* The voice's tone had been kind.

*"You have been silent lately."* Stakel wasn't going to ask when he would return. He feared that his going home would mean he had to leave Rathian and he wasn't sure he was willing to do that.

*"You didn't need me around while you learnt about each other."* Laughter sounded in his mind. *"I would have been in the way and things were going well enough without me."*

*"Now we are moving back to the front lines. Do you think he'll ask me to fight against my own people?"*

*"It could happen, but if it was kill one of your countrymen or risk Rathian's life, what would you choose?"*

There was no hesitation in his answer. *"I'd kill him them to save the prince. Rathian has given me a world I never believed in before. I won't lose him."*

"Stakel, are you coming to help me get dressed?" Rathian's voice drifted down the hallway.

He smiled. "I'll be right there. I'm sure Darius can help you until I arrive."

*"You won't be losing him any time soon."*

A gentle breeze swept over Stakel's cheek and he felt oddly comforted.

# Chapter Fifteen

Rathian stood in a corner of the ballroom. He hadn't been able to talk to Travi before the dinner and ball had begun, but they had made plans to meet the next morning for a ride. He smiled. Most of his life had been filled with training to be the Imperator and learning the ways of the ducenti, but he and Travi had managed to spend a great deal of time together while growing up. He missed having his older brother nearby.

His father caught his eye and gestured for him to join the group of men gathered around the king. Sighing, he left his comfortable hiding spot and strolled over there. He didn't like the lackeys who fawned over his father and hung on every word the king said. They never told the man he was crazy for having started this damn war. Just once, he wanted one of them to speak his mind and tell his father what he really thought of him.

"Rathian, I'd like you to meet..."

Before the king could finish, a page came rushing up to Rathian. "Your Highness, you're needed back at the manor."

"What's wrong?" Rathian didn't acknowledge his father or the men. He focused on the page.

"Not sure, sir. Just received word that your presence is needed. I took the liberty of ordering your horse saddled. He should be waiting outside for you."

He clapped the young man on the shoulder. "Thank you."

Stalking through the crowd, he made his way to the entrance. Travi caught him there.

"Where are you going?"

"Something's happening at the manor. I have to go." He smiled at his brother. "Congratulations, brother."

"Thank you, and I'll be at the manor in the morning for our ride." Travi nodded but didn't try to detain him any longer.

Rathian raced down the steps and leapt into the saddle. Swinging his horse around, he pointed his mount towards the manor. He nudged it once with his heels and they took off. His charger was used to travelling at speed and didn't fight him. It settled down into a ground-covering gallop. The moon was high, lighting the road and making it easy for Rathian to see.

What could have happened that Excelsie would pull him away from a court function? No matter that his second-in-command knew how much Rathian hated those things, Excelsie would never have summoned him unless it was an emergency. Events rolled around his mind, but the only ones he could think of involved Stakel.

He clenched the reins and his horse's head came up slightly. Relaxing his grip, he urged the gelding on.

Things had been calm for the most part since he had punished the men for the first attack on Stakel. Whoever hated his lover must have been biding his time.

Thundering up the manor's lane, he noticed a large group of men standing outside the arms practice arena. His mount plunged to a stop and he flung himself off, reaching for the man closest to him. It turned out to be Antioc.

"Report, Sub-commander," Rathian ordered.

"Sir." Antioc saluted. "About forty minutes ago, your honoured guest was dragged from your room and brought here to the arms arena. Inside are about twenty armed men. After being thrust in, someone locked the doors and we have been unable to break them open."

"These men? Are they of the ducenti?" He studied the oversized wooden doors, wondering if the best way to enter would be to break them down or find a second way in.

"No, sir. We obey your orders. We would never touch Stakel." Antioc's protest sounded sincere.

Rathian nodded. He'd worry about how Stakel had been taken later. At that moment, his first concern was to get into the arena and help save his lover.

"There's a hallway running the perimeter of the arms arena. We should be able to see what's happening." He glanced at Martin. "Lancer, take four of the best archers, grab your bows and get up to that walkway. Shoot to kill. That's a direct order."

Martin saluted, his blue eyes solemn. Rathian knew the seriousness of his order. It would be the first time the ducenti had ever fired upon their Launioc army brethren. He didn't say that order lightly, but again his authority had been questioned. Not by his own men—though one of his men had to be involved.

He gathered Antioc and the other men to him. "There's another way in. Gather your swords and come."

Before they could round the corner towards the second door, hidden behind a tapestry, Martin called to them.

"Sir, you should come and see this."

"Lancer, we don't have time for this," Rathian pointed out.

"I don't think Stakel needs our help, sir." Martin's voice had held a measure of respect for the Villious.

Rathian took the stairs two at a time and joined Martin at one of the viewing windows. His jaw fell open at the sight greeting him.

Stakel stood in the middle of the arena, surrounded by five men. Fifteen other bodies were scattered around the floor. Rathian couldn't tell if they were all dead or injured. He tried to hide his glee at the thought that Stakel might have killed them. It would mean less work for Rathian in punishing them.

His lover held a short double-edged blade in his right hand and a longer curved blade in an under-handed grip in his left. Stakel weaved his swings together, making the blades blur and sing in the air. It was like watching the most intricate and deadly dance Rathian had ever seen. The Villious flowed from spot to spot, stopping only long enough to see if any of the soldiers would challenge him. The ones left standing were the intelligent fighters. They had seen their fellow soldiers die quickly at the hands of this man. They were re-thinking their strategy.

Stopping, Stakel held the short sword to his chest and seemed to say something. Rathian was too far away to hear what it was. Some movement must have clued his lover in to an attack coming from the man right in front of him. A burst of gold light blinded them all. Rathian blinked, trying to clear his vision.

When the flash dissipated, another man was down on the floor, Stakel standing over him. Stakel raised his head, meeting Rathian's eyes. Even from his distance, he could see Stakel's brown eyes glowed with anger and the power surging through the man's body.

*"You must end this,"* a strange voice commanded him.

*"Why? Stakel has it under control."* He wasn't sure why he was arguing with a voice in his head. He stared down at Stakel, arousal flaring to life in his body. This was a side of his lover he'd never seen before. The fierce warrior more than capable of holding his own in battle. Rathian longed for the day when Stakel would join him on the battlefield.

*"If you don't stop this, more will die. His control is wavering and the power will consume him. Innocents will die."* The voice was compelling.

Rathian gestured for Martin and the archers to ready their bows. He stepped into the gallery overlooking the arena.

"Stop." His order ripped through the room, causing a wave of shock to shake the Launioc soldiers. "Drop your weapons and kneel."

Stakel didn't take his eyes off the soldiers in front of him. "It's about time you got here."

"Sorry. Can you unlock the door?" He pointed to where they stood.

"Don't let them stab me in the back." Stakel tucked the short sword into his belt and strolled to the exit. With a twist of his wrist and a push, they swung open.

Antioc and the other members of the ducenti rushed in, gathering the weapons and checking all of the fallen soldiers. Stakel crossed his arms and glared at the men.

"None of them should be hurt too badly. I knocked most of them out. Though there is one with a very deep chest wound. I hamstrung one as well." Stakel's voice was dispassionate.

Rathian knew killing was second nature to the Villious. "Why didn't you kill them?"

Stakel shot him a look. "Because they aren't my enemy. They were obeying orders from someone else. I won't kill the messenger, just the man who sent them."

A cold shiver raced down Rathian's spine. The promise in Stakel's voice gave the prince pause. He didn't know much about Stakel, but he did know the man was powerful enough to fulfil his promise. Rathian had a feeling things were going to get interesting in his world.

Stakel made no move to help the Lancers carry the unconscious men out of the arena. He picked up the long sword from where he'd set it and wandered over to where a cloth lay on a bench. Straddling the bench, he placed the long and short swords next to each other and started cleaning the blades. He ignored the noises behind him, allowing the power swirling in him to dissipate in the earth below him.

Silence filled the arena and he knew there was only one other person left with him. He didn't acknowledge Rathian. Stakel's anger wasn't directed towards the prince. Rathian didn't believe in subterfuge. If he wanted Stakel dead, he would have killed him when Excelsie had first brought him to the manor. It was silly to think that the prince wouldn't do whatever he had to do to keep Launioc safe, even seducing an enemy, but Stakel hoped deep in his heart that the pleasure they'd shared during their love making wasn't based on a lie. Footsteps approached from the doorway. He continued wiping the blades. When Rathian paused, Stakel felt the heat of a hand hovering above his shoulder. He sensed the prince's reluctance to touch him.

"It seems I have made an enemy among your men, Imperator," he commented, checking the short blade for nicks along the edges.

"So it would seem, though the men who attacked you were regular army. Not my men." Rathian's voice held fury in its depths.

"I know who they were, but it makes no sense for the regular army to attack me without some instruction from one of the Vanguard." He placed the swords on the cloth farther down the bench and swung around, facing the prince who had been standing directly behind him.

"True. I promise you I'll find out who ordered this and I'll punish them swiftly." Rathian's hands were clenched and resting on his hips.

Stakel's gaze rested on the bulge at Rathian's groin. The height of the bench placed him at the perfect level. He reached out and hooked his finger into the waistband of Rathian's linen trousers. Tugging Rathian forward, he found his interest in the attack waning for the moment.

"We'll deal with the transgressor together, but later. Right now, you're going to fuck me here for the entire world to see." He leant forward and blew a hot, moist puff of air over the prince's straining erection. Looking up into Rathian's blazing green eyes, he grinned.

"Then we're going back to your room and I'll fuck you."

# Chapter Sixteen

Rathian's eyes widened and Stakel chuckled. "Never been fucked before, my prince?"

"Um...no." Rathian shook his head.

"Don't worry. I think you'll like it." Stakel pushed Rathian back a little so he could stand up. He stripped his pants off with quick, efficient movements. His chest was covered with dirt and blood, but he didn't think either of them cared about that. He stepped forward to whisper in Rathian's ear, "I promise no one will know."

He trailed his hands down Rathian's chest and unbuttoned the sleeveless tunic his lover wore. He jerked it off and flung it aside, not caring where it ended up. Rathian's linen pants were light and Stakel tore them off with deft twists of his hands. Rathian gasped. Stakel fondled the prince's balls, playing with them. He pressed the pad of one finger against the soft skin behind them, caressing it lightly. Rathian's large hands gripped Stakel's waist, but Rathian didn't stop his assault on the man's body.

Stakel placed kisses and bites down Rathian's neck. In so many ways, he'd been rather passive during their lovemaking. Never initiating anything. He wouldn't fight if Rathian made any moves, but he'd let the prince take the lead. Somehow Stakel'd sensed it was what he was used to. The adrenaline racing through him wouldn't allow submissive behaviour tonight. As he had said, he'd let Rathian fuck him out in the arena, but he then would show the Imperator the glory in allowing him inside his body.

Stroking up and down Rathian's shaft, Stakel bent to take one of Rathian's nipples in his mouth. A gentle nip caused Rathian to jerk and moan. The cock in Stakel's hand twitched.

He winked up at Rathian who stared down at him in stunned silence. "I think you liked that." He did it again.

"Stakel," Rathian groaned.

He tightened his grip on Rathian's cock, pumping hard and fast. "I want you to take me against the wall, prove to your men that you control me, not the other way around."

His own cock filled and throbbed. He didn't care if the entire world watched this coupling. He needed Rathian like he'd never wanted another man before.

"Stakel, if you keep doing that, I'll take you and it won't be gentle or slow," Rathian warned him, cupping his chin with a shaking hand and lifting it so their gazes met.

"I know and that's fine with me. I don't want gentle, Your Highness. I want it rough and hard."

He dropped to his knees in front of Rathian and swallowed the man's shaft down to the root. Rathian grunted, flexing his hands on Stakel's shoulders. Stakel started moving, making sure to keep the suction tight and strong. He took a firmer hold on Rathian's balls, squeezing just to the point of hurting then easing off. Soon Rathian was thrusting deep into his mouth, each stroke hitting the back of his throat.

"Stakel, close." Rathian tapped Stakel's shoulders.

Stakel pulled away from the prince's thick cock. Climbing to his feet, he kissed Rathian quickly, backing up towards the wall. Rathian followed him with a stalking stride. Rathian's eyes burned with desire. Stakel felt another pair of eyes watching him.

Without moving his head, he swept the arena with his gaze. There was no one else in the room with them, but he didn't doubt someone was watching them and it was that person Stakel was doing this for. He wanted whoever had plotted against him to realise he wasn't going anywhere. Letting Rathian fuck him out in public was his silent declaration of war.

When his back hit the stucco wall, he turned and braced his palms on the rough surface. He tilted his hips, enticing Rathian to take him. Callused fingers traced the crease of his ass and delved in between his cheeks to tap his hole. Rathian pressed the tip of a finger into Stakel.

Stakel glanced over his shoulder at Rathian and shook his head. "No, just take me."

"I don't want to hurt you," Rathian protested.

"Just fuck me, Rathian. Don't worry about discomfort. I can deal with it." Reaching behind him, he managed to get a hold of Rathian's shaft. He encouraged Rathian to step closer.

Placing the head of Rathian's cock at his opening, he pushed back as Rathian pressed forward. The burn was fierce, threatening to overwhelm him, but he took a deep breath and relaxed. He wasn't a stranger to pain. The priests and the other Consorts had taken him harder.

Rathian's balls brushed the back of Stakel's thighs as Rathian settled deep inside him. He rested his forehead on the wall and Rathian's chin dropped onto his shoulder. After a second, he contracted his inner muscles as tight as he could.

"Now, fuck me."

With those words, it was like he'd broken a chain holding Rathian's control in check. Rathian pulled almost all the way out before ramming back in. Stakel met each stroke with a backward thrust of his own. The scent of sweat mixed with sex filled the air. Their grunts rang through the empty arena. Stakel felt Rathian's fingers digging into his hips and he knew he'd have bruises there tomorrow. He didn't care. This savage coupling was what he needed.

Rathian's smooth, rocking movements became jerky as Rathian grew closer to his climax. Stakel massaged the thick cock inside his passage. His own climax tingled at the base of his spine, but he grasped a hold of his pleasure. He wouldn't come until he was buried deep in Rathian's ass and Rathian was begging for him to flood him with his seed.

"Come now. I want to feel your seed filling my ass," Stakel ordered him, keeping control of their lovemaking.

A loud grunt and Rathian's seed bathed Stakel's inner channel. Stakel kept moving, encouraging Rathian to give him every drop of his essence. Finally, Rathian's hold loosened and his head landed on Stakel's back.

"What about you?" Rathian slid his hand around to grasp Stakel's cock.

Stakel pulled the hand away and turned to face Rathian. Both men moaned as Rathian's softened cock slipped from Stakel's ass.

"You can take care of me in a few minutes. When we're in your bed and I fill your ass."

A hint of fear showed in Rathian's eyes. Stakel brushed a kiss over his lips.

"I'll be gentle with you and you'll love it." He stepped away from the wall and looked around. "I've made love to men before, though I was drugged and didn't care about how my partner felt. This time is different. I want you to like it."

The ruined fabric of Rathian's pants rested on the end of the bench. Stakel snatched it up and cleaned them off. He gave the prince a wink.

"I think you proved to them who was in control." He nodded towards the door. "Now I want that ass."

Rathian headed off towards the manor. Stakel didn't bother to get dressed, but he did pick up the short curved blade. He wouldn't be caught unarmed again.

Rathian wasn't sure what he should do except walk to his suite. None of his men reacted to the fact that both he and Stakel were naked. He held his head high. There was no reason he should be embarrassed. As the Imperator, he had every right to walk around the manor sans clothing, if he wanted.

Rathian never thought he'd be uncomfortable in his skin, but knowing all eyes were on him was unnerving. The footsteps following him kept him moving along at a steady pace instead of hurrying. He stopped, allowing one of his men to open the manor door for him.

"Sir, I need to speak to you."

He turned and saw Excelsie standing in the hallway to his left. "Now isn't a good time, General."

Stakel remained close but didn't say anything. Rathian moved and his lover's hand came to rest at the small of his back. Rough fingers caressed the soft skin there. Shivers chased down his spine, but his focus stayed on Excelsie.

"I'm afraid it is important." Excelsie's gaze shot over Rathian's shoulder to land on Stakel. "We have some new information about Villious and how the battle goes." The general's eyes were cold and ugly.

Duty warred with desire. He longed to go with Stakel to his rooms. Stakel seemed to enjoy their lovemaking and he wanted to experience it as well, even though he'd been taught that the Imperator never makes himself submissive to anyone. Yet he didn't think Stakel would take advantage of that.

"Darius, bring the Imperator a set of clothes and food to the war room." Stakel's orders shocked all of them.

"Who are you to give the prince's page orders?" Excelsie's body tensed.

Stakel pushed into the general's personal space. Rathian saw the scowl marring his lover's face. Stakel's brown eyes glowed with a golden light. He started to reach out and stop the Villious from confronting Excelsie.

*"If he means something to you, you must let him fight his own battles. Do you want him to stay with you?"*

Who the hell was this voice talking to him? He'd never had it happen before Stakel had arrived.

*"Yes."*

It was a simple answer, but it had been spoken from the heart. Rathian didn't want to lose Stakel.

*"Then you must allow him to fight his own battles and establish his place in the ducenti. He'll not be a subservient lover. As a Consort, he fought against the chains and whips of the priests. They couldn't break his pride. He won't allow you to put him in that same position."*

Rathian bit his lip and let Stakel deal with Excelsie. Glancing around, he saw Darius standing on the bottom stair. The page gave him an askance shrug. The prince nodded.

Stakel had clearly decided that the war was more important at that moment than their pleasure. In a way, it made Rathian happy to know his lover understood the demands placed on Rathian as the Imperator.

"I don't have to explain anything to you, General. You aren't my commander, so your authority doesn't extend to me." Stakel pointed at Rathian. "The only one I'll ever take orders from is Prince Rathian. My loyalty is his and no one else's."

Excelsie snarled, but something in the set of Stakel's shoulders or the fact that the Villious' hand gripped the curved blade convinced the general not to lose control. Rathian joined them.

"One of these days, the prince won't be there to protect you and your evil plot will be revealed." Excelsie spun around and marched off to the war room.

Rathian started to chase after him. Anger boiled in him at the threat Excelsie had levelled towards Stakel. His lover's hand stayed his movement and he looked at Stakel, who shook his head.

"Don't. This is between him and me. When the time comes, he'll make his move and discover that I don't need anyone's protection." A bruising kiss landed on his lips. "Go. Talk about the war. I can wait."

Stakel stroked his naked cock roughly and Rathian groaned. Stakel might be able to wait, but he wasn't sure if he could.

"I'll try to return as soon as possible," he promised.

"You know where to find me."

Stakel pumped his cock again then headed up the stairs. Rathian watched his lover's tight ass flex with each step. For the first time, he cursed the responsibilities of being the Imperator.

# Chapter Seventeen

Rathian glared at Excelsie, knowing the general had picked that moment because his friend didn't like him spending more time with Stakel. He stalked down the hall to the war room. Entering, he went to the side table and poured himself a glass of wine. He turned to find Excelsie staring at him.

Lust flashed quickly in Excelsie's eyes, but the emotion made his skin crawl. It didn't inspire the same feelings that Stakel's desire did. When Stakel looked at him with desire, he wanted to give himself over to the man and lose the world he ruled for a while. To see passion in Excelsie's gaze made Rathian feel like an object to be conquered and owned. If they were ever to come together, there would always be a struggle for who the leader was.

He heaved a silent sigh of relief when Darius raced in with an armful of clothes. "Thank you, Darius. I know Stakel told you to bring me some food, but take a tray to my suite instead. I don't plan on this meeting taking that long."

"Yes, Imperator." Darius bowed and ran from the room.

"You baby him." Excelsie presented his back to Rathian as the prince got dressed.

"I treat him the way my uncle treated me while I was training to join the ducenti." Rathian left his shirt unbuttoned and gestured to the maps strewn over the table. "What did you need to talk to me about?"

"Our spies have brought information that the Queen's Army is getting ready to launch a major offensive all along the front. We're not sure when it will start, but we need to have our troops in position and ready." Excelsie ran his finger over the line that marked the border between Launioc and Villious.

"Thank you for informing me, but we knew this was going to happen. My brother is back. So we'll be leaving for the front lines within a day or so." He met Excelsie's gaze. "Is there anything else you wanted to talk to me about?"

"You've been spending a great deal of time with the Villious prisoner." His friend had made the comment rather causally, but Rathian could tell Excelsie wasn't happy with the situation.

"It's none of your concern who I spend time with," Rathian stated.

"You're my leader and my prince, but you're also my friend. I feel like I should be the voice of reason to warn you." Excelsie touched Rathian's arm. "He's not one of us. Stakel doesn't understand our world."

"Do you think he's doing this to deceive me?" He kept his voice level. To be honest, he couldn't be angry with his friend. He understood why Excelsie felt he had to mention his problems with Rathian's relationship.

Unlike Rathian, Excelsie didn't accept others who were different, even if it merely meant being from another country. The general had never been able to see that change was good. Rathian closed his eyes and remembered the night time visit he'd had from Xasel. Change was good and he embraced everything new Stakel would bring to him.

His cock stiffened at the thought of allowing Stakel to take him like the prince had done to Stakel.

"Yes, I do." Excelsie frowned. "You've given him access to all areas of the manor. He can watch us train and learn our ways. How do we know he won't disappear when we get to the front and tell them where our weaknesses are?"

"There had better not be any weaknesses in the ducenti, Excelsie, or both of us are to blame for it." Rathian shrugged. "There's no way we can know. I trust him. You don't. I guess we'll deal with what we find out. If you feel the need, keep an eye on him. Just remember that I won't tolerate you treating him like a prisoner or a monster. He's my lover, General. My companion and maybe something more."

A shocked expression chased over his friend's face. Excelsie started to say something but Rathian shook his head.

"I won't argue with you about this. If you find some proof that Stakel is plotting against us, then bring it to me and I'll consider it, but don't expect me to toss him aside simply on your word alone. I'd like to believe you have the ducenti and Launioc's best interests in mind." Rathian scowled. "I don't, though. I think you have ambitions beyond your station. You need to remember who's in charge here, General, and don't push me. You might be my friend, but I am your

Imperator and won't take your advice as anything other than a challenge."

"Yes, Your Highness." Excelsie saluted, face inscrutable.

Rathian looked at the maps. "We'll meet tomorrow to plan our departure and you can finish briefing me on the Villious troop movements."

He left the war room, trying to keep from running down the hall. Excitement rushed through him. He wanted to crush Stakel against him and plunder the man's mouth. He wanted to know how it felt to be filled like Stakel was every time they made love.

\* \* \* \*

Stakel finished cleaning up and went to stand by the window. While he knew the information Excelsie was telling Rathian was important, he also knew that the general had chosen that precise moment to interrupt them on purpose. There was a growing feeling in Stakel's gut that Excelsie was responsible for the attacks. He didn't have proof—the general was a clever enemy and it would be hard for Stakel to get the man to show his true colours.

It might be hard to get Rathian to believe him as well. Excelsie had been a close friend of the prince's for most of their lives. No one wanted to believe a friend would try to hurt someone they cared about. Yet Stakel knew the truth, that not even your closest friend or lover could be trusted to sacrifice anything for you. He'd learnt it in the Temple, watching the Consorts jockey for position with the queen. Brother cheated brother. Lover turned on lover. Trusting didn't come easy to him, but he had a feeling that if he had proof, Rathian wouldn't doubt him.

He turned when the door opened. Darius entered, carrying a tray. Another page came behind him with two glasses and a bottle of Milinan wine. Darius set his tray down then took the wine from the boy. Stakel hid his smile as Darius dismissed the boy. Rathian's page had come to think of Stakel as his second master, though Stakel had never claimed him.

"I took clothes and food to the war room, but His Highness told me to deliver the food here. He doesn't plan for the meeting to take too long." Darius gestured to the tray. "It's just fruit and cold meats. They'll last until the prince comes."

"Thank you, Darius. I appreciate how well you do your duty." Stakel went to the table and poured a glass of wine for himself. "Would you like some wine?" He held the bottle up.

Darius shook his head. "I'm honoured to care for the Imperator and his Custos."

Stakel frowned. "Custos?"

"Yes, sir." Darius nodded.

"I'm not Rathian's Custos. I'm simply his lover." Stakel gulped his wine and poured another drink.

"Why do you think you were attacked earlier this evening? Why do you think the general doesn't like you?"

"Excelsie hasn't liked me since he brought me here. I think that has more to do with me being Villious than me being the prince's lover." Stakel moved back to the window, rested his hip against the sill and stared out into the garden.

"To his credit, the general doesn't like anyone except the prince." Darius eased closer to him. "I've always believed the general wants the position of Custos. He's managed to break up every relationship the Imperator has had."

"How do you know this?" Stakel shot the page a startled glance.

"No one pays attention to us. People forget we're in the room and say things. Or we see them do things that they think are private." Darius shrugged. "Plus, it's not hard to see the general is jealous of you."

"You might be right about Excelsie, but I think you're very wrong about the Custos issue."

The door swung open again and Rathian strolled through. Stakel moved to meet the prince in the middle of the room. When they came together, it was like the earth shook. Their mouths met in hungry kisses, devouring each other with fierce determination.

Stepping back as his lungs began to burn from lack of air, Stakel met the prince's gaze. "Why are you here? I thought you would be longer."

"Excelsie was wasting time. I'm sure he has crucial information to tell me, but he wouldn't get to the point. I told him we'd meet tomorrow in the afternoon. Right now, I have other far more important things to take care of." Rathian ran a thumb over Stakel's swollen lower lip. "A personal training session."

Stakel glanced over Rathian's shoulder at the page. He nodded at the door. "That'll be all for tonight, Darius. We'll see you in the morning."

"Yes, sir."

Darius' exit went unnoticed by either man. He laughed silently. Stakel might deny his status as the prince's Custos, but Darius knew the Villious was already far more than just the Imperator's lover.

# Chapter Eighteen

Rathian trembled slightly. Stakel pressed close to him and he found his nerves were getting the better of him. He knew Stakel planned on taking him, but he wasn't sure he could do it.

Stakel stepped away to pour a goblet of wine for him. He took it and drank it down then held the empty glass for more. Stakel shook his head.

"You should eat if you intend to drink any more. I want you relaxed, not drunk." Stakel cupped his cheek. "It'll be all right, my prince. I promise you'll like it."

Taking a deep breath, Rathian mentally let go of his concerns. Stakel would never hurt him or take advantage of him. There had been plenty of opportunities since the man arrived for Stakel to do something and Stakel had always stayed true. He nuzzled the rough palm against his face.

"I trust you."

"Thank you, Imperator." Stakel kissed him gently. Taking his hand, his lover led him over to his personal bathing chamber. "Try and let go of everything you were ever taught about what you should do. There is joy in allowing someone else to take control."

He stood, letting Stakel undress him. When Stakel's hard cock brushed his ass as Stakel leaned in to tug his tunic off, he realised Stakel was naked. He chuckled.

"You don't like clothes, do you?"

Stakel's laugh bathed his ear with warm breath. "I've learnt to live without them. It's hard to start wearing anything constricting."

He nodded. He hated the feeling of being confined as much as Stakel seemed to. "What are you doing?"

"I'm getting ready to bathe you." Stakel helped him step into the warm water.

"I thought you wanted to fuck me." He cringed inside because he knew his words were crude.

"I do, but first I must make sure your needs are met. Your body is tight. If I don't loosen you up a little, it will hurt and I don't want that for your first time." Stakel scooped up some of the soap kept close to the pool. "Close your eyes and let me take care of you."

He did as his lover had commanded. No one else had bathed him since he was a child. Surrendering control of his body, he shivered as Stakel's callused hands slid down his right shoulder to grip his hand. The slick soap caused Stakel's touch to be smooth and soft. Each finger was cleaned and rinsed.

He gasped as he felt a warm, moist mouth sucked each finger and thumb in. Stakel's tongue teased along their lengths as it had played with Rathian's cock during their other encounters. Sharp teeth nibbled lightly and shivers racked his body. Water replaced Stakel's mouth.

"Oh," he moaned.

Within seconds, he was immersed in the sensations of Stakel's hands and body all around him and rubbing on him. Over his shoulders. Down his back. Strong fingers gripped his ass and massaged the flesh there. Rathian jerked as one of his lover's fingers trailed down over his puckered opening. Pleasure shot through him. A tap and he pushed back.

"Not yet, my prince." Stakel's voice was low and heavy with lust.

He groaned, giving everything over to Stakel. He lost himself in the feelings and let go of all thoughts about what lay outside the doors of his suite. Those problems would be there when he left the room, but all that mattered at that moment was what Stakel was doing to him.

The water waved around his ankles and Stakel knelt to wash his legs. His feet and toes were treated to the same attention as his hands had been.

"No," he protested when Stakel's hands disappeared.

"Don't worry. I'm still here," Stakel reassured him.

He opened his eyes to find Stakel standing in front of him. The combination of gentle caring and burning desire in Stakel's eyes fuelled Rathian's lust even higher. A firm touch on his chest played with his nipples, twisting and pinching them until they were red and aching. He reached out and tangled one of his hands in Stakel's dark hair.

"I want your mouth," he begged, arching his back.

Stakel's lips settled over one of his nipples with hard suction.

"Gods," he breathed as teeth scraped over his flesh and Stakel's hands cradled his ass.

He didn't try to pull away this time as Stakel tapped a fingertip against his hole. No one had touched him there before this man. It was a vulnerability he'd never allowed himself, but from the very beginning, Stakel had been breaching walls Rathian didn't even know existed. Stakel's talented mouth moved up Rathian's neck to fasten on to the sensitive spot behind his ear. Their bodies rubbed together, cocks aligned perfectly.

A finger pressed against his lips and he opened, sucking it in without hesitation. After getting it as wet as he could, Stakel removed it and stroked it over Rathian's ass. There was a question in that touch.

"Yes," Rathian answered, with a tilt of his hips.

Moans filled the steamy air as Stakel thrust his finger into Rathian. He shifted, even that small invasion uncomfortable at first, but with each deep, steady retreat and advance, his inner muscles relaxed and he began to move. A brief emptiness, then two fingers pushed into him. Stakel's mouth worked to keep him less focused on his ass and more intent on the feeling of teeth and tongue.

"One more," Stakel warned.

His hands gripped Stakel's shoulders as his ass was taken. Full. He was so full. His eyes met Stakel's in surprise. His lover gave him a tight smile.

"Feels good, doesn't it?"

It was all he could do to nod. His entire body was caught up in the feel of Stakel moving inside him. A twist of the fingers and a bolt of pure lightning shot through him.

"Wasis. What was that?" he panted.

"That is the spot you hit every time you take me. It's the spot that will make you forget your name and the world around you." Stakel bit his earlobe.

"More," he pleaded.

Stakel gave him what he wanted, nailing that spot with each thrust until Rathian's cock ached and his balls were tight. His release settled at the base of his spine and exploded from him in great bursts.

"Stakel," he grunted, spilling his seed into the swirling water at his feet and on the stomach of his lover.

Stakel kept moving until Rathian stopped rocking his hips. A lassitude followed the tension of his climax and he blinked at the grinning man. He tightened his muscles, trying to keep Stakel from removing his fingers.

"I like it," he admitted.

"Good. Then you'll love this."

Stakel spun him around and bent him over. He braced his hands on the side of the pool. Stakel's body rubbed against his back as the man reached for a small bottle at the edge. A pop, then a trickle of cool oil ran down between his ass cheeks. Rathian widened his stance when Stakel started massaging the oil into his relaxed opening.

Soon something blunt pressed against his hole. Stakel gripped his hips, urging him to push back. His breath stuttered then stopped as Stakel's cock impaled him. It was thicker and longer than Stakel's fingers, and it filled him. Stakel didn't stop until his balls brushed the back of Rathian's thighs and the prince could feel the curls at Stakel's groin caress his ass.

There was no movement for a few seconds. Rathian realised Stakel was waiting for him to tell him it was all right to move. Tilting his hips and nodding, he clenched his inner passage and milked the cock in him. It was like the chains holding Stakel still had broken and the man slammed into him. He was being taken rough and hard, but he didn't mind. He found it thrilling to think that he was the one to destroy Stakel's control.

Skin slapping skin and grunts were the music to which they made love. Rathian met each thrust with his own push. He took Stakel in as deep as he could. His own cock stiffened and a second, weaker climax washed over him.

"Ah," he shouted, his seed painting the pool's edge.

Once. Twice. On the third deep stroke, Stakel's own release flooded Rathian's inner channel with heat. The hands gripping his hips tightened until they hurt. He would have bruises there.

"Mine," Stakel growled.

Rathian nodded. His body trembled. He was Stakel's and Stakel was his. There was no way they could let each other go. No other option than to be together until the gods separated them.

* * * *

Rathian woke up when he heard a noise. Searching the room, he realised Stakel wasn't there. It must have been the door shutting that had startled him. He climbed out of bed and tugged on a pair of trousers. When his eyes adjusted to the darkness, he left the room and spotted Stakel at the end of the hall. Frowning, he wondered where Stakel was going.

They made their way downstairs. He noticed that the guards didn't react to Stakel's passing, but saluted him as he went by. Outside, he followed as Stakel headed towards the Temple of the High God. A shiver chased down his spine. Why was Stakel visiting the temple in the middle of the night?

He slipped into the sanctuary just as Stakel knelt in front of the altar. The flame flared brightly and Rathian gasped. Dropping down beside his lover, he bowed his head. Their hands entwined, and they found comfort and simple joy in each other's touch.

"Whose temple is this?" Stakel's voice was low and rough.

"Xasel, our High God. We of the ducenti have always prayed to him." Rathian nodded towards the altar. "All Imperators pledge to keep Xasel's laws before the entire ducenti and the altar. Look at the flame."

Stakel stared at the basin filled with oil. A faint golden glow surrounded the basin. The flame burned even brighter. Rathian remembered the flame so incandescent only when Jelviut and Carius were in the temple.

"Why does it burn?" Stakel inclined his head towards the altar.

"It was lit the night the first Imperator died and has never been allowed to go out."

Stakel stood, moving towards the flame. He held a hand over it. Gasping, Rathian raced up to try to tug Stakel's hand out of the fire. Their hands fused together, not allowing either of them to pull apart.

Stakel's gaze met his and he saw an emotion strangely like love sparkling in the man's dark eyes. He leant forward, not fighting the urge to kiss Stakel's lips, but Stakel turned to stare up at the statue of Xasel behind the altar.

"Life and soul I pledge to you, Xasel, High God and Creator."

He shut his mouth and stiffened. How had Stakel known the oath every Custos spoke before the flame?

Stakel turned to look at him, placing their hands over his own heart.

"Heart and body I pledge to you, Imperator, Leader of the ducenti. Everything I am exists for you, until Xasel calls us home."

The flame shot high into the air, burning bright white for a second before settling back to the same small flicker. Rathian knew what he had to do.

"Life and soul I pledge to you, Xasel, High God and Creator. Heart and body I pledge to you, Custos, Protector of the ducenti. Everything I am exists for you, until Xasel calls us home."

Their eyes closed as warmth waved through him. Stakel wrapped his arms around Rathian's waist and they embraced. Their mouths fused together, tasting and teasing each other. They were sealing their pledges with a kiss.

*"Imperator and Custos. Together, you are legend."*

They broke apart. The eyes of the Xasel statue glowed and Rathian swore that the statue smiled.

Suddenly tired, he yawned. "We should go back to bed."

Stakel nodded but didn't say anything. They made their way back to their suite and settled down under the blankets. Rathian felt a sense of rightness deep inside his soul. He snuggled closer to his lover, wrapping his arms around Stakel's waist and laid his head on his broad shoulder.

# Chapter Nineteen

Rathian strolled out of the manor, grinning up at his brother. Travi was sitting on his horse waiting for him.

"Everything work out all right last night?" Travi asked as Rathian swung up into the saddle.

"It was pretty much over by the time I arrived." He gestured to his decem to follow them. His bodyguards would arrange themselves around the princes but wouldn't listen or interfere in their conversation.

Stakel stepped out on the front steps and leaned against one of the pillars. Rathian felt his cheeks flush as his lover winked at him. He waved and Stakel nodded back. Antioc moved up beside Stakel, letting Rathian know the sub-commander would keep a causal eye on the man. Not that Stakel needed any protection. Last night had proven the ex-Consort could take care of himself.

"Let's go."

Travi led the way out of the courtyard onto the forest trail. They rode quietly for a few miles before Travi dropped back to ride beside him. He missed spending time with his older brother. Even when they weren't talking, it eased him. He didn't have to be the Imperator or the prince. He could simply be himself.

"That man who watched us leave? Is he someone special?" Travi's questions were neutral.

Smiling, he nodded. If it had been anyone else, he wouldn't have said anything. "Stakel is a Villious. Used to be a Queen's Consort. He was left behind by his comrades and taken prisoner by our army."

"Why is he so important to you?" Travi frowned. "He's the enemy, isn't he?"

He shook his head. "No. This is between you and I— I don't want my men to hear it because they shouldn't doubt my authority. The first couple of days Stakel was here, I couldn't sleep. My mind was all over the place, wondering about him and worrying about what to do with him."

"Understandable. We don't know much about the Queen's Consorts, so he was a mystery." Travi slowed his horse to a walk. "Did something happen to change your mind?"

"I never really considered him a threat. There was something about him and my reaction to him that told me he wasn't there to harm me. Then one night, I had a vision or a dream." He shrugged. "I'm not sure what to call it. The High God spoke to me."

"The High God? You mean Xasel?" A puzzled expression crossed his brother's face. "I didn't think anyone worshipped him anymore."

"The ducenti have always worshipped Xasel and always will. We owe our existence to the god."

"Xasel visits you and tells you what? That Stakel means no harm and you can trust the man? And then you take him to your bed?"

They drew their horses to a stop and Rathian turned to look at his brother.

"It wasn't that easy. I did think about the consequences, but there is something connecting us, Travi. I've never felt this way." He grimaced. "Bah, now I sound like a woman."

Travi laughed. "Stakel is an attractive man. I can see why you would desire him."

Rathian looked away, studying the trees around them. "It's more than that, Travi. Deeper than mere lust or passion. I like him. He treats me like an equal when we're alone, but when we're out where my men can see me, he defers to me. I think he can help us win this stupid war."

"What makes you think he'll want to?" His brother's horse shifted, bumping their knees together. "Maybe all he wants is to go home."

Rathian didn't say anything. His brother was right. Stakel had talked about the mountains and how much he'd missed them over the twenty years he'd lived in the Temple. Rathian wondered how far into the pass they could get before the Villious army spotted them. He wanted Stakel to be able to see if his village was still there, but he wouldn't allow him to go anywhere without him. No longer would either of them walk in the world alone.

"He's my Custos, Travi."

A sharp intake of breath was the only noise Travi made for moments. Then he asked, "Are you sure?"

Nodding, he looked over and caught Travi's concerned gaze. "We said the vows," Rathian admitted.

"Wasis. Does anyone else know?" Travi looked worried.

"It was early this morning, before sunrise. We spoke them in front of the Flame. Stakel knew the right words to say." Rathian felt puzzled. "How did he know the oath?"

"You said he'd read Martin's mind to get our language. It's possible he could have read it in someone's head," Travi pointed out.

Rathian shook his head. "The oaths we spoke are the secret ones. The Imperator and Custos speak a second set of oaths when they pledge themselves in front of the ducenti. No one except the Imperator and his intended Custos would be able to say the true oaths."

"Really? Why didn't I know that?" His brother seemed confused.

"No one knows about it. I only know about it because Uncle Jelviut told me right before he left to fight on the borders. He must have known he and Carius weren't coming back. He told me that I would know my Custos by the oath he spoke." Rathian shivered slightly.

"Stakel was a Villious. The Villious have nothing to do with us, so we know it wasn't them who told him. They think we're demons—or worse—because of the way we love."

Travi shrugged. "Father isn't going to like this. He hates the Villious queen and he's always had a hope that you and Excelsie would bond."

Rathian laughed and shook his head. "Excelsie and I aren't meant to be anything other than friends. He longs for power and is rather cruel about enforcing his authority. None of the men respect or love him. The ducenti can't be ruled by fear and cruelty. Not any longer."

"I heard he doesn't like your Custos." Travi turned his horse around, heading back towards the manor.

"No. Stakel doesn't fear him and that drives Excelsie crazy. I'm reaching the end of my patience with him."

Rathian followed him. "I've been keeping an eye on the commanders and sub-commanders. I think I might have to promote one to general and demote Excelsie."

"He won't like that."

"No, he won't, but once Stakel is announced officially as my Custos, I can't accept his continuing disrespectful treatment." Rathian was firm in that belief. Stakel might not have started out as a Launioc, but he had become more important to the prince than anyone else ever had.

"You might have other problems besides Excelsie." Travi rode into the courtyard and dismounted.

"You're right." Rathian joined his brother on the ground and they headed into the manor. "So what's your fiancée like?"

Travi smiled a silly grin. "She's wonderful and the way she kisses…"

Rathian chuckled.

\* \* \* \*

Stakel glanced up as Rathian and the tall blond man he'd seen the prince leaving with that morning strolled into the breakfast room. They were laughing and his body perked up at the sound of Rathian's deep laugh. It had only been an hour since Rathian had kissed him goodbye, yet he wanted to drag the prince back to their bed and ravish the man.

He stood, catching Rathian's gleaming gaze. The prince held out a hand to him.

"Stakel, I want you to meet my brother, Travi. He's the next king of Launioc and future husband of a high-spirited Milinan princess." Rathian gestured to his brother.

Prince Travi smiled at him and shook his hand. He bowed, studying the older man. There was a family resemblance around the mouth, in the green eyes, and the blond hair.

"It's a pleasure to meet you, Your Highness." Stakel stepped back beside Rathian. "Congratulations on your forthcoming marriage."

"Thank you, and I'm sure you'll meet my bride-to-be at some point. Maybe this stupid war will be over soon." Travi sat down at the table.

Rathian leaned over and brushed a kiss over his cheek. He didn't seem to feel the usual urge to be discrete in front of others. Something had changed since yesterday. There would be no more hiding. He slipped his hand around the back of Rathian's head, pulling their mouths together. Stakel nibbled on Rathian's bottom lip, causing the prince to gasp. He thrust his tongue inside Rathian's mouth and the men duelled, tasting each other.

Travi cleared his throat. They pulled apart with a guilty look at each other.

"Sorry," he apologised to Rathian's brother.

"Don't be. I tend to lose my head when I'm around Melody." Travi winked at him.

He sat down next to Rathian and accepted the full plate Darius placed in front of him. He started eating, enjoying the banter between the brothers. Breakfast went by quickly and Stakel had never had a better meal. The Consorts weren't allowed to eat at the tables or anything civilised like that. Usually they fought over whatever scraps the queen threw to them.

Thirty minutes later, Travi wiped his mouth and stood. "Better be going or Father will get upset that I'm not at breakfast this morning."

"It was nice meeting you, Prince Travi." Stakel bowed before sitting back down.

He waited for Rathian to come back from escorting his brother to the front door. Darius took his plate.

"How are you doing, Darius?" He smiled at the young page.

"I'm fine, sir." Darius glanced around. He must have been checking to see if anyone else was near. When he saw no one else there, he sat next to Stakel. "You need to be careful, sir."

"I always am." He smoothed a lock of blond hair off the page's forehead.

A light pink blush touched Darius' pale cheeks. "I know you are, sir, but there are people in the ducenti who don't want you to be the prince's lover."

Stakel couldn't help but chuckle. "I know it, Darius. I think the general has voiced his opinions loudly enough."

Darius ducked his head. "Yes, but I'm worried they might do something to you. Rumours are shifting through the manor. Some are saying bad things will happen. You'll turn the Imperator's mind against him and us."

"I imagine some aren't happy because I'm a Villious." Stakel wasn't worried about it. He knew that Rathian wanted to believe his men would welcome him with open arms, but Stakel wasn't so naïve.

"It's more than you being Villious, sir," Darius informed Stakel. "Some of their hatred stems from your place in the Imperator's heart."

"We're lovers, Darius. No more than that." Stakel frowned, remembering the odd dream he'd had the night before.

"But you are more than that. I can see it. So can the others. You're more than a mere lover. You're his Custos."

Footsteps echoed into the room. Without looking up, Stakel said, "Rathian, your brother seems like a nice man."

The page appeared shocked. "How did you know it was the prince?"

He shrugged. "I'm not sure."

Rathian sat on the table, one hard thigh pressed against Stakel's shoulder. "The night we had sex in the hall, you came out of Antioc's suite to see me. I hadn't knocked or announced my presence in any way, yet you told me you knew I was outside. As Darius asked, how did you know it was me?"

Stakel thought about it for a moment. "I can't explain it. Just a feeling more than anything. I can always sense you. It's like energy runs between us. The closer you are to me, the stronger the energy."

"See, that's what I'm trying to tell you. No one but the Imperator's Custos would have that type of connection with him." Darius glanced at Rathian with a pleading expression. "Explain this to him, sir. He doesn't understand the implications or the truth of what he is."

"I will, Darius, but it'll have to be later. I need you to round up the pages and get them packing. We're heading back to the front tomorrow morning." Rathian stopped the page's protest with a quick frown. "Don't argue, boy. Stakel knows the danger. He's quite capable of dealing with any problems that might arise."

Darius stood and bowed. "Yes, Your Highness."

They watched the young page walk from the room. Stakel stood and moved to stand between Rathian's thighs. He cradled his lover's face, leaning forward to kiss him. Nibbling along Rathian's bottom lip, he took advantage of Rathian's gasp to thrust his tongue into the prince's mouth. He stroked his tongue along Rathian's, teasing it into his own mouth where he sucked on it.

Rathian slipped his rough hands under Stakel's linen shirt to trace the hourglass scar on his back. He arched as warmth trailed from the fingers on his skin throughout his entire body, pooling back in his groin. He rocked his hips forward, pressing against Rathian's erection. Shivers racked his body as Rathian caressed the top of his crease.

The prince tilted his head to the side, offering more skin for Stakel to taste. He kissed a line over Rathian's jaw to the soft spot behind his ear then scraped his teeth over it. Rathian moaned and his hips lifted off the table.

"I want you," Rathian murmured.

Stakel thrust once more with his hips and stepped back. "In what way?"

Rathian blushed. "I want you to take me."

His voice was low, so no one could overhear him begging for Stakel's cock. Stakel jerked, already imagining the tightness of Rathian's ass. He stepped back even farther, holding out his hand to him.

"I think it's time for a nap." He grinned and winked at Rathian.

The Imperator stood, slipped an arm around Stakel's waist and started to drag him from the breakfast room.

"My morning ride has worn me out, I'm afraid." Rathian chuckled.

"Mmm...and now I get my morning ride." He squeezed Rathian's hard ass.

Rathian glared at him and he couldn't help but laugh. They made their way back to Rathian's rooms, stopping only to salute the soldiers who were moving throughout the manor. Some had knowing smiles on their faces as they passed them.

"You're leaving tomorrow?" Stakel wanted to take his mind off Rathian's body or else he'd be stripping Rathian in the hallway and taking him without thinking whether anyone would see.

"Yes. With Travi back, I'm not needed here. The reports from the front lines haven't been bad, but I'm afraid that without me to stop them, the regular army commanders will use my men as fodder to wear out the Villious soldiers out." Rathian's frown seemed to hold worry for the rest of his men far away.

"It's like they're your children," Stakel teased.

"They are in a way. I've trained them and with them for years. When I turned eighteen, I took the oath of the ducenti and became a lancer. Even though I was the heir to the Imperator, I didn't get special treatment. I earned my promotions with hard work and determination. I hadn't planned on becoming the Imperator as soon as I did, but Uncle Jelviut's death accelerated my advancement." A hint of sadness showed in Rathian's green eyes.

Stakel looked around and didn't see anyone paying particular attention to them. He pushed Rathian into an alcove hidden from the main corridor by a velvet curtain the colour of dark wine. Rathian's head thumped against the wall as Stakel pinned him there with a deep hard kiss. Rathian buried his hands in Stakel's hair, keeping his mouth there as they devoured each other.

He slipped his hands between them and managed to get Rathian's pants unbuttoned. Hooking his fingers in the fabric, he tugged the pants down low enough to free Rathian's cock. He nodded, letting Rathian know he needed to loosen his hold.

Dropping to his knees, Stakel licked his way from the root of Rathian's shaft to the head. The bitter saltiness of the seed leaking from the slit danced on his tongue and he wanted more. He swallowed the length down to the base and pressed his tongue to the vein pulsing along the underside.

"Fuck," Rathian growled.

Stakel grinned up at his lover the best he could with his lips wrapped around Rathian's cock. This would take Rathian's mind off his troops for a while.

"No," Rathian protested as Stakel let his dick slide out, but drew a deep breath when Stakel sucked one of his balls into his warm mouth and swirled his tongue around it.

He let go and licked the other one. After sliding his hand around Rathian's hip, he trailed his fingers down his lover's crease, stopping to tap his puckered hole. Rathian widened his stance as much as possible with his pants around his knees. Keeping his gaze on Rathian's face, he took his lover's cock into his mouth while he pressed his finger deep into Rathian's inner passage.

Rathian threw back his head and bit his lip. Stakel saw the tendons in the prince's neck flex as Rathian tried to keep from crying out. He established a hard, fast rhythm, thrusting and sucking. Relentlessly, he drove Rathian over the edge into his climax. Salty liquid flooded his throat and he drank it down like a thirsty man at a well.

When Rathian stopped jerking, Stakel removed his finger and licked his softened cock clean. He placed a gentle kiss on the tip of the shaft before standing.

"Come here," Rathian whispered, cradling the back of Stakel's head in his hand and bringing their mouths together.

Their kiss was gentle to start with, then Stakel rubbed against Rathian's thigh, making the prince break their kiss and laugh.

"Let's go take care of that."

Stakel moaned softly as Rathian pressed his palm to Stakel's erection. "Yes. I can't wait to bury my cock in your ass."

A shiver racked Rathian's body. Stakel laughed, tucking Rathian back into his pants and buttoning them up. He peeked out from behind the curtain and didn't see anyone in the hallway. Grabbing Rathian's hand, he led the prince from the alcove towards their room.

# Chapter Twenty

Rathian chuckled when Stakel pushed him into their room and shut the door. He was still laughing while he started stripping his clothes off. Stakel finished getting naked before he did and shoved his hands away, impatient to get him naked. When the final piece of fabric hit the floor, Stakel bent, put his shoulder to Rathian's stomach and lifted, carrying him to the bed.

His back hit the furs and blankets, causing his breath to rush from him. He shifted, easing a pillow beneath his hips and spreading his thighs. Stakel crawled between his legs, his attention focused on Rathian's cock, which stiffened again under his hot gaze. Rathian let his head fell back on the pillows behind him as he enjoyed the way Stakel's tongue felt licking the entire length of his cock.

"Gods," he groaned, lifting his hips to try to thrust his cock into Stakel's mouth.

"Hmm…none of that, lover." Stakel fondled Rathian's balls before sliding a finger back to play with his hole. "I've sucked you once today. It's my turn now."

"Then get on with it." He glared down his body at Stakel.

"Still in charge, aren't you?" Stakel grinned up at him and pushed two fingers deep in his ass.

"Fuck," he cried out. The burn made him arch his back and he clenched the furs under his hand.

Stakel pumped his fingers in and out of Rathian's ass, nailing the spot inside him that caused him to shudder. Three fingers stretched his hole until he begged for Stakel to take him.

"Please." His voice was rough. "Now."

"If you insist." Stakel smirked at him.

He watched through narrowed eyes as Stakel knelt and grabbed a small jar off the stand next to the bed. Stakel poured oil into his hand and coat his shaft with it. They moaned in unison. He hooked his hands behind his knees, pulling them back towards his chest. Stakel's blunt head pressed into his puckered opening. He relaxed, bearing down, and Stakel's cock slid in.

Wrapping his legs around Stakel's waist, he met each thrust with a snap of his hips. Stakel entwined their hands, pinning them to the bed beside Rathian's head. Their bodies were close enough that Stakel's hard stomach rubbed against his cock, creating enough friction to bring his climax exploding from him.

Stakel slammed into him, riding him harder and faster. His lover's smooth rhythm disappeared with each stroke. His inner passage clenched tight around Stakel's cock, encouraging him.

"Wasis." Stakel grunted and impaled him one more time before freezing.

Warm liquid flooded his ass and he kept flexing his muscles to make Stakel's pleasure last as long as possible. Finally, Stakel gave one last jerk before crushing Rathian into the bed. He unwrapped his legs and embraced Stakel. Pressing a kiss to Stakel's sweating brow, he traced the man's spine, soothing him.

Their breathing eased and Stakel slipped out of him. He tossed the pillow onto the floor while watching Stakel walk to the bathing chamber. He closed his eyes and sighed, relaxed and tired. Maybe they should take a nap.

A wet cloth trailed over his stomach as Stakel wiped his seed off his skin. He hummed his thanks as it worked down between his legs, washing him clean. Stakel joined him in bed.

"I think a nap is in order. You'll be busy this afternoon, making sure everything is organised." Stakel brushed a kiss over his lips.

They spooned under the blanket Stakel had pulled over them. His ass was cradled against Stakel's groin and his lover's hand rested on his stomach. He wondered how he had ever managed to sleep alone before now.

\* \* \* \*

A soft knock woke Rathian about an hour later. Sitting up, he scrubbed his hand over his face and called out, "Come in."

Darius pushed open the door and peeked around it, a smile on his face. Rathian waved for him to enter. The page backed into the room, balancing a large tray in his arms. Rathian jumped out of bed and cleared off the trunk at the foot of it.

"I thought you might be hungry, Your Highness. Also, General Excelsie is looking for you." Darius frowned. "I told him you were busy in a private meeting. I'm to tell you he wants to speak with you as soon as possible."

"Thank you, Darius." He ruffled the boy's hair. Turning back to the bed, he chuckled. Stakel's bare ass was sticking up in the air. He pinched the tempting sight. "Come and eat, amator."

Stakel mumbled something and buried his face deeper into the pillows. Both Darius and Rathian laughed. Rathian jerked the blankets off the naked man. The cool air shocked Stakel into opening his eyes and glaring at Rathian.

"Why are you waking me up?" Stakel reached for the blankets.

"You need to eat and we have to get packed." He went over and sat at the table, lifting covers off plates.

"We have to pack?" Stakel climbed out of bed and hugged Darius before joining Rathian at the table.

Darius poured them cups of wine. Rathian took a cup then gestured towards the empty chair.

"Have you eaten yet?"

The page nodded. "Yes, sir. I ate before I brought you your food."

"Bring Sub-commander Antioc and Lancer Martin to me. Then tell Excelsie I'll meet him in the war room in an hour. That should keep him happy for a while."

Darius bowed then raced from the room. They smiled at each other.

"I don't remember ever having that much energy when I was his age," Rathian said fondly.

"I was too busy enduring another beating or training session. I didn't have extra energy. I was simply trying to survive." Stakel frowned. His brown eyes darkened as he obviously remembered his past.

"The priests tortured you in the guise of training sessions?" Rathian piled several different foods on a plate and handed it to his lover.

"Sometimes. Mostly they tortured us for their own enjoyment. I know when you hear me call them demons, you think I'm saying it because of their treatment of me." Stakel shook his head, taking the plate. "I believe they really are demons. They certainly don't look human."

"What do they look like?"

"Red glowing eyes. Fangs and claws. Their skin is sallow. No hair. Voices from the bowels of hells. There is a stench that follows them of decaying flesh." He shivered. "They are the things nightmares originate from."

"Where did they come from? Or have they always been in your country?" He leant back in his chair, eating slowly.

Mysteries surrounded the Villious priests. Launioc legends mentioned them and he'd long thought the demons talked about in the legend of the founding of the ducenti were the same priests.

"We aren't allowed to speak of them." Stakel gave him a small grin. "Doesn't stop the children from whispering about them in dark corners, trying to scare each other though."

His lover stood, before moving towards the window. Rathian admired Stakel's high tight ass and broad shoulders. He could see the tension in them and knew the man wasn't comfortable with talking about the priests.

"You don't need to tell me anything, Stakel. You can work on forgetting about them." Rathian sipped his wine but kept his focus on Stakel's back.

"No. I'll tell you what I can. You need to know what you're up against because if the war continues, the queen will bring them down from their mountain temple. They are far more difficult to kill than you would think."

Stakel rested his hand on the glass. "Our legends speak of an order of priests formed up in the mountains near to the Launioc border. Around where my village was. They searched for knowledge, believing that to be the source of all power. As they gained power, they wanted more of it. It is said they turned to dark magic. They prayed to the dark gods, asking for their favour and promising their very souls as payment."

Rathian shivered. The dark gods weren't mentioned in Launioc for fear of drawing their attention. He said a silent prayer to Xasel.

"Their souls were already corrupt, so the dark gods asked for the sacrifice of an innocent. They stole a prince from a neighbouring country. One of beauty and purity, I guess. Instead of killing him outright, they drew out his death. His blood and tears painted the senior Rector's chamber." Stakel glanced over his shoulder at Rathian. "I don't know who the prince was."

He had an idea. It would seem their countries' histories were connected further back than anyone knew.

"They were waiting for the darkest night. Winter solstice when the night is the longest. They held their black blades to his body, ready to cut and drain him dry when the gods demanded it." Stakel's voice was vague and sad, as if he could see the scene before him in the glass.

"Did they kill him?" Rathian's hands trembled.

Stakel shook his head. "No. The prince was rescued. Five men died trying to save him. They sacrificed their lives to slow the priests down long enough for the others to escape. The dark gods were furious. They unleashed demons from their hells. The demons possessed the priests, but instead of returning to their prison, they chose to stay here."

"How can they do that?"

"I'm not sure. It has something to do with the queen and her Consorts. I believe our blood helps chain the demon priests to this world. That is why they torture and beat us. The more blood they pull from us the stronger they are."

Rathian stood and went to his lover. Slipping his arms around Stakel's waist, he pulled him back against his chest. He brushed a kiss over the nape of Stakel's neck. Shudders racked the Stakel's body and Rathian knew his lover was reliving some horrible moment in his life.

"No more, love. You're mine now and I won't let them have you back. I'll die before I let them take you." He spoke his promise in a deep voice, tightening his arms around Stakel's waist.

Stakel sighed, relaxing in his arms. "I know."

Those two simple words warmed Rathian's heart. Stakel trusted him to keep him safe. He laughed silently. It was strange that this man would trust him when Stakel could more than take care of himself.

"Am I really going with you to the front?" Stakel turned in his arms and encircled his neck.

He nibbled on Stakel's bottom lip for a few seconds before replying, "Yes."

Stakel shot him a sceptical glance. "I'm not sure that would be a good idea. Some of your men don't trust me. How can you be sure I didn't seduce my way into your bed just so I could lead you into a trap?"

He shrugged. "I was told you would change my life and I'm not going to doubt the vision I had."

"Hmm…maybe we should come back later." Martin's amused voice interrupted their kiss.

Martin and Antioc burst out laughing as Stakel waved at them to leave. Rathian broke away from his lover and turned to wink at his men.

Both saluted. Rathian returned the salute then gestured for them to sit. He tugged on Stakel's hand, pulling the man from the window to join the others at the table. Pausing for a moment, Stakel then tossed a pair of pants at him. He slipped them on but left them unlaced.

"Eat." He poured some wine for them.

"You wanted to see us, sir." Antioc filled a plate for Martin before gathering his own food.

"Yes. Stakel is coming to the front with us." Rathian checked both men's expressions to see how they reacted.

Martin smiled over at Stakel and Antioc nodded to him. Good. He'd figured he wouldn't have a problem with these two.

"I told him I'm not sure it's a good idea for me to go." Stakel waved a hand at him.

Antioc shrugged. "There are a few who wouldn't like you with us, but their minds are closed to the possibility of change. You're Villious, so you will always be our enemy. No matter what your position in the ducenti turns out to be."

"You need to come with us, Stakel. Your place is next to the Imperator's." Martin tapped Stakel's hand.

"Besides, I need someone to keep me company when Antioc's in meetings all day."

"Don't lie just to make me feel better." Stakel shook a finger at the younger man. "We'll be on guard when we're closer to the front. I doubt there will be much free time."

"Would you be willing to train with us?" Martin took a sip of wine. "I think we could learn from you. Your sword use is different from ours."

"I can't teach you much."

"Don't be modest. You took on twenty men and won," Rathian pointed out.

"Yes, but some of that has to do with the fact that I'm a Queen's Consort. The ritual changes our bodies. We become faster and stronger. Whatever natural ability we have increases along with our magic." Stakel saw their confused looks. "I'm a natural healer. I could heal myself without a problem, but after going through the rituals, I can now heal anyone."

"You might be right, but still by training with you, my men can learn some of the moves specific to Villious soldiers. We don't fight the same."

Stakel thought for a second and nodded. "You're right. It'll give me something to do while you're meeting with your generals."

"You'll be in a lot of those meetings. I need your knowledge of the mountains and the terrain." He planned on utilising every advantage Stakel could give him. He gave Antioc a serious stare. "I expect both of you to keep Stakel company while I'm not around."

"You can count on us, sir." Antioc saluted.

"Hey, I'm not a child needing to be protected or entertained," Stakel protested.

"Maybe it's my men I'm worried about. You've already charmed my page and these two are taken with you. I don't want all of my men falling in love with you." He leant forward to give Stakel a quick kiss. "I plan on keeping your charms all to myself."

"Can you ride?" Martin asked.

"Yes. Not as well as you do, but I've ridden before. You won't have to worry about me with that."

"Good." Rathian stood. "I'm going to clean up and go meet Excelsie. Will you two escort Stakel to the stables and help him pick a mount?"

"Yes, sir." They both said before standing.

"Finish your meal."

He gave Stakel a hard kiss before heading to the bathing chamber.

* * * *

Martin, Antioc and Stakel wandered the stable, looking for a mount for Stakel. Stakel thought about how strange it was that men who should have been his enemy were becoming his closest friends.

Stopping in front of a stall where a dark bay gelding stood, Martin patted the horse's neck. "Have you ever been back to your village, Stakel?"

He shook his head. "No. I don't even know if it's still there. The priests came and took me away during the night. It's when their power is strongest. From the moment I was imprisoned in the Academy, my old life ceased to exist for me. Once I was at the Temple, my world narrowed to the rector's chamber, the queen's bedroom and the fighting arena."

The gelding bunted its nose against his shoulder. He smiled up into the liquid brown eyes. "I'll take this one."

"Are you sure? There are others in the stable more fitting for the Imperator's amator." Antioc nodded towards the other end of the stables where the commanders' horses were housed.

Stakel looked over the rough gelding. "He has some mountain pony in his ancestry, I think. I don't need a fancy mount, Antioc. He's a bit like me and we'll get along well."

"Fine." Antioc turned the stable boy who had been following them. "Make sure this horse is moved into the stall next to the Imperator's stallion. His grooming gear should be packed for the trip to the front."

"Yes, sir." The boy bowed then ran off to tell the stable master.

"What was it like?" Martin asked as they wandered off towards the front gate.

"Living at the Temple?"

"No. Your village. The mountains." Martin gestured to the flat farm fields spread in front of them as they left the manor grounds. "I've never been to them. Our headquarters at the front rests in their shadows, but I've never had to go up into them."

Stakel thought about his home and the countryside around his village.

"The mountains can be harsh and unforgiving. You make a mistake while you're in their midst, you die. Yet there is beauty there as well. Wild streams rushing down to the plains, filled with cold water and brightly coloured fish. Cognaki trees flourish there, filling the air with their musky scent. I used to play among them as a kid while my parents harvested the bark." He smiled.

"Do you have any brothers or sisters?" Antioc held Martin's hand as they meandered down a trail into a small stand of trees.

"I have a brother. I don't know if he's alive or dead. I guess it doesn't matter now. I've been gone so long, I probably couldn't find my village again, even if it still existed." He tried not to let the thought depress him.

"We'll be your brothers now, Stakel." Martin squeezed his shoulder. "You're no longer alone."

He grinned at the two men. "Thank you. I have to admit you've made me feel welcome when I didn't expect anything but hatred from you."

Antioc laughed. "I wasn't exactly nice to you at first, but Martin set me straight. Now that I've seen how you handle a sword, I realise that you could have killed all of us without trying, if you had really wanted to."

"That's true. I wasn't interested in killing anyone. I figured the queen and the priests would be happy if I had killed Rathian. I wasn't going to do anything they would have wanted."

They wandered around the forest for a while, enjoying the late summer warmth. As they made their way back to the manor, Stakel thought about the dream he'd had the night before.

"Do you have a temple here?"

"Yes. The Temple of the High God." Martin nodded to the left where a small stone and wood building stood.

"Xasel, right?" Stakel headed towards it.

"Who do you pray to?" Antioc followed him.

"I don't pray to any spirit. In Villious, the priests are the only connection we have to any god and the dark gods aren't ones I want to pray to. They exact terrible payments for answering any request."

He pushed open the wooden door and stepped into the sanctuary. It looked just like it had in his dream. A flame burned in a basin on the altar in front of him. As he approached, it flared bright gold and shot into the air. He dropped to his knees. Martin and Antioc joined him.

"It's true," Antioc whispered.

He didn't know what his friend was talking about, but he stared into the flame and saw a face. It appeared to be Rathian, yet he sensed it wasn't. There was deep suffering and sorrow in the green eyes staring back at him. This man in the fire had seen demons—Stakel could tell by the scars on the man's cheeks and the tears in his eyes. A loving smile broke over the man's face and the man nodded to him. He nodded back.

"Stakel?"

Someone shook his shoulder. He came out of the trance to find Martin and Antioc kneeling beside him, staring at him. He glanced at the flame—it was back to normal and there wasn't a face in the fire.

"What happened?" Stakel asked.

"That's what we want to know. We knelt to pay our respects and the next thing we knew, you fell over. It was like you were in a trance." Martin seemed puzzled.

"Didn't you see it?"

"See what?" Antioc glanced around the temple.

"The face in the flame." Stakel gestured to the altar.

"There wasn't anything in the flame, Stakel."

He saw the look they exchanged. Standing, he rubbed the back of his head and sighed.

"Maybe there wasn't anything there," he hedged, knowing it wasn't true, but not wanting to make them worry.

"I think you need to go and lie down for a little while. The Imperator will be done soon and he'll come for you." Antioc gave him a leer. "You should be rested for that."

"Antioc, stop it." Martin punched the sub-commander, then agreed with him. "You should go lie down. I'm sure it hasn't been that restful around here."

"You're right. I think I'll go back to my room."

"Do you want us to go with you?" Martin escorted him to the Temple door.

Shaking his head, he gave the younger man a hug. "No. You have other things to do and I'll be fine."

"We'll see you at supper tonight."

Stakel made his way to the room he shared with Rathian. It was funny how quickly it had come to feel like home to him. He stripped and slid under the light silk blanket. Curling onto his side, he closed his eyes.

*"The face was there."* The voice was soft, like it didn't want to bother him.

*"I know. Who was he?"*

*"His life has brought you to where you are now."*

He rolled onto his back and sighed. *"More mysteries and secrets. Why can't you just tell me?"*

A chuckle skated through his mind. *"That isn't how we operate, my son. You must figure it out for yourself. Just know that he is pleased with you. He doesn't show himself to just anyone, you know."*

*"I don't know why I encourage you."* He relaxed and said aloud, "I'm going to sleep now."

*"Sleep well, my son."* A gentle breeze caressed his cheek as he drifted off.

# Chapter Twenty-One

*The next day*

Rathian sat on his mount, watching his men form up. It was time to head back to the front. Excitement caused his hands to tremble slightly—he didn't like being away from the majority of his men for so long. Excelsie joined them, but Rathian didn't look at his second-in-command.

"The men are ready to go, sir," Excelsie informed him.

"Are the pages and wagons packed?" His stallion shifted away from Excelsie's mount.

Darius rode up, leading another horse. "Here's the mount for Master Stakel, Your Highness."

Out of the corner of his eye, Rathian saw the general stiffen. He waited for the outburst. It didn't take long.

"You can't bring the Villious with us." Excelsie grabbed his arm.

Rathian's mount shifted a few inches away again. "Why not?"

He didn't look at his friend, keeping his gaze on the Lancers before him. He inspected the saddles and bridles. The fifty-five men in the yard were some of the best the ducenti had to offer. There wasn't anything wrong with their equipment.

"He's the enemy. No matter how long he's been here or how many times you fuck him, he's still a Villious and we can't trust him." Excelsie's voice was cold. "We can't risk him escaping and going to tell them our weaknesses. Leave him behind. Fuck one of the pages if you need to, but don't let your prick make mistakes that will cost us our lives."

Rathian whipped around, glaring at Excelsie. "Never accuse me of allowing sex to confuse my mind. I'm the Imperator and my entire life has been dedicated to the ducenti. I know my responsibilities." He reached out and fisted his hand in Excelsie's shirt, pulling the man forward until they were inches away from each other. "Don't push me, General. My patience is running out and just because you're my friend, doesn't mean I won't deal with you like any of the rest. Stakel will be going with us and I'll not hear any more words against him."

Anger flashed in Excelsie's eyes for a second before the general lowered them in submission. Rathian pushed him back in the saddle.

"Yes, Your Highness." Excelsie moved his horse to the head of the Lancers.

Stakel strolled from the manor, brown hair gleaming in the sunlight. His eyes were sparkling when they met Rathian's and the prince noticed the happiness leeching out of Stakel's gaze. Rathian tried to stifle his anger. It wasn't Stakel's fault that Excelsie was a closed-minded soldier. He would have to keep an eye on the general and make sure nothing got said to Stakel.

"Sorry to keep you waiting, sir." Stakel stopped by the dark bay gelding Darius had brought. His lover bowed slightly to him, showing respect in front of his men.

"It's all right. We had some issues to work out before we could go."

He watched Stakel mount, tracing the firm line of Stakel's ass and thighs with his gaze. Stakel settled easily into the saddle, back straight and proud. Those dark eyes skated over to Excelsie and back—Stakel knew who had the problems Rathian spoke of. Stakel's eyes asked a question, but Rathian shook his head.

"You'll be riding up at the head of the columns with me." Rathian gestured for the columns to form up.

"Are you sure you want me where they can see me?" Stakel nodded back towards Rathian's men.

"Yes." He wouldn't back down and no one would dare argue with him about his decision.

"They aren't going to be happy with a Villious as a companion to their Imperator." Stakel eased his horse up next to him.

"You are no longer a Villious or a Consort. You are a member of the ducenti and have proven yourself loyal to me." Rathian nudged his horse into a trot.

"Is that why you told Darius to give me a Lancer uniform?" Stakel waved a hand towards the black pants and red sleeveless fitted vest he wore.

"I told him to give you the uniform of a Custos."

He could see shock hit Stakel when it made his lover rock in his saddle.

"A Custos?" Stakel shook his head. "I don't think you know what you're doing."

"I do know, but I don't want to discuss this with you at the moment." Rathian touched Stakel's thigh. "We'll talk later at camp. Trust me, I know what I'm doing and I think the gods have smiled on this union."

Stakel nodded, silent.

* * * *

Twilight was just kissing the sky as Rathian brought the column to a halt. Stakel sighed. He hadn't ridden so far over several days in his entire life. His legs were tired and his ass was numb. Shoulders slumping slightly, he waited for Rathian's order to set camp.

"Dismount," Rathian ordered, swinging off his horse.

Stakel dismounted as gracefully as possible. He leaned against his horse for a moment, letting his legs get used to standing on the ground instead of being wrapped around the horse's body. Darius walked up to him.

"I'll take care of your horse, sir." Darius reached for the reins in Stakel's hand.

"I can do it." He didn't give up his hold.

"I know you can, sir, but I'm your page as well. The Imperator's guards are setting your tent up now." The blond page gave him a quick smile. "As the Custos, you are entitled to the same treatment as His Highness."

He let the younger man take the horse. Stepping aside, he allowed the Lancers to do their jobs. He'd spent the month during his time with the Vanguard watching the fifty-five men at the manor train. They fitted like pieces of fabric sewn together to make a blanket or a tunic.

Each man had a job and he knew how to do it without interfering with the others. Stakel knew he'd have to find his own place within the Vanguard, though he figured it would be right beside Rathian.

"Your tent is up, sir." One of the Lancers approached him and saluted.

"Thank you." He smiled but didn't salute. He would have Martin show him the proper dismissal of the men.

Rathian turned from the discussion he was having with Excelsie. The general glared at Stakel. "I have some orders to give the general. I'll join you in our tent for dinner. We'll talk then."

The gleam in Rathian's eyes told Stakel that there might not be many words spoken, but he would eventually have a conversation with Rathian. He needed to convince Rathian that making him his Custos was a mistake.

*"Why do you think it was a mistake?"*

Stakel sighed. The voice had been silent for most of the day and he'd been glad in a way. It was hard trying to adjust to a new life without having to deal with a strange voice in his head as well.

*"I'm not Launioc. I'm the enemy."*

*"You need to talk to someone about the history of the Vanguard. Not all of the Custos were Launioc. Some were from other countries, brought here by fate or the gods to be the most important person in the Imperator's life."*

He ducked down to enter the tent. *"I think Excelsie might have something to say about that."*

*"Yes, we'll need to keep an eye on him. I think he's learning to be subtle now. No longer will he challenge you face-to-face. His attacks will all be secretive."* The voice didn't sound concerned.

*"Thanks for the warning."* He sank onto the cushions placed on the floor. A bottle of wine rested in a bucket of water. Testing the water, he found it cold enough to keep the wine chilled.

*"Your purpose here is more than just to cause problems between Rathian and Excelsie. It's more than just to be the prince's lover. You are here to save innocents from an evil darker than they've ever seen."*

Laughing, he shook his head. The voice spoke in riddles at times and he didn't have the patience at that moment to figure out the meaning.

He studied the tent he was sitting in. The four walls were a dark greyish purple with a white trim. From what he'd noticed on the outside, there was nothing to prove the tent belonged to the prince, but inside, luxury abounded. Richly woven carpets in brilliant colours covered the floors. Jewel-toned pillows were tossed around the single room, providing comfort and places to rest.

Stakel glanced up as Rathian entered. A small smile flirted with the corners of the prince's lips. His lover started stripping his white and purple tunic off as he walked forward.

Sitting up, Stakel reached out, grabbing his lean hips and pressing his mouth to the bulge under Rathian's pants. He blew a hot puff of air over it. Rathian threaded his hands through Stakel's hair and moaned.

He looked up at Rathian. "What kind of discussion would you like to have, my prince?"

Rathian's eyes gleamed with lust. "One where we moan and groan. Where skin slaps skin and you're buried deep in me."

Stakel's gaze went to the tent entrance. There would be two members of Rathian's bodyguard right outside the flaps, guarding their leader. He pulled back slightly and urged Rathian to his knees in front of him. Tracing Rathian's lips with his fingers, Stakel shook his head.

"I'd love to talk to you that way, but our conversation must happen differently. Until we are inside a room with a door we can lock, you will be taking me. Here on the road, anyone can come in." He stopped Rathian's protest. "Your authority is absolute and no one would say anything to your face if they saw you in that submissive position, but whispers would spread. Those who would harm you wouldn't hesitate to take advantage."

He pressed his lips to Rathian's mouth, placing his hand on Rathian's chest over his heart. "I won't risk harm coming to you because of me."

Rathian's eyes widened and Stakel realised his lover never thought about the problems that could arise if they were caught. While the men didn't have an issue with Rathian fucking Stakel, they might not accept his submission to Stakel. Not even with Stakel being Rathian's Custos.

He slid his hands around the back of Rathian's head, bringing their mouths together. They could talk about it later. Now he wanted Rathian to bury his cock deep and fill him. Rathian asked for entrance by stroking his tongue along the seam of Stakel's lips. He opened for him and shivered as Rathian teased the roof of his mouth.

Stakel allowed Rathian to push him onto his back and settle between his spread thighs. Running his hands over Rathian's shoulders and back, he traced the scars marking the battles Rathian had fought in. He thought about the wounds that had caused them and shuddered. Some were ragged and told of deep injuries that Rathian might not have survived. Stakel made a silent vow to guard Rathian with his life if necessary. There was no way he wanted to lose Rathian now that he'd found him.

"What are you thinking about?" Rathian's voice was low.

He blinked, realising he'd been touching one jagged scar continuously while he had thought. "Nothing that matters at the moment."

They kissed again, fingers fumbling with buttons. Stakel needed more skin. He wanted to feel all of Rathian pressed against him. Finally, they were naked and Rathian aligned their cocks, moving his hips in long smooth strokes. The rhythm was eased by the liquid leaking from their erections.

"More. Faster," he cried.

Rathian looked surprised and Stakel winked at him. A sly smile crossed Rathian's face. "So that's how you want to do this."

Rathian's move was so sudden that Stakel found himself gasping, lying on his stomach with a pillow stuffed under his hips. Rough hands parted his ass cheeks and he jumped when cold oil trickled down his crease. Rathian's fingers stretched Stakel's opening, teasing and tormenting him for only a few seconds before pulling out.

"I don't think you need much preparing, not the way you're begging for it." Rathian's voice wasn't low now. It held determination and a hint of laughter.

Stakel nodded. With the oil Rathian had spread around and inside him, he would be fine. He looked over his shoulder to see Rathian kneeling between his legs and he rose up to his knees, bracing himself on his hands.

Rathian hesitated for a moment. "Are you sure?"

He knew his lover was worried about hurting him. He lowered down to his elbows, offering his body to Rathian. "Use the oil and take me."

Their eyes met briefly and Rathian nodded. More oil was poured over his hole. Rathian covered his cock with a handful as well. Stakel pushed back as the flared head of Rathian's dick pressed in. He was still rather tight and pain burned through him, making him hiss.

Rathian paused, but Stakel shook his head. It would be better if they didn't take it slow.

"Fuck me," he shouted.

A gleam shot through Rathian's eyes. With one hard thrust, Rathian buried himself balls deep into Stakel's ass, making them both cry out. There was no softness or finesse after that. Their coupling was savage. Rathian's grip on his hips hurt.

Grunts and groans filled the tent. The harsh rasp of their breathing surrounded them when the pleasure grew so hot they couldn't make any noise. Arousal and sweat scented the humid night air. The sound of their bodies coming together with each violent thrust became all he could hear.

Stakel tried to balance on one hand. He needed his cock to be touched, but each stroke of Rathian's dick shook him to his core. He could only prop himself up and take it.

"You'll spill your seed just from me fucking you," Rathian growled.

He shuddered, knowing that Rathian was right. Each thrust was deeper and nailed that magical spot inside him, the spot that made lightning shoot through his blood and pool at the base of his spine. His cock stiffened until it ached and his balls drew close to his body.

"Please," he pleaded, not caring anymore who might be listening.

"Now," Rathian ordered, leaning forward and biting Stakel's shoulder hard enough to draw blood.

His climax exploded from him. His ass clamped down on Rathian's cock, milking Rathian's own completion out of him. Stakel felt the flood of wet heat fill his inner passage and a silent sigh issued from his lips.

When their bodies stopped shivering, Stakel's arms gave out and the two of them collapsed in a heap on the pillows. He grimaced, pushing several wet ones out from under him. Rathian chuckled wearily.

Stakel didn't move when Rathian pulled out and stood. He kept his eyes closed and he enjoyed letting Rathian clean him. A drop of cold water hitting his heated skin caused him to open his eyes. Rathian knelt beside him, holding out a dripping glass of wine.

"Have some wine and then we'll sleep. Darius can bring us food later."

They shared the glass, not talking, but letting their hands drift over each other's skin. Rathian set the glass aside and curled up behind Stakel, wrapping an arm around his waist and pulling him back to snuggle with him. In an odd moment, Stakel realised he enjoyed the feeling of protection he got from being surrounded by Rathian's large body. It was an odd position to be in, though, since usually it was Stakel who wrapped himself around Rathian. A noise outside the tent made him tense, but when no one came in, he relaxed. Even as he slipped into sleep, Stakel's instinct told him to rest lightly. Danger lurked beyond the tent walls and it wasn't just from the Villious.

# Chapter Twenty-Two

"Explain to me why you told Darius to dress me in the uniform of a Custos?"

They were lying together under the furs in Rathian's tent. It was the second night of their journey. They hadn't had time to talk during the day since Excelsie had done his best to keep them apart.

Stakel had kept his irritation hidden. There wasn't any point in dealing with the general at the moment. He didn't want to usurp Rathian's authority.

"Because you are my Custos." Rathian's voice was low and sleepy.

"How can I be?" He rolled onto his side and eased up on his elbow, staring down at his lover. "Don't I have to swear an oath or something?"

Frowning, Rathian blinked up at him. "You did."

"No, I didn't. I think I'd remember doing that."

The prince sat up, resting his hands on his knees. "The second to last night after you fucked me. You went to the Temple of the High God. I followed."

"I did?" He remembered the strange dream he'd had that night. "I thought that was a dream."

"If it was, we shared it. We spoke the oaths, binding us as Imperator and Custos. You knew the words."

He was stunned. How could he know the words? How could he be Rathian's Custos?

*"You were meant for each other. Fated to find each other from the beginning."* The voice startled him.

*"How do you know this?"*

A chuckle echoed through his brain. *"It's my job."*

*"Who are you?"*

*"Aren't you tired of asking that question yet? All in due time, my son."*

"Our oaths were accepted?" He still wasn't convinced. "Don't they need to be witnessed?"

"It was witnessed. The oaths we spoke are private ones, said between two men and the High God. Xasel caused the flame to surround our hands without burning us. That is his sign of acceptance." Rathian cupped his cheek and kissed him gently.

"What do I have to do?" Stakel didn't know his responsibilities.

"What you've been doing. Watch my back. Deal with problems if I'm busy with other things. Didn't you wonder why more of the men were coming to you for orders?" Rathian eased them back down on the furs.

"Yes, but I thought it was because Antioc and Martin come to me," he murmured.

"They come to you because you are my Custos. Your words carry my authority." Rathian spooned close to him. "Stop worrying about it and try to sleep. We're travelling the last leg of our journey tomorrow and it's the roughest."

Stakel nodded and closed his eyes. He fell asleep quickly. He was unwilling to struggle with his thoughts anymore.

\* \* \* \*

Fog rolled in during the night, covering the camp in heavy silence. In the Imperator's tent, Stakel's eyelids fluttered and a grimace marred his face while he dreamt.

*He stood in the corner of a horrifyingly familiar room. The walls were curved and carved from the mountain. The floor was etched in an elaborate seven point star. Pillars of obsidian stood in the centre of the room with a small white marble bowl in the middle.*

*It was the rector's chamber, but not exactly as Stakel remembered. There were few stains on the walls and floors. It was like the room had just been created and hadn't been turned into the portal of hell it had become.*

*A noise drew his attention to an opposite corner where a man lay, chained to the wall. Glancing around, Stakel didn't see anyone else in the room, so he stepped closer to the prisoner. The stranger sobbed and the pain in his voice broke Stakel's heart. There was no way he could help him, since he was well aware that he was dreaming.*

*Stakel dropped to his knees next to him and a gasp left his lips. He had been tortured. Strips of skin peeled away and burn marks marred his pale skin. His head was bald with scars – like his tormentors had scraped his hair off.*

*Stakel had seen the priests do this to other captives. He reached out, wanting to comfort him, but his hand went through the image, as if the prisoner was a ghost. The man whispered something. Stakel leaned closer to hear what he had to say.*

*"Aurelius, I loved you. I wish I had told you before, but I was afraid."*

*Tears formed in Stakel's eyes as anguish tore through his heart.*

*"They're going to sacrifice me soon. In a matter of hours I fear, and I'll never have known what it's like to kiss you or to feel your body above me or in me."* His hand clutched at a small gold figurine of a lion. *"You always watched over me like a lion, protecting me, but you can't protect me now. I love you."*

*The man's voice failed him and Stakel realised it had been hoarse, probably from screaming when he had been tortured. He wanted to scream. To beg any god that might be listening to save him, even though Stakel knew the dream wasn't real and no matter what he wished, the man would die anyway. Tears coursed down his cheeks as he watched those thin shoulders shake with silent sobs.*

*"Don't cry," Stakel spoke without thinking.*

*The man's head whipped up and brilliant green eyes stared at him like he could see him.*

The scene around him faded and he found himself kneeling beside Rathian, reaching out to him. Stakel's eyes were wet.

"Damn," he swore, jumping to his feet and fleeing the tent.

The night fog was receding, creeping away as quietly as it had arrived. Men and horses stirred. Stakel made his way to the small creek they were camping by. He waded into the freezing water, hoping it would clear his head. He closed his eyes and breathed deep of the chill morning air. The eyes from his dream greeted him behind his eyelids—he'd seen them before. They were the same colour as Rathian's, but they hadn't been his lover's.

The crackle of a fire drew his attention and he turned to see the orange gold flames devour the logs in the campfire. He remembered. He'd seen those eyes the day he'd seen the face in the altar flame at the Temple. It was the same man. He frowned. Why was he dreaming about a man he'd never met? One he was pretty sure never existed, or if he did, it was long ago and Stakel had never heard of him.

Tears pricked his eyes again at the memory of the heartbreak in the man's voice at never having told Aurelius he loved him. He leaned over and splashed his face with water. More men woke as he headed back to Rathian's tent. It would be time to ride soon. Darius was making his way to the cook tent when Stakel called to him.

"Darius, eat your breakfast first and then bring some for the Imperator and I."

"Yes, sir." Darius grinned at him and saluted.

"What are you doing out here?"

He turned to see Excelsie glaring at him. The general's hard gaze trailed over him and Stakel wished he'd remembered to pull on his pants before leaving the tent, but he stood there, letting the general look his fill. With a moue of disgust, Excelsie averted his gaze.

"I went to wash in the creek." Stakel crossed his arms in front of his chest. "Why are you asking? I have the right to walk the camp."

Excelsie's jaw clenched at Stakel's challenge. The general stepped closer to him, but he wouldn't back up. Showing weakness to Excelsie would be giving him satisfaction. Stakel didn't fear Excelsie. He didn't trust him either. There was something going on behind those angry eyes and he didn't think it was for the good of the Vanguard.

"One of these days, you'll reveal your true being. Villious and I'll be there to stop you," Excelsie hissed.

Stakel held his arms out from his body, offering Excelsie a clear shot. "Why not get rid of me now? I'm unarmed and no one is close enough to stop you." He dropped his arms and clenched his hands into fists.

"But you better kill me with the first blow because I'll rip you apart before you get another swing in."

Excelsie snarled at him, but Stakel could see the apprehension in the general's eyes. Excelsie spat at him then whirled, stalking away.

"General Excelsie," Stakel called.

The general stopped, still facing from him.

"Don't ever threaten me again unless you plan on killing me right then and there. Remember, I don't make idle threats."

Stakel continued on to the tent. Rathian stood outside and Stakel could see that his lover had witnessed the confrontation. He bowed and saluted. Rathian returned the salute then kissed him.

"What was that all about?" Rathian gestured to the retreating Excelsie.

"Just his usual growling and threatening." Stakel ducked around Rathian and entered the tent.

"He threatened you?" Rathian followed him in.

Stakel dug through his packs to find a clean pair of pants and tunic. "Yes. He has ever since he brought me to the manor. Obviously making me your Custos doesn't mean anything to him."

He jerked on the pants, lacing them tight. The tunic slipped over his head and he turned, offering his side to Rathian. "Can you lace me up?"

"He knows better than to challenge you." Rathian pulled the laces, making the tunic fit Stakel's chest like a glove.

"Why?" He tugged on his boots before clipping the belt—with his sword's sheath attached—around his waist.

"No one can challenge the Custos. To do so is to challenge the Imperator." Rathian tossed him his blade.

He caught it and slid it home. "So he'd have to fight both of us?"

"Yes." Rathian held the tent flap open for him as they walked out into the camp.

Darius greeted them with a smile. "Your breakfast, Your Highness. Custos."

"Thank you, boy." Rathian ruffled Darius' hair.

Stakel led the way over to a small table and two chairs. Food and wine rested on top of it. "I can take care of myself."

"It's not that. It has always been the custom of the ducenti. If either the Imperator or the Custos are challenged, the other must fight with them."

"Unity and loyalty," Stakel murmured.

"Yes." Rathian sipped from the cup of wine Darius poured for him.

Antioc approached them and saluted.

"Yes, Sub-commander?" The prince nodded in acknowledgement of Antioc's salute.

"The men will be ready to go in under an hour's time, sir."

"Good. Make sure Custos Stakel's mount is ready."

Stakel swallowed down his last bite of breakfast. "No. I'll get him ready."

"You don't have to take care of him. That's the grooms' jobs."

Leaning over, Stakel kissed Rathian before standing. He smiled down at his lover. "I need something to do. I'm used to working. At the Temple when we weren't being tortured or used as studs for the queen, we worked." His gaze traced over Rathian's muscular form.

He leaned in to whisper, "Besides, if I stay around much longer, I might drag your ass back into the tent and have my way with you."

Rathian laughed and punched him. "Get out of here then. We don't have time for that, no matter what my cock says."

He winked and wandered over to the picket lines where the horses had been tied for the night. His gelding whinnied at him as he approached.

* * * *

Stakel swore his horse sighed in relief when they reached the top of the trail and saw the Launioc camp before them. Tents were spread out with men sprawled everywhere. Rathian growled softly and Stakel knew the prince wasn't happy to see the disorganisation of the army. He held his horse back as Rathian moved off. Glancing around, he noticed one section closest to the fortress.

This section was organised in neat rows. The weapons were hung neatly and any armour was rested on low tables, off the ground. The soldiers of this section were sparring against each other until they saw Stakel's group. They snapped to attention and saluted as Rathian rode past.

"Vanguard?" Stakel nodded over to the men when he noticed Antioc riding next to him.

"Of course." Antioc lifted a hand to the men. "Even without our Imperator, we maintain discipline. His Highness won't be happy with the way the regular army looks. I'd hate to be the army generals."

"Does Rathian outrank them?" Stakel dismounted as their unit halted in front of the stable. He patted his gelding and let the groom lead the horse away.

"He's the king's son, but even if he wasn't, as the Imperator, he is their commander." Antioc gave him a wicked grin. "And as the Custos, you outrank them now as well."

"I'm sure that news will thrill them." He turned to see Darius directing the pages to unload the wagons. "Who does this manor belong to?"

"Some noble who ran to the capital when the Villious got too close." Antioc led the way into the main house.

Darius pushed past them and Antioc grabbed the page.

"Remember to put Custos Stakel's belongings in Imperator Rathian's suite."

He started to protest. "Give me the rooms closest to the prince."

"No. The Custos and the Imperator always share a bed. It's expected and it's not like any of us will think less of you. Hell, we'll all be envying you." Antioc winked at him.

Rathian stood in the entrance of the manor, talking to some disgruntled soldiers. The prince reached out and wrapped a hand around Stakel's wrist as he walked past. Stopping, he waited quietly while Rathian finished giving the men orders. After the men stalked out of the manor, Rathian turned to him with a weary smile.

"I have to meet with the regular army generals. I'm not sure how long it will be, so why don't you settle in and after have Antioc or Martin show you around the manor and the camp. I'll meet up with you at the late meal where you'll meet the rest of my commanders and the army leaders." Rathian leaned in and kissed him. Stepping back, Rathian said, "Starting tomorrow, I want you to sit in on the meetings. You need to be brought up to speed. We'll formulate strategies based on your knowledge."

Stakel kissed him back, then saluted. "At your service, Imperator."

He followed Darius up the stairs and into the west wing of the manor. He had a feeling he'd be far busier than he'd thought.

# Chapter Twenty-Three

*A few days later*

Stakel sat with Martin and Antioc. Rathian ruled the head of the table where he and his top generals discussed the war. Stakel had asked to be allowed to sit with his friends instead of with the commanders. Grinning, he watched Antioc bully Martin into eating. The young soldier was still recovering from the slight illness he'd caught when they'd arrived at the camp.

Stakel saw annoyance flash in Martin's eyes and decided to distract Antioc with a question.

"How was the Vanguard founded?" He'd never been told the story before.

Antioc's eyes brightened and he turned to face Stakel with an eager grin. He knew the history of Launioc's most famed and feared military unit was the sub-commander's favourite topic. Martin's 'thank you' was mouthed silently. Stakel nodded.

"When the country of Launioc was founded, King Rathian the First had three sons. Hardisa was the heir. He was a solid, responsible sort of man and destined to become a great king after his father." Antioc stopped and checked Martin's plate, frowning when he noticed his lover wasn't eating.

"Stop glaring at me," Martin complained. "I'm full."

Antioc pushed Martin's food closer to him and the Lancer turned to appeal to Stakel.

"Please, Stakel, tell my overbearing mother-hen of a lover that I'm fine."

He touched Antioc's arm. "Martin's fine. He's survived the worse of the illness. Now he must regain his strength, but that doesn't mean stuffing him full of food."

Stakel gestured to a waiting footman. "Take Lancer Martin's plate. He's done for the night."

The footman took the plate away and returned with a small glass of Milinan wine.

Sighing, Martin toasted them. "The best wine in the world comes from Milina. Maybe it's a good thing Prince Travi is entering into marriage with the Milinan princess."

Stakel wasn't interested in politics. He caught Antioc's gaze and brought him back to the previous subject. "You said Rathian the First had three sons."

"Aye. Hardisa was the oldest and heir. Theray was the second son and a more beautiful man didn't exist." Antioc looked down the table where Rathian sat. "If you believe the legends and stories, Prince Rathian is the exact image of Theray."

Martin narrowed his eyes, gazing at the prince. "Now that I think about it, all of the Imperators look remarkably alike. Mirror images of each other."

Stakel met Rathian's bold green eyes and shifted as a flare of desire burned through him. Wasis. He wanted that man.

"It's because they're related to each other. Resemblance is strong in most families, especially since their paternal line is the purest of all the world's royal lines." Antioc took a swig of ale and gathered his thoughts.

*"Or could the resemblance be god-given?"*

Stakel pushed the voice to the back of his mind. A court dinner wasn't the place to discuss anything with the voice in his head.

"The third son, Dixet, was the senior priest in the service of Xasel, the High God. Though the king loved all his sons, it wasn't a secret that Theray was his favourite. His second son's beauty reminded him of his beloved queen who had died while giving birth to Dixet." Antioc fiddled with his silverware.

"Theray was beautiful, kind and smart. He helped establish the system of government we have now. His gentleness kept wars from breaking out. The prince helped create learning centres and guilds." Martin waved a hand at their fine clothes. "What we wear is a direct product of the guilds Theray founded.

"Still even the most perfect of souls had enemies. Theray was kidnapped. The prince was rescued by a soldier who swore Xasel sent him a dream."

Antioc leaned towards Martin and the lovers said the name together, "Aurelius."

*Yes.* The voice rang in Stakel's head.

The name sounded familiar in the same way Stakel's own did. Soul deep, like he'd heard it every day of his life. He frowned, wondering why it seemed that familiar.

The plates were cleared from the table. When he looked around, he saw the prince, General Excelsie and the high commanders were still deep in discussions about strategy and troop movement.

Stakel had already given them his recommendations and wasn't interested in getting glared at by Excelsie.

Stakel saw Martin cover a yawn. He stood, attracting everyone's eyes. Bowing to Rathian, he smiled.

"May I have your permission to leave the table, Imperator?"

Rathian's green eyes gleamed with pride. Stakel wasn't sure if it was for the respect he was showing or for some other reason, but he did know he liked the happy look on the prince's face.

"Permission granted." Rathian waved a hand at Martin and Antioc as well. "You all may leave."

"Thank you, sir." Antioc saluted and helped Martin out of the room.

Rathian winked at him and Stakel knew the prince would update him when Rathian came to bed later that night. He nodded.

Turning, Stakel made his way from the room. His skin burned with the weight of two pairs of eyes. He knew one was Rathian's, because it trailed over his back and caressed his ass. Anger and malicious intent fuelled the second stare. It had to belong to Excelsie.

Antioc and Martin waited for him outside the dining hall. He smiled, gesturing for them to lead the way.

"I think we should continue our discussion in your suite, Sub-commander. If Martin falls asleep, you won't have as far to carry him."

The younger man glared at him, but Stakel sensed Martin's exhaustion. It had been the first time since his illness that the Lancer had joined them for dinner.

"Stakel's right, amator. I don't want to cart your ass all over the place." Antioc's arm went around Martin's waist and he urged his lover forward.

Stakel kept silent as he followed them. He reflected on what he'd seen in the month since his capture – or liberation, depending on how he chose to look at it.

He'd seen the training that went into creating the Vanguard and why this unit of men were considered the best in the Launioc army. Yet what impressed him the most was the bonds that held the Vanguard together. The reasons they fought went beyond simple pride and honour. The Vanguard's doctrine played to the deepest emotions a human could feel. The doctrine of love. The idea that a man will fight hardest for those he loved the most.

Stakel had grown to understand the idea behind allowing the men to engage in sexual activity with other soldiers who wasn't their brother-lover. It was another way to strengthen the ties. The images of lancers mourning fallen lovers were seared in Stakel's mind. The depth of their loss proved that more than shared moments of battle and bloodshed chained them together. Martin mumbled something and Antioc laughed. There was a purity of joy between the couple walking in front of him. Stakel smiled. The two men had come to be his closest friends, next to Rathian.

"Here we are." Antioc threw open the door.

Stakel headed for the chair to the left of the fireplace. It had become his favourite place in their suite. He stripped, letting his fine clothes drop to the floor. He wore them to make sure he didn't embarrass Rathian with his barbarian ways, but he was far more comfortable in bare skin.

He wrapped a grey wolf fur around his shoulders and settled in the chair. He'd stolen the fur from Rathian's bed. It smelt like the prince, and Stakel loved being surrounded by that scent.

One of the many footmen had started a fire to ease the evening chill. The Growing Season faded into the Harvest Season much quicker in the northern Launioc provinces. Martin and Antioc joined him. The sub-commander sat on the floor and leant back on Stakel's chair. Martin curled up against Antioc. They all watched the flames flicker for a few minutes.

Finally, Stakel shifted, touching Antioc's shoulder for a moment. He wanted more of the story.

"Who was Aurelius?"

Both men laughed, but it was Antioc who answered him.

"Aurelius had been in the service of King Rathian since he was a young man. He'd watched the princes grow into men. No one knows how he really felt about Theray before the kidnapping. Maybe he'd always loved the young man but didn't believe he was worthy. It didn't matter." Antioc stared into the fire and Stakel wondered if the flames were revealing the story.

"An enemy kidnapped Theray from his suite in the royal palace. No one knew how he got past the guards, but somehow he'd managed to secret Theray out. When it was discovered, King Rathian was beside himself with rage and fear. He didn't want to lose his beloved son." Martin turned, resting his chin on Antioc's shoulder and looking up at Stakel. "Not quite the same story with our prince and his father."

Stakel agreed. King Barkuc was filled with jealousy towards his son. The king hated the idea that the Vanguard obeyed only one man and that it was Rathian.

"Does the king not like Rathian simply because he is the Imperator?" Stakel didn't understand the reasoning for it.

Antioc shrugged. "Who's to say? There are quite a few generals in the regular army who hate us and it could be they that are filling the king's ear with lies."

"The way of the court is the traffic of lies," Martin mumbled.

"Aye, love, you're right." Antioc gave a full body shake as if ridding himself of bad thoughts. "When all hope was lost, Aurelius came before the king and spoke about a dream he'd had. The soldier had seen Theray chained to posts in the middle of a stone chamber. The prince had been alive in Aurelius' dream, for Theray met his gaze and asked to be saved."

Stakel thought about the dream he'd had while making the journey north. "How could Aurelius know where the prince was if he wasn't in on the original plot?" Stakel wasn't sure he'd like the answer.

"Aurelius swore the dream had been sent from Xasel, the High God. Remember, Theray's younger brother was the senior priest in Xasel's religion. Wouldn't the god do all in his power to save his favourite worshipper's brother?"

"I know of no gods who do any good in their believers' lives," Stakel said, ignoring the twist in his stomach that came from the mention of any god or priest.

"Maybe your gods are vindictive, evil creatures. I don't blame you, considering all you've been through at the hands of the priests." Antioc's hand reached under the wolf skin and gave Stakel's ankle a squeeze. "In Launioc, the gods interfered in our lives all the time. Good or bad. The outcome was determined by how you prayed. Or at least, it was like that in Theray's time. So it was possible Xasel chose to help Theray."

Stakel wasn't convinced but didn't feel like arguing. He patted the sub-commander's hand and smiled.

"The king was desperate to find his son, so he was willing to take a chance. He asked the soldier if he knew where Theray was. Aurelius admitted he didn't know the exact spot, but he had a feeling he should go north. So he and a hand-picked squadron of his ten best men rode out to find Prince Theray." Antioc paused for a moment before he continued, "Several months later, after all hope had disappeared, five beggars stood at the palace gates, demanding entrance."

A soft snore interrupted the story. They glanced down to see that Martin had fallen asleep. Antioc shifted slightly, getting to his feet and cradling Martin in his arms.

Stakel stayed seated as Antioc put Martin to bed. The crackle of the wood burning soothed him. Antioc returned and settled on the floor again with a sigh.

Gripping the man's shoulder, Stakel reassured him. "Martin'll be all right. The worst is over. He just needs to recover. The prince is making sure he does by keeping him with me."

Antioc's hand lay on top of his for a moment. "I know, but the thought of losing him is frightening to me."

Stakel traced the blue slashes on Antioc's arm. "Yet you have lost lovers before."

"Aye. In battle where they were given an honourable death by a worthy opponent." Antioc waved back towards where Martin slept. "Illness isn't a glorious death. It isn't something I know how to fight. Besides, Martin is different." The Launioc ducked his head. Stakel detected a blush on the sub-commander's cheeks.

"Martin is special to us, Antioc," Stakel murmured, brushing a kiss over Antioc's neck. "Were the beggars Prince Theray and Aurelius?"

Antioc seemed relieved for the renewal of the story.

"The beggars finally made enough commotion that the king was summoned. Rathian took one glance at the smallest beggar and burst into tears. He ordered the gates to be opened and the royal physicians awakened. The king and Theray's brothers were appalled at Theray's appearance. The only way his father recognised him was from his eyes and a small figurine that had disappeared when Theray was kidnapped." Antioc grimaced. "Just the descriptions could make you ill. Scars and open wounds that festered. Where once glorious golden curls cascaded from his head, there was only rough skin."

An image arose in Stakel's mind. A man who in many ways looked like Rathian, but was thinner and younger stood there. Pain and fear haunted those brilliant green eyes. Yet he could see insanity smouldering deep inside Theray's mind and Stakel wondered if the prince really did survive his abduction.

Antioc leant forward, elbows at rest on his knees. He lowered his voice. "Every time anyone asked them what had happened while they were on their mission, their eyes would go blank and the most gruesome grimace would twist their lips. They never told. Not even when ordered by the king. Whatever happened in the North changed them deep in their souls."

"Not one word was told about their rescue or flight back home?" Stakel found it hard to believe.

The Launioc soldier nodded. "No official account can be found in the royal archives, but the five who survived remembered. On the longest night of the year, every year since they'd returned home, they would gather together. It was the night the world was frozen in endless winter. The five would tell the story to each other, making sure they would remember their fellow soldiers sacrificed for the prince's life. All the long centuries since, the wind howled, snow blew and the coldest parts of Hell seemed to open to spit forth a demon on that night."

Stakel rested his head on the side of his chair. "There are nights when demons walk this world."

He'd had personal experience with demons. He understood the pain they caused. He'd endured the price they asked and he had a strange feeling that Theray had gone through the same torture.

The click of the doorknob turning had Stakel and Antioc facing it while moving to stand between the door and the bed. They tensed as a shadow started to slip in. As the intruder turned, Stakel relaxed.

Rathian looked at their protective placement and flashed a rueful smile. "Sorry. Being a prince tends to make a person forget his manners."

"Sir." Antioc saluted, fist to chest.

Rathian returned the salute and turned to Stakel. "I went to our bedroom and you weren't there."

"I'm sorry, sir. I didn't mean to keep him so long," Antioc apologised.

"Don't be sorry, my friend. You kept me no longer than I wanted to be kept." Stakel hugged the soldier then faced Rathian. "I thought Excelsie would keep you in discussions all night."

Rathian frowned. "There were a lot of decisions to be made if we're to move the units tomorrow."

"Hmm..." Stakel didn't want to make a big deal about it.

His dislike for Rathian's friend was founded on nothing but instinct and jealousy. Stakel shook his head in disgust. He was the prince's Custos. If Rathian had been inclined to take Excelsie to his bed, he would have done so before now.

Antioc's gaze caught his and a knowing gleam showed in them. He knew the sub-commander had his own misgivings about the general, though neither of them had discussed it with each other.

Stakel moved to the prince and pressed his body tight to the muscular one in his arms. A hot burst of air grazed his lips as he took Rathian's mouth. Stakel was tired of talking about Excelsie. Rathian cradled Stakel's ass, fusing their groins together, making him moan.

He stepped away and took Rathian's hand in his, not wanting to lose contact. "I think we should go to your room."

Rathian's cheeks were flushed and arousal showed in his eyes. "Probably a good idea. Don't want to keep Antioc awake."

"Oh, please don't stop on my account," Antioc protested.

They turned to see the younger man leaning against the foot of the bed. His cock stood out from his nest of auburn hair, proud and firm.

"As beautiful as they are together, lover, I don't think they're interested in giving you a show." Martin sat up, his blond curls matted from sleep. "Let them go and come to bed."

Antioc sighed and bowed. "I'm sure you'll shut the door behind you." He climbed into bed, snuggling close to Martin.

Stakel headed out, pulling Rathian. Before he opened the door, the prince stopped him.

"Here." Rathian handed Stakel the deep purple tunic he'd worn at dinner. "You shouldn't wander the halls naked. My men might like it too much."

Stakel hesitated. "Only the royal family may wear purple."

"And those we say can." Rathian shoved the tunic into Stakel's hands. "Take it. Trust me, you won't be wearing it for long."

Stakel chuckled at the leer on his lover's face. "All right, but if someone complains, you'll have to explain."

"I'm the Imperator and no one would disobey my orders. If I say you can wear purple, you will wear it."

Stakel stared at the prince. "There's not a humble bone in your body." He pulled the tunic on.

The silk clung to his chest and shoulders. It barely covered his ass. He headed out of the room back towards the suite he shared with Rathian. The entire time the prince stayed close enough for Stakel to feel the heat from his body.

# Chapter Twenty-Four

Reaching out, Rathian cupped Stakel's firm ass. His Custos stopped and pushed back. He snaked his arm around Stakel's waist, pulling his lover tight to him and rubbing his erection against Stakel's ass.

Stakel brought one arm up and encircled Rathian's neck. The prince slid his hand down and stroked the hard cock jutting up from Stakel's dark curls. He pressed his lips to Stakel's neck, sucking up a mark on the golden skin.

"Are you sure you want to do this here?" Stakel's voice held lust.

"No." He stepped back and let Stakel go. "You better get moving. That ass of yours is far too tempting for me to keep my hands off much longer."

Stakel grinned at him then turned and moved down the hall, ass swaying. He wondered how he managed to keep his hands off Stakel during the day. One of his Lancers saluted to him as he went by. He nodded to the soldier who had a knowing look in his eyes. Shaking his head, he hurried after Stakel.

Entering their suite, he turned to shut the door and found himself pinned to it by Stakel's hands. He shivered as Stakel licked a wet trail down his spine to the small of his back.

"Gods," he moaned, arching his back when Stakel blew warm air over the wetness.

"The gods might have had something to do with this," Stakel murmured, "but they aren't here with us now. It's you and me, lover, and I want you to take me."

He growled softly, whirled around and flipped Stakel over his shoulder. He caressed Stakel's ass as he carried him to the bed. Rathian tossed Stakel onto the furs and pillows. Laughter filled the air as he landed on top of him. Stakel bent up into him.

"Love that feeling," Rathian groaned as their cocks rubbed together. "I could spend all day doing this with you."

"Your men might not like that," Stakel grunted, moving faster.

Rathian rolled over onto his back, helping Stakel straddle his hips, and settled his cock in the crease of Stakel's ass. Stakel braced his hands on Rathian's shoulders, rocking their groins together, causing the head of Rathian's dick to rub over Stakel's hole.

"Where's the oil?" Stakel glanced down at him.

"On the stand there." He pointed to the small table next to the bed. "Darius must have refilled it and left it out."

"I think the boy knows too much." Stakel reached out to grab the jar.

Rathian ran his hands over the lean body stretched out above him. He pinched Stakel's nipples, twisting and tugging. Stakel undulated, begging with his body for Rathian to continue his teasing. He wrapped his hand around both their cocks and starting pumping.

Stakel opened the jar and poured some of the oil over Rathian's hand to ease the friction. Rathian coated their lengths, stroking and squeezing. When he got to the head of Stakel's cock, he pressed his thumb into the slit at the top.

"Wasis," Stakel swore, spilling oil on Rathian's stomach. "You keep that up, I'll be spilling more than oil on you."

"Get yourself ready. I want you to ride me." He slid his free hand down and fondled Stakel's balls.

"Yes, sir." Stakel gave him a wink and leant forward, reaching behind him to start thrusting his fingers in and out of his opening.

Rathian watched Stakel's eyes grow bigger, and his lover bit his lip. He wanted to feel what Stakel was doing. He covered his fingers and pushed them inside Stakel, impaling him in counter-point to Stakel's own fingers. Stakel was never empty. The movements still rubbed their cocks together and Rathian could feel his climax building at the base of his spine. His balls were tightening and drawing close to his body.

"Please, Stakel. I need to be in you, and I'm not going to last long." Rathian pulled his fingers away from Stakel's ass and gripped his hips.

"Slick yourself up." Stakel held out the oil jar.

Rathian poured more out and coated his cock. Stakel rose up on his knees, reached back and positioned Rathian's head against his relaxed hole. Stakel lowered his body while Rathian braced his feet against the bed and pushed up. He buried himself as deep as he could, nailing the spot that caused Stakel to cry out.

"Gods. Again." Stakel's body jerked.

Rathian gripped Stakel's hips tight and slammed into him. Stakel rode him hard, milking his seed from him. His climax shot through him and he flooded Stakel's ass.

"Rathian," Stakel cried out, his release covering Rathian's stomach and chest. Stakel leant forward and kissed him. Their tongues twined together, teasing and tasting each other as their bodies jerked, spilling their pleasures out. Soon their breathing calmed and their heart rates eased.

Arms giving out, Stakel flopped on top of Rathian. The prince helped his lover to roll off and he moaned as his softened cock slid from Stakel's ass. He forced himself to climb to his feet, before going to the bathing chamber and getting a cloth to wash their bodies. He cleaned up then wiped Stakel off. He tossed the cloth back towards the bathing room before sliding next to Stakel under the blankets. Stakel wrapped his arms around Rathian's waist, pulling him close. Rathian sighed, letting his eyes drift shut.

\* \* \* \*

Stakel jerked awake, a scream ringing in his ears. He glanced around, searching for the person crying out for help. The room was dark and Rathian breathed deeply beside him. There was no one else in the suite.

He slipped from the bed and walked to a side table where a pitcher rested. Pouring a glass of water, he took his drink and moved to a set of chairs in front of the fireplace. He stirred the fire up and curled in the chair, staring into the flames.

The fire died down again and he wasn't sure how long he'd been sitting there before Rathian joined him.

The prince sat on the floor by the chair, his head resting on Stakel's knee.

"Couldn't sleep, amator?" Rathian's voice was rough.

"Had a dream." Stakel ran his fingers over Rathian's head.

"Bad dream?" The blond man nuzzled closer.

"I think it was a combination of dream and nightmare." He offered Rathian the glass.

"What was your dream?"

"It was a vision I'd had before. The second night on the trail, I dreamed of the rector's chamber. Only it looked like it had just been created. There was a man there. He'd been tortured. He was crying."

"Crying? Who was he?" Rathian frowned up at him. "One of your fellow Consorts?"

"No." Stakel shook his head. "I'd never seen him, or at least I didn't think I had. The day before we left to come up here, Martin, Antioc and I went to the Temple of the High God."

"Antioc told me."

"While we were there, I saw a face in the altar flame. It was the face of the man I've been dreaming of." Stakel returned his gaze to the embers. "Tonight I think I figured out who he is."

"Who?" Rathian's hand squeezed his thigh.

"Prince Theray."

Rathian looked confused. "The first Imperator of the ducenti? Why would you be seeing him in your dreams?"

Stakel shot to his feet and paced. "I don't know. I didn't even know for sure until Antioc told me some of the history of the Vanguard."

"He told you about Theray being kidnapped and Aurelius going after him?"

"Yes and how only five came back, but he didn't get a chance to explain why Theray founded the Vanguard." He whirled to face Rathian. "Will you finish the story?"

"The five who came back understood the danger the men who had taken Theray represented. They fought against the evil and learnt how they thought." Rathian stood and went to the trunk set at the end of the bed. Bending down, he opened it and dug around inside.

Stakel watched as his lover found what he was looking for and turned back to him. He took what Rathian handed him. It was a small golden figurine of a lion. He glanced up at the prince.

"Theray was holding this in my dreams."

Rathian trailed a finger over the mane of the lion. "Aurelius gave Theray this lion the night before the prince was taken. Theray held on to it throughout the entire ordeal. Said the only way he kept his sanity was by keeping it in his hands. It reminded him that Aurielius cared for him and would come for him."

Stakel started to hand it back, but Rathian shook his head. "It's a tradition now for the Imperator to give his Custos the lion as a token of his love. The lion has also become the symbol of the Imperator."

Stakel cupped the back of Rathian's head and brought their lips together in a soft kiss. Rathian embraced him. Their lips and tongues danced with each other. When they broke off the kiss, Rathian tugged him back to the chair and they curled up together.

"Only those who are members of the ducenti know the full story of the rescue. The men who had taken Theray had him for a month or so before Aurelius had arrived. They'd done terrible things to him." Rathian's hands rubbed over Stakel's arms.

"I know. I have a feeling that the men who kidnapped Theray were the priests the Villious legends speak of. His escape is the reason why the demons were unleashed." Stakel rested his head on the prince's shoulder.

"I can't say I'm sorry."

"Don't. The dark gods demand a steep price when their wishes aren't answered. I'd rather have to deal with the demons than have your ancestor die." Stakel closed his eyes, thinking about the legends he'd learnt. "Our legends spoke of the prince being freed by an event the priests couldn't understand or deal with."

"Seven of the eleven men who went sacrificed their lives for Theray. They loved the prince so much they were willing to die for him. Something tells me the priests and demons didn't understand that kind of love and loyalty." The prince caressed Stakel's back. "There aren't many people who grasp the depth that men can love each other, even if it wasn't a sexual love."

"True. The priests only understand pain and fear. They don't love anyone, not even each other." He looked up at Rathian. "Is that why Theray made the Vanguard a unit of lovers?"

"Yes. All of the men who returned from the North were lovers. Aurielius helped Theray heal as best as he could. The Imperator had nightmares and flashbacks for the rest of his life. He would have moments when he lost touch with the present and seemed to lose his sanity. Aurelius was the only one who could bring him back to reality." Rathian pulled him closer. "That's why the Imperator's lover becomes his Custos. Commanding the ducenti is difficult and troubling at times. Dealing with my father and the regular army commanders could drive me to murder. I need someone to help me relax."

Stakel laughed. "I think we've got the relaxing part covered."

"True. Sex does ease things a little." Rathian entwined their fingers around the lion figurine. "We seem to fit. My weaknesses are your strengths."

"I'm more suspicious and you're naïve in some ways. I guess it has to do with our backgrounds. I've had to watch my back with the Consorts every second of the day. You've never had your authority questioned. Your men love you and will do anything you want them to do."

"There were times when I didn't think I'd find my Custos," Rathian admitted. "There are several men in the ducenti that I liked, but none of them ever touched me deep inside. It might sound silly. I feel like something is missing when you're not around."

Stakel felt a surge of happiness such as he'd never felt before. It was almost as if he were back in the mountains of his childhood, lying in the Cognaki grove. Though he had to confess, he'd never dreamt his lover would be male, but he gave a mental shrug. It didn't matter. He wouldn't turn his back on Rathian for all the beautiful women in the world.

"It's not silly. That's how I feel about you as well." He cupped the prince's cheek and kissed him.

"From now on, you'll be joining me in the morning planning sessions." Rathian's finger pressed against Stakel's lips when he would have protested. "I don't care what Excelsie or any of the others say. You're my Custos. You're my true second-in-command. It's about time we all start treating you like that."

Stakel wondered how the generals and commanders were going to react, but he'd learnt in the few months they'd been together that once his mind was made up, Rathian couldn't be talked out of a position. "If you're willing to risk their disapproval, I'll be there to back you up. I have some ideas. There are several mountain passes close by that I think we need to send scouts down. If the queen's army has any clue the passes are there, they'll use the trails to move troops to flank us."

Rathian nodded. "See, I knew I kept you around for a reason."

They laughed then grew quiet, watching the rising sunlight creep into the room. Footsteps sounded outside the door. Stakel knew they would have to stir before too long. The world beyond their suite wouldn't stop for them.

# Chapter Twenty-Five

*Three days later*

In the war room, Stakel and Rathian bent over the map of the mountain passes. Even though Stakel had been away from his village for twenty years, he remembered much about the trails leading through the mountains. They were plotting some scouting trips for the men to take. Tension was running high in the camps — there hadn't been much fighting since they'd returned from the capital, and everyone believed the Villious were just regrouping and getting ready to mount a new offensive.

They looked up as the door burst open and Antioc raced in. The sub-commander went directly to Stakel and fell to his knees in front of him.

"Where is he?" Antioc grasped Stakel's hand. "You have to help me find him."

A wave of fear and despair washed over Stakel, swamping him with Antioc's emotions. He hadn't had this reaction to the emotions of others since he'd been captured by the Launiocs. He'd hoped it was because the drugs the priests had given him had worn off.

"Antioc, what are you talking about?" Rathian grabbed the hysterical soldier and pulled him away from Stakel. "Who are you looking for and why does Stakel have to find him for you?"

"It's Martin," Stakel whispered, picking that clear image out of the jumbled mess.

"What about Martin?" Rathian glanced between him and Antioc.

"He's gone. I had guard duty last night on the front lines and Custos Stakel was with him when I said goodbye at moonrise. When I got back, he wasn't in our room." Antioc shot to his feet and paced.

"Maybe he's with his squadron. Have you checked with them?" Rathian asked.

"First place I went. They told me Martin hadn't shown up for sword drills." Antioc shook his head. "Martin never misses training. You know how we almost had to tie him down when he was ill to keep him from going to them."

Stakel sat on the edge of the table. He closed his eyes and reached for the voice, hoping it would answer him. There wasn't anyone else he could think of to help him.

*"Martin's been taken,"* the voice answered his unspoken question.

*"Do you know who took him?"*

*"No, but go to his room. Maybe we can find a trace. Nothing will have happened to him yet."*

Stakel drew the others' attention by standing. "I have to go to your room, Antioc. There might be traces of the men who took him."

"He didn't go on his own?" Rathian followed them, only taking the time to lock the door.

"No. Martin was kidnapped. I don't know why or by whom, but we'll figure it out." Stakel squeezed Antioc's shoulder.

"I don't understand. Why would anyone take him?"

Stakel had to run to keep up with his friend. "It has nothing to do with Martin." Rathian started to protest and Stakel held up his hand to stop him. "I think Martin's disappearance was engineered to flush me out. I don't believe any of the Vanguard had anything to do with this."

"Flush you out? Why?" Antioc skidded to a stop outside his room.

Stakel didn't answer. He touched the door. A blinding light shot through his brain and he fell.

*Wasis.* Rathian caught Stakel as his Custos' knees buckled and his eyes rolled back.

"Open the door," he barked, lifting Stakel in his arms.

"Damn. What happened?" Antioc got the door open before clearing a bed off.

"He touched the door and passed out. Do you think we should get the medicus?" Rathian set his lover on the bed before taking a hold of Stakel's hand.

"No. You know our healers can't do anything for him. I have some headache powder. I'll mix it up. He'll probably need it." Antioc headed to the bathing chamber.

Rathian nodded. Once the sub-commander got his emotions under control, he could deal with problems without panicking. Rathian wished his mind was as clear, but his heart still raced after seeing Stakel drop.

"I'm getting weary of this," he murmured.

"Imagine if it was actually happening to you," Stakel spoke without opening his eyes. "How tired would you be then?"

"Are you all right?" Rathian cupped Stakel's stubble-covered cheek. "What the hells happened to you?"

Stakel grimaced as he sat up, resting his head on the back cushion. "Just a headache."

"Here. Drink this." Antioc returned and handed Stakel a mug of steaming tea. "We found it tastes better mixed with tea and honey."

"Thank you, friend." Stakel sipped twice and sighed. "Let me focus, Antioc, and then I'll tell you what you need to know."

"I already know enough." General Excelsie stepped into the room.

Antioc saluted. Rathian rose to his feet but didn't move from Stakel's side. He sensed tension radiating from his lover.

"One of the guards saw two men carrying another off house grounds. He didn't think much about it. Figured it was a drunk who needed help back to the barracks." Excelsie moved closer. "This morning after hearing about Lancer Martin's disappearance, he thought about those men."

"What did he remember?" Antioc asked, seeming to forget he wasn't supposed to address a superior officer without being given permission.

Rathian didn't reprimand the younger soldier. Excelsie glared at Antioc but let it pass.

"Two of the men were very dirty. They wore their hair in braids. The third man had a coat thrown over his head and stumbled like he was drunk."

"So why are you here?" Stakel's question was terse.

"The guard swears they stepped outside the gates then vanished." Excelsie's smirk was smug.

"What the hells does that mean?" The prince stared at the general. "They probably stepped off the road into the shadows. Why would he think it had anything to do with Martin's disappearance?"

"When he went to investigate…"

"They were gone and the only thing left was the coat lying on the ground. No footprints. Nothing. They'd vanished." Stakel pushed to his feet, facing Excelsie with a defiant air.

"How did you know that?" Rathian shifted slightly, uneasy with the direction the conversation was going.

Stakel turned to Antioc, ignoring both Rathian and Excelsie. Rathian watched as Stakel took a hold of Antioc's hands. "I believe Martin was taken by Consorts."

"Wasis." Antioc jerked away and snarled at him. "Consorts? How the hells would they get in here?"

"Someone had to let them in. There are no signs of broken doors or locks," Excelsie commented, narrow-eyed gaze settling on Stakel.

Rathian had a feeling he knew where the confrontation was heading. "Don't blame Stakel. He was in my bed all night."

Rathian wasn't going to allow the general to accuse Stakel of Martin's kidnapping.

"Then how did they get into the house if this Villious didn't let them in?" Excelsie frowned.

Stakel shook his head and moved away from them, going to stand by the far wall. He placed his hand on the stone next to the door. "Very few of the Consorts have the ability to move through stone, but there are at least two that I remember who are powerful enough to do it."

"No one walks through stone. Those are only myths and tales people use to scare their children at night," Excelsie scoffed.

Rathian studied Stakel's face. Stakel was serious. "Can you do it?"

The grimace forming on Stakel's face told Rathian all he needed to know about what he thought about it, but Stakel nodded.

"I can. I hate it. As you slip through the stone or wood, whatever surface you travel through, you can feel the weight or pressure of the object. It isn't easy and should never be done lightly." Stakel pressed his hand against the wall.

Rathian started to protest, wanting to tell Stakel he believed him and didn't need a demonstration. He was too late. Stakel's hand began to slowly sink into the stone until he was up to his elbow in the material. Antioc gagged and turned away. Rathian's stomach roiled, but he forced his gaze to stay. This was a part of Stakel and he wasn't going to deny it, even if it went beyond his realm of understanding.

Excelsie took a step closer to Stakel, his hand on the grip of his sword. An uneasy shiver moved down Rathian's back at the sight of the expression on his friend's face. Hatred and disgust gleamed in Excelsie's eyes, tainting them with an insane edge. There might be something to Stakel's insistent belief that Excelsie hated him.

Refocusing on Stakel, Rathian was shocked to see his lover's body was half inside the stone and half out. It was a slow process, but no one spoke during the entire ten minutes it took him to disappear into the wall. Another ten went by before Stakel stepped into the doorway, sweating and pale. Rathian rushed to his side, wrapped an arm around his waist and helped him to the bed.

"Neat trick. What else can you do? Maybe put a spell on Prince Rathian, so that he slept while you helped your friends smuggle Lancer Martin out of the royal house." Excelsie reached out to grasp Stakel's shoulder and pull him away from Rathian.

Rathian didn't have time to protest or react. Stakel spun around, driving his fist deep into Excelsie's stomach. The general started to sink to the floor. Grabbing him, Stakel thrust a knee into the man's face. Both Rathian and Antioc grimaced as Excelsie's nose broke with a crunch. Blood spurted from the mangled flesh. Stakel pushed the injured man from him, a disgusted snarl on his face.

"I told you never to touch me, Excelsie. Never threaten me without killing me. If I were so inclined, I'd kill you here and the other commanders be damned." Stakel turned to meet Antioc's gaze.

Rathian was torn between helping Excelsie and letting the man lie on the floor. He settled with calling for two guards and having them take the general to the medicus. When he had finished that, he found Stakel pacing the small room Antioc and Martin shared.

"What happened to Martin?" Antioc didn't seem surprised at the swift and brutal fight, or concerned about the general.

"Excelsie is right. A spell was cast to cloud the minds of the guards, but it wasn't from me. I believe one of the Consorts crept close enough to cast the spell. It's something we have the ability to do." Stakel scrubbed his hand over his face and sighed. "Martin was smuggled out of the fortress to force me to go to the priests."

"Then you can't go." Rathian folded his arms over his chest and glared at Stakel.

Stakel quirked an eyebrow at him and he felt like an idiot. Of course, Stakel would be going. There wasn't any doubt about it. No matter how much the man inside Rathian wanted to lock Stakel up and not allow him to leave fortress, the Imperator in him understood and would be helping Stakel pack.

"I'll go with you." Antioc pulled out a rucksack and started stuffing clothes into it.

"I'm not sure that's a good idea." Stakel reached out, bringing the sub-commander to a halt. "I know where I'm going and I don't want to have to worry about you. I know you can take care of yourself during a fight, but the demon priests are another story."

"Why do they want you? The Consorts left you for dead months ago." Rathian frowned, not liking the thought of that.

"The Consorts hated me. Every chance they got, they tried to kill me. My defiance brought me torment and torture, but the power inside me was so strong, I became the priests' favourite." Stakel shrugged. "It wasn't a privilege, but somehow they managed to make the other Consorts hate me. It was their jealousy that led to my capture."

"The priests want you for your power."

Stakel nodded. "Yes. They would have to drain two or three men to make up what they lost when I was taken."

Rathian was surprised by that revelation. He'd seen Stakel's power at points during the months they'd been together, but Stakel had never done anything to indicate he had that much magic in him. "Why risk losing you by letting you be part of the Consorts?"

"They still have to keep the queen happy. It's her people they torture. I think that she could change her mind and block them. As powerful as they are, they won't risk losing access to their prey." Stakel glanced at Antioc. "All right, you can come with me. I'll need help with Martin after I free him. You'll stay outside the room, though. Things get twisted in the rector's chamber."

Antioc nodded grimly.

"Go and saddle your horses," Rathian ordered the sub-commander. "I'll help you pack, amator."

He headed out of Antioc's rooms towards their suite. Entwining their fingers together, he held Stakel's hand and bit his lip. As Imperator, he'd been taught that one man wasn't more important than the entire unit. He liked Martin and didn't want anything to happen to a man he considered more than just a soldier, but a friend as well, yet he couldn't afford to chase after him and leave the rest of the ducenti without their Imperator.

"I have to admit I'm afraid to let you go." He looked at Stakel as they entered their suite.

Stakel headed over to one of their trunks and jerked out his own rucksack. "I know, but you can't go. First, you aren't used to dealing with the priests. Second, the Vanguard needs you here to lead them."

Darius came in. He glanced from the rucksack to Stakel then over at Rathian. "Your Highness?"

"Go and pack some food for Custos Stakel and Sub-commander Antioc. They'll heading out to find Lancer Martin."

"Yes, sir." Darius saluted and raced from the room.

"Wait, Darius," Stakel called.

The page stopped and turned.

"Make sure you pack a medical kit for us. I don't know what kind of injuries Martin has and I can't be sure I'll have enough energy left to heal him." Stakel stuffed a vest into the pack.

Rathian nodded at Darius and the boy left. Turning, he went to the table next to their bed. He picked up the lion and took it to Stakel. "Take this with you."

"I don't want to lose it." Stakel cupped his hand, pushing it back towards him.

"Theray had this with him and he survived. I'll be happier knowing you have it."

Stakel stared at him for a moment. Smiling, he tucked the figurine in a side pocket of the sack. "I didn't think you were superstitious."

"I like to think of it as being traditional. The Custos always carries the lion into battle and I have a feeling this is going to be the biggest battle you've ever had."

Rathian wove his fingers through the braid at the back of Stakel's head and tugged him close, pressing their lips together. He poured all of his love and worry into the kiss, wanting his lover to feel how much he needed and cared for him. Stakel answered him with a fierce embrace of his own.

Putting a few inches between them, he rested his forehead against Stakel's and sighed. "Don't get yourself killed, love. I'll be useless if you do."

"The same goes for you. I won't be here to watch your back. Remember, don't trust anyone." Stakel's intense brown eyes bored into Rathian's.

He knew his lover was talking about Excelsie and he nodded. "I'll make sure to stay safe."

A cough sounded from the doorway. They turned to see Antioc standing there with Darius, holding two more sacks.

"The horses are ready, sir." Antioc bowed.

"Thank you, Sub-commander." Rathian nodded at the younger man. "Be as safe as you can and we'll see you when you return with Martin."

He didn't follow them as they left the room. It might be weakness, but he wouldn't watch Stakel ride away. If Stakel died, Rathian didn't want the last sight of his lover to be Stakel's back. He turned to face their bed — he hoped he wouldn't be sleeping in it alone for long.

# Chapter Twenty-Six

*Four days later*

Stakel held up a hand, gesturing for Antioc to stop. Dismounting, Stakel stood and studied the trail they'd been following. Antioc had stayed quiet since they'd ridden out. He knew the soldier trusted him to find Martin. Whether Antioc believed they would all be able to escape from the priests, Stakel couldn't tell. He had his own doubts but chose to keep those silent.

A faint sense of fear filtered into his mind and it came from the left fork of the path. He nodded. Martin had been taken in this direction. He knew the trail led farther into the mountains, up a canyon and ended at a sheer rock face.

The Queen's Temple had been carved in the mountainside centuries ago. When it had first been created, it had been merely the monastery where the priests had lived. After the demons had come, it had turned into a Temple and worshippers of the dark gods had come from countries near and far to pray at its altar. He wasn't sure why it was called the Queen's

Temple, since this queen rarely came there. She would only come on the longest night of the year to renew her ties to the demon priests and the dark ones. He'd participated in most of the ceremonies for the last ten years.

He turned to look at Antioc. "They took Martin to the Temple. I figured they would. The priests' powers are strongest there."

"Why do they want you? Why take Martin?" Worry tainted Antioc's words.

"They need my power and they chose Martin because they knew I'd come after him. Unlike Rathian, I've never learnt to keep perspective about things like this." Stakel swung back on his horse. "Rathian understands that one man isn't more important than the entire Vanguard."

Antioc started to say something and Stakel shook his head.

"I'm not blaming him, Antioc. As Imperator, his duty is to all of the men, not just one. If he found himself focusing on one, he'd lose the detachment he needs to command. I don't have many friends, so I can't afford to lose one." He smiled at the sub-commander.

"Good, but if we all don't get back safe, the Imperator will kill me."

"I think Rathian is the least of your worries." Stakel headed down the trail, trying to keep his focus on sensing Martin.

"When we reach the Temple, how do you want to do this?" Antioc's voice was low.

"I'll need to enter the rector's chamber alone."

"But..."

"You don't have what it takes to defeat the demons, Antioc. No matter how well you're trained. They are more than men. I'm not sure I can do anything against them, but I'll at least make sure I free Martin before it's over." He pointed to a stand of Cognaki trees, the only kind of plant that lived this far up the mountain. "We're only a few yards from the entrance. We'll hide the horses in there. Take just your short sword with you. There will be guards and I'm sure the priests will have alerted them that we're coming."

Antioc grinned at him and nodded. "Don't worry about me. I can take care of myself and Martin once you get him to me."

Stakel tied his horse loosely to a Cognaki tree. He wanted to be able to get away fast when they left the Temple. The horses would stay. There was a small water hole and some other vegetation around, so they would have no reason to stray.

As they crept from the trees, he stroked the lion tucked in an inside pocket of his vest. Touching the figurine gave him a sense of calmness and strength. It helped remind him that there was someone out there in the world who would miss him. For the first time in his life, he wasn't alone.

They made it to the entrance of the Temple. The door stood open in invitation. The priests knew he was there. Leaning close to Antioc, he pressed his mouth to the man's ear.

"The guards will come after you. They've probably been given orders to allow me to pass through. Can you take care of them?"

Antioc gave him an indignant glare and nodded.

"Good. We'll more than likely get separated. I'll make sure that Martin meets you back here at the entrance and you can escape." He started to step inside.

Antioc took hold of his arm and pulled him close. His friend gave him a quick hug and kiss. "You both better meet me back here."

He smiled. He'd try his hardest to join back up with Antioc. It wasn't a suicide mission he was on. He didn't want to give up his life, though if it ended up being the only choice, it was the one he would make. "We will."

Stepping into the Temple, he braced himself for the flood of memories he was sure were going to swamp him. Only anger and hatred surfaced. The fear he sensed belonged to Martin and wasn't as strong as when they had begun to follow the trail. The priests had either drugged him or he had been starting to think and plan. Stakel knew Martin's training. The young Lancer would be plotting an escape route. At least until the torture ensued, then he would focus on the pain. Not begging and screaming would be the centre of Martin's attention then.

Stakel didn't look around. He knew the Temple wouldn't have changed in the months since he'd been gone. Lit torches were sparsely placed along the walls of the sanctuary, lending little light to the room. He headed for the door leading down into the chambers beneath the Temple.

He rested his hand on the handle and a noise made him tense. The guards were moving in. He'd sensed them from the instant they'd entered. Antioc's hand touched his back.

"I'll deal with them. Get to Martin."

He didn't reply, just plunged into the darkness beyond the door. Stakel heard a harsh grunt then the hiss of Antioc drawing his sword. He couldn't worry about the sub-commander.

Darkness seemed to swallow him. No lights were down there, but then he didn't need light to hear the screams coming from the chamber of his nightmares. Martin. Stakel resisted the urge to rush in. He needed to get an idea of where all the priests were. He inched down the corridor, each scream of pain making his muscles tighten further. Memories tried to push in, but he wouldn't allow them space in his mind.

Closing his eyes, he pictured the chamber. Martin would be hanging in between the pillars, one arm chained to each. His feet would be manacled together under him. His blood—from a thousand cuts and wounds—would be funnelled into the basin beneath him. It was a position Stakel had found himself in hundreds of times over the years as a Consort.

The rector would be closest to Martin. He was the only one who wielded the sacrificial blade. The other four priests would be at the four elemental points. East and Fire. West and Water. North and Air. South and Earth. There wouldn't be any more guards in the chamber. Mere mortals weren't allowed in unless they were to be killed.

Standing to one side of the doorway, Stakel breathed in and steadied his nerves. There wasn't any time to think about what could go wrong or what was at stake. He had to take out the priests without giving them time to think. If they banded together, they could kill him with just a thought. He drew on all of his power and silently wove a spell. He'd have one chance to take them out. After that, he would be in danger of losing his life.

A quick caress of the lion in his pocket, then he plunged through the doorway. He threw his hands up and spoke the words of the spell. A bright gold net appeared, landing on three of the priests as they stood in front of the pillars. They shrieked as the net encircled them and started to pull them down into the large black hole that had appeared in the floor under where Martin was hanging.

Shock caused Stakel to pause. His spell was meant to ensnare them, not send them back to where they had come from. He didn't have enough power to do that, or even the right kind of power.

"But I do." The voice rang through the chamber.

"Who are you?" The rector stalked around the other three.

Stakel knew he wasn't talking to him. He tried to see Martin. His friend hung from the columns, just as Stakel had imagined. Blood flowed from several open wounds. He took a step towards the pillars.

"Stop."

The priest threw out his hand and Stakel froze. He fought to move his feet.

*"Gather your power, Stakel."*

*"I don't know what to do."*

*"I'll take care of it. Just give me control."*

For most of his life, Stakel had hated giving over control of his life or body to anyone, but after spending time with Rathian, he'd learnt that not everyone was out to hurt him. He had a feeling that the voice belonged to someone who could deal with the priest. Closing his eyes, he ignored the fear building inside him and let his walls down.

*"Thank you."*

Stakel felt his power ease from him. There wasn't any pain. It was taken a little bit at a time until he was empty. Dropping to his knees, he opened his eyes and saw a tall, dark shape appearing before him. The demon's eyes widened and true fear grew in them.

When some strength returned, Stakel eased his way to a wall and leaned against it for a moment.

The figure solidified and he realised he was looking at Xasel the High God. He'd seen paintings in the Temple at the Launioc capital. Could the voice he'd heard all his life be the god? There was no time to question. He ducked as the demon threw another bolt of fire towards Xasel.

"You'll have to do better than that, demon." Xasel caught the flame in his hand and tossed it back at the priest. "You survived last time because I didn't have enough power to destroy you, but this time, I have the strength to return you to the hells you came from."

"You're relying on this feeble human for help." The demon gestured to Stakel, who dodged a bolt of lightning.

His reflexes kicked in and he ran, grabbing a dagger from his boot as he headed towards the pillars. While the god and demon battled, he was going to get Martin down and try to sneak away without being noticed. Another bolt singed his hair as it tore past. Stakel skidded to a halt next to Martin.

The young lancer's eyes cracked open. "Stakel?" His voice was torn and rough, as if he'd ruined it with screaming.

"Yes and Antioc's right outside." He reached down to saw at the ropes holding Martin's ankles in place.

"Shouldn't have come." Martin's head lolled.

"He wouldn't stay home. Had to come with me." He grimaced. The ropes were soaked in years of blood, making them almost as hard as iron.

"Won't want me. Damaged."

Stakel took a moment to look his friend over. Shallow cuts decorated the man's body, blood trailing from them down his skin. Bruises and burns marred his arms and Stakel could imagine what other forms of torture Martin had had to endure for the four days it had taken them to arrive at the Temple. With the help of the demons, the Consorts had probably travelled straight to the Chamber instead of having to travel the mortal way.

"Don't talk nonsense, Martin. Your injuries are wounds received in battle." He grunted. "One done."

Martin's ankles were free. The blond winced as he twitched his legs. Stakel glanced behind him. Xasel and the demon were enveloped in a golden haze, though the god's eyes met his in a quick glance. Approval shone in Xasel's eyes. The next blast of energy drove the demon away from the door. The god was going to try to clear their escape route.

He reached up and sliced through the rope holding Martin's right hand up. Moving quickly, he caught his friend's arm on his shoulder, wrapping his own arm around Martin's waist. The angle made it difficult, but he managed to stretch and cut the other one as well. Both dropped to the floor as Martin's body collapsed.

Shooting another look over his shoulder, he saw the demon was doubled over and Xasel stood, staring down at the creature. Xasel gestured for Stakel to take Martin out of the Chamber.

"This will hurt, but it's the only way I can think of to get you out of here. You can't walk." Stakel slung Martin over his shoulder and stood with a grunt.

"Do what you have to do. I'm in no position to stop you." Martin's voice was strained and tight, like he had spoken through gritted teeth.

"Don't look back, son. Take your friends and get out of here." Xasel gripped the demon's scaly neck and lifted it off the floor. Shaking it like a dog with a bone, the god held out his other hand towards the hole in the floor.

Antioc met them at the chamber door. "Is he?" Fear coloured the sub-commander's words.

"No. Here." Stakel offered Martin to Antioc. "Take him and get out of the Temple. I'll be following you."

"I can't leave you in here alone. The Imperator would kill me if I didn't bring you back as well." Antioc looked like he wanted to argue more, but a groan from Martin stopped him.

"Just get him out of here. Don't worry about me. I'll be all right." Stakel turned Antioc around and pushed the man down the hallway. He slunk back into the chamber.

Xasel dangled the demon over the pit in the floor. Stakel noticed bright red and orange flames shooting from it, licking the demon's feet. The creature whimpered, struggling against the god's hold.

"It's time for you to return to your spawning place, demon." Xasel touched one of the pillars, causing it to explode.

Stakel ducked and Xasel whirled to look at him.

"Get out of here. You can be no more help to me."

A strong wind roared through the chamber, pushing Stakel out of the room. As he left, the last sight he had was Xasel reaching for the second pillar and it exploding as well. The mountain moved. Ominous cracks appeared on the walls of the passage leading away from the chamber. Dust and rocks poured from the stone around him and he ran. The god was right. There was nothing Stakel could do now that the mountain was collapsing around them.

He caught up to Antioc and Martin at the entrance of the Temple. Relieving Antioc of Martin's body, he gestured to the soldier. "Go get the horses. Have them ready on the trail. We must get as far away from here as we can."

Antioc didn't argue this time. He took off at a dead run, leaping rocks and dodging boulders as the pieces of earth rolled down from the top of the mountain. Stakel followed as quickly as he could. He knew Martin had to be in a great deal of pain, but there wasn't anything he could do for him until they were safe.

He got to the horses, giving Martin to Antioc before swinging up onto his mount's back. "Ride, Antioc. This place is going to fall down around us."

Wrapping his arms around Martin to hold him in place, Antioc kicked his mount's sides and the gelding shot off down the trail like lions were chasing him. Stakel held the reins loosely and his horse galloped after his herd mate. Trusting the animal to take care of both of them, he turned back for one last look at the Queen's Temple.

Flames shot from the entrance as the grand façade of stone and earth imploded on itself. Dust rolled in blossoming clouds, covering everything in a film of dirt. The ground beneath his mount's feet shook and heaved. Numbness settled into his heart as he watched the destruction of the origins of his nightmares. By the time they'd got to the bottom of the trail, there was nothing left of the Temple except piles of rubble and flames painting the sky red.

Antioc pulled his horse to a stop and waited for Stakel to catch up. "So that's the end, huh?"

Stakel shook his head. "No. The priests are gone, but the Consorts and the queen still exist."

"Wouldn't the Consorts lose power if the priests are dead? It seems to me they provide the others with the abilities." Antioc stroked a hand over Martin's drooping head.

"I don't know for sure and we shouldn't linger. Martin will need healing attention. I don't want to provide it here out in the open."

"You're right."

He took the lead, ignoring the words Antioc whispered to Martin as they rode. Martin's outside wounds would heal fine, but Stakel worried that his friend would close his emotions off and not allow the others to help him.

When they had got far enough away from the landslide, Stakel led them off the trail into the Cognaki forest lining the route. He didn't want to risk camping out in the open. The Villious army might send soldiers to investigate the fire and dust. It was too dangerous having to fight them again that day.

They made camp, encouraging Martin to rest against one of the saddles. The Lancer wasn't in the mood to argue. After dinner, Stakel knelt beside the younger man and laid a hand on his shoulder.

Martin's blue eyes opened and his friend smiled at him. "Exciting, wasn't it?"

"Very. Now let me see what I can do for you."

He closed his own eyes and condensed his power into a smaller ball inside his hand. There wasn't much there. Most of it had been given to Xasel. He needed food and rest before he could do anything on a larger scale, but he could do a little healing.

Martin hissed as Stakel pushed the power into him. Stakel had felt the heat of healing before and knew it burned as badly as having a fresh ember pressed to his flesh. His friend's muscles tensed from the pain.

"Just another second," Stakel murmured, letting the last of his power ease into Martin's body.

Rocking back on his heels, he opened his eyes and looked at what he'd done. None of the wounds were fully healed, but none of them were bleeding anymore. He brushed a lock of sweat-drenched hair off Martin's forehead and grinned.

"You'll be okay." He pushed to his feet, turning to see Antioc standing there with a bowl of steaming water and some clothes. "Wash his wounds and make sure they're clean. I'm sure he'd like a wipe down as well."

Martin started to protest.

**"Let him do this for you, Martin." Stakel pointed out towards the darkened forest. "There's a small creek at the edge of the camp. I'm going to wash."**

# Chapter Twenty-Seven

*Five days later*

Darius burst into the war room where Excelsie and Rathian were planning another attack on the Villious front line. Rathian merely had to look at the joyous smile on the boy's face to know that Stakel had returned.

"We'll discuss the rest of this tomorrow, General." He didn't wait to hear Excelsie's response.

He waved at Darius to lead him to his Custos. "Is Lancer Martin with him?"

"Both Sub-commander Antioc and Lancer Martin have returned with Custos Stakel, Your Highness." Darius skipped ahead.

"Good. Has the medicus been summoned?"

"Yes, sir. As soon as we received reports of them approaching. Lancer Martin was taken to the healing tent." Darius stopped in front of Rathian's suite. "He's in the bathing chamber, sir."

"Thank you, Darius. Make sure no one disturbs us until sun fall and then I would like Sub-commander

Antioc to join us for a late meal. I need his report." Rathian pushed open the door, dismissing the boy.

"Yes, sir."

Water splashing greeted him as he entered the room. Stakel's voice could be heard over the washing sounds.

"You used me."

A pause and Rathian frowned, trying to hear who his lover was talking to.

"What would you call it? Forcing me to return to the Temple? You knew I would go after Martin. That's why you didn't stop him from being taken."

Stalking into the bathing chamber, Rathian demanded, "Who are you talking to?"

Stakel looked up from where he sat submerged up to his chest in the warm water, a fierce scowl marring his strong face. "Xasel, the High God."

A quick glance around the chamber let Rathian know there wasn't anyone else in the room with Stakel. "Where is he?"

"Hell, I'm sure if he were so inclined he could show himself."

*"Come to the grove just west of the camp and I will discuss this with you."*

Rathian couldn't stop his jerk of surprise as a voice echoed through his head. It sounded familiar.

*"Yes. I've talked to you before as well, Prince Rathian. You are my Imperator and in many ways my voice to the ducenti."*

"Why haven't I heard you earlier in my life?" He sank onto one of the benches that were placed around the bathing chamber.

*"I don't waste my energy talking to my worshippers. For the most part, they are perfectly capable of taking care of themselves. I had to wait until your Custos arrived."*

"Did you have something to do with my being brought to the manor after I was captured?" Stakel surged to his feet, water sluicing off him and distracting Rathian.

*"I might have pushed Excelsie to bring you to Rathian, but Excelsie is hard-headed and mean-hearted. His interests aren't the same as ours and I'd advise you to keep an eye on him."*

"We know that," Stakel grumbled as he dried off.

"Where are you going?" Rathian stood, watching Stakel pull on clean clothes and stomp into his boots.

"I'm going out to this grove because I have questions that need to be answered. I'm tired of being a pawn to demons and gods." Stakel left, his shoulders stiff with anger.

"I'll come with you."

A chuckle filled his head. *"Good idea, Imperator. I never thought you might have to talk some sense into your Custos. I do believe he is really angry with me."*

Rathian raced from the suite to catch up with Stakel. He took his lover's hand in a tight grip, but he didn't try to stop him. He flagged down Darius, who looked surprised to see them out of their bedroom.

"Go tell the grooms to saddle our horses," Rathian ordered the page.

"Certainly, sir." Darius whirled around and headed out of the building towards the stable.

"You should eat something," Rathian suggested in a mild tone.

"Eat something? I really couldn't care less about food at the moment." Stakel stopped and glared at him. "All my life I've been dragged one place or another by the whim of people who didn't care about me at all. Now I find out that this whole thing has been planned by a god I didn't even know existed."

*"I do care for you, Stakel, or I wouldn't have done what I did."*

Rathian stopped another page carrying a tray of meat pies. He grabbed two, handing one to Stakel. "You and Antioc probably didn't halt for food, wanting to get back to us as soon as possible. Maybe part of your disgust comes from hunger."

His lover snatched the pie from his hand but didn't say anything about his comment. Rathian didn't speak. He stared at Stakel, tracing his gaze over the beloved face of his Custos. Only in the dark of the night had he allowed himself the uneasy thoughts of failure. What would he have done if Stakel hadn't returned from the Temple?

Without thought, he stretched out a hand and rubbed his thumb over Stakel's bottom lip, cleaning a crumb off. Stakel's tongue sneaked out and licked his skin. He sucked in his breath. The wet rasp of the tongue went straight to his dick, which swelled behind his pants, pressing against the leather, begging to get free.

"We could go to the grove later," he whispered, sliding his finger into Stakel's warm mouth.

Stakel sucked it in all the way down to the base and pulled back in the same slow motion the man used while sucking Rathian's cock. A nip at the fleshy part of his palm and Stakel stepped away from him, shaking his head.

"I don't want to put this off. When we get in bed, I want to stay there for a while." Lust burned in the man's brown eyes.

"Wasis. Did you have to say something like that?" He reached down and adjusted himself, looking for room in his pants.

"Both of our asses will be sore by tomorrow night," Stakel promised under his breath.

"Imperator, your mount is waiting outside along with the Custos'." Darius bowed in front of them.

"Let's go. I want to get back before too long."

Stakel laughed and led the way to the courtyard where their horses stood. Rathian watched Stakel swing up into the saddle before he mounted and they rode off.

"Do you know where this grove is the god spoke of?" Stakel glanced around in the mid-afternoon sunlight.

"Yes, I think I do. If it's the right one. We've used it as a secret place for us to conduct our prayers to Xasel. It's been a sacred place in the ducenti history since we were founded."

Rathian turned left out of the gate and headed towards the lone stand of Cognaki trees off to the side of the camp. Stakel followed him.

"I wondered why there were Cognaki trees growing this far down the mountain. Did you plant them?"

He shook his head. "No. In our legends, these trees sprung from the ground to protect Theray and Aurielius as they escaped the demons. They were running back home and the prince was weak. Aurielius knew he couldn't stand much more without rest and food. The soldier prayed to Xasel. As they came over the last hill, there was this stand of Cognaki trees."

"It hadn't been there before?" Stakel sounded sceptical.

"No. This trail is the only one leading into the mountains from the Launioc side. There was no way they were lost or anything like that. The trees hadn't been there when Aurielius and his men rode through to rescue Theray." Rathian saluted the guards. "Theray believed it was the work of Xasel in answer to Aurielius' prayer. So it was named sacred and no one but a member of the ducenti may enter it."

Rathian stopped at the edge of the grove, dismounted and found the hidden entrance to it. Pushing back the brush, he gestured for Stakel to go ahead of him. He stared at Stakel's firm ass as he went by. He dropped the brush and moved through the narrow path. The darkness within the grove made it hard to see his lover in front of him.

"Damn." He slammed into Stakel's back. "Why'd you stop?"

"Because I'm here and he's trying to decide whether he should kneel or hit me." The new voice surprised him.

He nudged Stakel in the back to get him to move. Stakel strolled into the grove, hands clenched. Rathian stepped out and saw a tall man standing in the middle of the clearing, where the altar and Xasel's statue usually stood. Blinking, Rathian tried to figure out what was wrong about the figure. As he got closer, Rathian realised that he was blurred. No feature was distinguishable.

"Why can't we see you clearly?" Stakel demanded.

"It takes a great deal of energy to manifest in this world. I used up a lot of mine during the fight with the demon." Xasel waved his hand at his body. "This is the best I could do."

"Wasn't it mostly my power that you used back there?" Stakel didn't seem interested in showing respect to the High God.

Rathian dropped to one knee. "Xasel." He bowed his head and touched his hand to his chest.

"No need for that, Imperator, though I do appreciate the gesture." A heavy weight rested on his head for a second. "Stand and join your Custos."

Rathian rose and went to Stakel, who was staring at the god with narrowed eyes.

"I first heard your voice when I was young, running around my village. You always warned when danger threatened, but you were strangely silent the day the Villious soldiers came to recruit." Stakel shook a finger at the god.

"You needed to go to the Temple. The first step was to get you inducted into the army." Xasel shrugged. "I don't have a lot of power outside Launioc now. Without more worshippers, my power is waning. At one time, I could affect things farther beyond our borders. Unfortunately I only had enough strength to free Theray from the priests, but not to destroy the demons they became."

The slump of the god's shoulders hinted at disappointment. Rathian felt odd reassuring a god.

"You did everything you could." Well, he assumed that the god had.

"I know, but not destroying the demons at that moment plunged Villious into such dark and terrible times. Their queens became sacrifices to the demons along with her Consorts. I had to bide my time until a soul was born that had the power I needed to end their reign." Xasel pointed to Stakel. "That's why I started talking to you. I was hoping I could help prepare you for what was going to come."

"All you ended up doing for me was get me tortured and raped. You didn't do anything for me." Stakel's hands clenched into fists.

"Ah, but I managed to get you captured by the Launioc army. They took you to the ducenti where you met the man meant for you." Xasel nodded towards Rathian. "I'm sorry you had to endure the pain, but hasn't finding the Imperator made up for it?"

Rathian watched as Stakel thought about what the god had said. He wasn't sure what Stakel would say, but he didn't think love would make up for all that pain and torture. Sliding his arm around Stakel's lean waist, he pulled his lover close.

"I thank you for getting us introduced." Stakel's hand touched Rathian's. "He's great, but I don't think even he makes up for what I went through."

"Sorry." Rathian squeezed Stakel's hand.

"You could have stopped the Consorts from taking Martin, but you needed a reason for me to return to the Temple." Anger burned in Stakel's eyes. "I'm not sure I could forgive you for putting him in danger like that."

"He's a soldier, Custos. He knows the risks during war."

"This is your war, between you and the demons. He shouldn't have to deal with the nightmares he'll have because of this." Stakel relaxed, leaning against Rathian.

"You can help him. You've learnt how to live with the memories." Xasel crossed his arms and Rathian assumed the god was staring at Stakel.

"I would never give them the satisfaction by not living my life and not risking things because I was afraid of getting hurt. Martin doesn't have to prove anything to anyone. He's lived a rather sheltered life. The ducenti have morals and have never used torture to break a man. They offer their enemies an honourable death, quick and relatively painless."

"You will help him. Yes, I used you, Custos, and I allowed Martin to be hurt so I could get you to the Temple. I can't very well lie to you about it. I needed you and now the demons are gone. All that needs to be done now is for the queen to be destroyed."

It was Rathian's turn to shake his head. "I won't kill her."

"Get over the fact that she's a female. One of the things the demons and dark gods did after Theray escaped was to tie themselves to the Queen of Villious. Did you ever wonder why it was always a female born to the queen? Why there has never been a male heir to the Villious throne?"

He tightened his hold on Stakel. Women might not rate high on his sex scale, but he respected and liked most of the ones he'd met. Killing one didn't sit right with him.

"If she survives, there is the possibility she could raise the demons again." Xasel started to fade. "Try to get over your own moral code, Imperator. Sometimes lives must be sacrificed to allow millions of others to live. Male or female, either will kill you if it means they might live to see another day."

"So says the god who can't die," Stakel mumbled. "I don't like the fact that you used me by hurting my friend, but I understand why you did it. If we get a chance, we'll take the queen out. I have no hesitation in ending her life."

"That's all I can ask." Xasel smiled at them. "I have to go. My hold on this world and this form is weakening. Thank you, Custos, for giving me your energy."

"You're welcome, but I get the feeling it wouldn't have mattered if I gave it to you or not. You would have taken it." Stakel bowed, touching his hand to his chest.

Xasel chuckled. "You're right as usual."

"High God." Rathian saluted.

"Imperator."

A heavy weight rested on his shoulder and he knew Xasel had left. Stakel shifted next to him. He looked at his lover.

"Are you satisfied?"

Stakel shot him a glance. "Do you really think hearing him tell me he'd have taken my power whether I agreed to it or not satisfied me?"

"Probably not, but I believe it's the best you're going to get." He released Stakel's waist and took his hand. "Let's go back."

"I know it's all I'm going to get. I don't even know why I complained," Stakel mumbled as they trudged out of the clearing. "Explanations mean nothing to a god."

Pulling Stakel to a stop, Rathian burrowed his hands into the dark curls at the nape of his lover's neck and kissed him hard. Tongues duelled. Teeth bit and lips sucked. They broke apart only when both of them needed air.

He panted, leaning forward and pressing a quick kiss to the base of Stakel's throat. "I know something that could take your mind off all this."

"When we get back to the fortress, have Darius bring Antioc to us. We'll get the reports out of the way and then you can distract me all you want." Stakel's eyes held a wicked glint.

Rathian had a feeling it was going to be one of the quickest debriefings he'd ever done.

\* \* \* \*

The door shut behind Antioc and Stakel flopped down on the bed. He stared up at the unadorned stone ceiling of their room. Rathian's movements could be tracked by the sound of his footsteps as his lover moved about.

"I'll give Martin seven days. If he doesn't snap out of it by then, I'll step in," he promised.

"Aren't your expectations a little too high?" Rathian came to sit next to him. "You said yourself that he'd never experienced anything like the torture the demons did to him."

"True, but seven days is long enough to wallow in self-pity." Stakel rolled over onto his side, curling around Rathian's hips. He stroked the man's naked thigh. "I'm willing to give him some space. If he comes to terms with it, I'll leave him alone. If he doesn't, I'll show him how."

Rathian ran his fingers through Stakel's hair, letting the strands fall back to rest against his cheek. "I'm not sure he can be as strong as you, love."

"Martin will be. I won't allow them to win again."

He nibbled along the curve of Rathian's hip, causing Rathian to shift on the blanket. His lips and his hand met at the base of Rathian's cock.

"Maybe Antioc will convince him without your help." Rathian gasped as Stakel pumped the thick cock in his hand.

"I'm not interested in talking about it anymore." He squeezed tightly.

"All right."

He let Rathian push him over, sprawling onto his back as Rathian leaned above him. Reaching up, he wrapped a hand around Rathian's neck and pulled him down for a kiss. Stakel sucked on Rathian's tongue, tasting the wine they'd had for their late meal. He trailed his free hand down Rathian's spine, caressing the soft skin at the top of his ass.

Rathian inched away. "I want to taste you."

"Swing around and lay beside me," he instructed, applying pressure to Rathian's hips.

Rathian got the message and lay down, presenting him with the perfect view of the man's erection. Stakel eased forward, surrounding the head with his lips and sucked the liquid leaking from the slit. Rathian gasped and arched his hips, pushing his cock deeper into Stakel's throat.

He swallowed Rathian's shaft. Jerking, he moaned as his own cock got sucked into Rathian's moist, warm mouth. He swirled his tongue around Rathian's shaft, tasting the unique flavour of his lover's skin. He bobbed back and forth, helping build Rathian's climax. He slid his hand between muscled thighs to cup and fondle Rathian's balls. He used his other hand to encourage Rathian to fuck his mouth.

His lover's thumb teased Stakel's hole and he pushed back, impaling his ass on the digit. Soon they were rocking and thrusting, driving each other closer and closer to the edge. His balls tightened and he could feel his climax start to explode. He tapped on Rathian's hip to warn him. Rathian took him deeper and swallowed.

Stakel pulled off Rathian to cry out as he flooded Rathian's mouth with his seed. He closed his eyes as his pleasure swept over him. When he came back to himself, he glanced down his body to see Rathian licking his cock clean. He nudged Rathian with a knee. Rathian looked up at him.

"Come here," he said, gesturing that he wanted Rathian to kneel over him.

Lying on his back, he gripped Rathian's hips as the Imperator knelt over him, pressing his cock to Stakel's mouth. He relaxed his jaw and allowed Rathian to slide in without resistance. As the spongy head hit the back of his throat, he added suction.

"Gods, I love your mouth," Rathian rasped, rocking in and out slowly while Stakel grazed Rathian's opening.

He stared up the solid body into Rathian's green eyes while savouring the salty, bitter seed pouring out of Rathian's cock. Drinking it down, he milked his lover dry.

"Wasis," Rathian breathed as he lay beside Stakel. "I've missed you."

Pushing up to lean on his elbow, Stakel looked at Rathian and smiled. He cupped the man's cheek, saying, "I missed you, too."

Their kiss was soft this time, a pledge of love and honour. They snuggled together. He wrapped his arms around the prince's waist, pulling Rathian's back against his chest. For the first time in ten days, he fell asleep fast and didn't dream.

# Chapter Twenty-Eight

*Seven days later*

"Clear everyone out," Stakel commanded Rathian. "Even Antioc."

"But I want to stay. Martin needs me," Antioc protested, his face pale.

Stakel shook his head. "No. You've encouraged this by pitying him. Martin needs a firm hand."

"Stakel?" Rathian asked for reassurance.

"I've been where Martin is and I'm the only one who can help him deal with it." Stakel squeezed Rathian's hand and gave Antioc a hug. "Trust me."

Antioc looked over to where Martin sat in the corner. "I love you, Martin."

Stakel waited until he and Martin were the only ones in the room. He stalked over and jerked open the curtains. Martin growled and blocked the light from his eyes. Stakel went to his friend and gagged at the stench coming from him.

"Gods, when did you bathe last?" Stakel breathed through his mouth.

"Doesn't matter. No one will touch me now," Martin mumbled.

"Hell no, not even self-respecting lice would get near you. Come with me. First thing is getting you cleaned up."

He reached down and grabbed Martin's arm, pulling the younger man to his feet. His friend fought with him every step across the bedroom. Finally, he tossed Martin over his shoulder, and then carried him. Martin yelled, fists pounding on Stakel's back.

"Is everything all right? I'm having trouble keeping Antioc away." Rathian's voice eased in through Martin's shouts. The prince didn't sound convinced that these actions were the best way to handle things.

"Either feed him Milinan wine until he passes out or get the medicus to give him a sleeping draught. I can't deal with two hysterical men." He shot a warm smile to Rathian. "Antioc won't like how I plan to help Martin work through the trauma."

"I'll do my best, amator."

Stakel pushed through the door of the bathing chamber. Several men were in various states of undress.

"Out," he snapped.

No one argued. They took one look at the Imperator's Custos holding the struggling man over his shoulder and they didn't want to get involved.

He didn't wait for the room to empty. He entered the first pool and dropped Martin into the water, clothes and all. The filthy man broke the surface, swearing and punching. Stakel dodged the first couple of swings, then he calmly pushed Martin under again. When Martin came up for the air the second time, Stakel held out a bowl of soap.

"First you take off your clothes and clean yourself. I'll help you wash your hair."

Martin stared at him, a wild look in his blue eyes. "Why does it matter if I'm clean or not? No one wants to touch me or be near me."

"Of course not. You smell and look like you wallowed in a sty." Stakel threw a cloth at Martin. "If you allowed him, Antioc would hold you no matter what. He loves you, Martin."

"He wouldn't if he knew what had been done to me." Martin shuddered.

"I know what was done to you and I'm still here. I've touched you and am willing to help you."

Stakel stripped and sat on one of the benches ringing the pool. Martin started scrubbing and then frowned.

"No way can you know what they did. I was there for three days."

"And I was with them for seventeen years. Do you really believe I've never felt their whips? Have never endured their touch?" Stakel felt the memories pounding in his mind, wanting to get out.

Martin's eyes skittered away, but Stakel could tell Martin wasn't convinced. He sighed.

"Only Rathian has heard some of this." He shut his eyes, collecting his thoughts. "You had twenty-five years of life and love to help you figure out that what the priests did to you wasn't what will always happen. Antioc's touch never burned like theirs. He never gave you pain without pleasure. Your amator never made you beg to make himself more powerful." He took a deep breath and opened his eyes.

"I know." Martin's voice was so low, Stakel almost hadn't heard it. "But the bad memories are piled up on top of the good ones and I can't find the path through to how things used to be."

"You never will. That path has been closed to you." Stakel shook his head. "You can't go back, Martin. Everything is different now."

"The rest of the ducenti will pity me. They'll see me as broken." Martin waded over to where Stakel sat and curled up on Stakel's lap.

"They'll pity you if you continue to act this way, but if you clean up and allow Antioc to love you again" — he caressed Martin's shoulder — "you'll prove to them that you're not broken. They'll see that you've experienced hell, quite literally, and survived."

"What doesn't kill me has made me stronger," Martin murmured.

"No. You've always been strong. What doesn't kill you simply doesn't kill you. It has nothing to do with who you are on the inside. All the torture and pain you went through has refined you. Now you'll no longer rely on others. You know you can deal with anything." He slipped his hand under Martin's chin, lifting the younger man's face so he could look into his eyes. "You're Antioc's equal. He has fought more battles than you but he's never gone through what you have."

"I'm afraid," Martin admitted.

"Of what?"

"That I won't be able to let him touch me." Martin's eyes dropped.

"Let's wash your hair." Stakel eased the blond man off his lap, reaching for the soap again.

"All right." Martin got his hair wet again and knelt for Stakel to soap up his hair.

"When I had time to think about it, I used to worry about the same thing. Though I didn't think I'd ever be free of the priests, I did dream about finding someone who might care for me." He pressed on

Martin's shoulders, signalling for the man to dunk under the water. He sluiced the water away from Martin's hair, making sure the suds were rinsed off. "I didn't know what love was and to be honest, I still don't have much of an idea. What I do know is the first time I let Rathian touch me, I had a choice. I could turn away and never risk finding out if he might be someone I could trust. Or I could accept what he was willing to give me and let him teach me what caring for someone would feel like."

"Why did you choose to trust him?" Martin scrubbed his hands over his face.

"I wasn't going to let them win. Freedom from the Consorts and the priests meant I could do as I pleased. By staying isolated, they would have succeeded in breaking me. The priests might not have got my power, but they would have taken my life without killing me. I wasn't willing to allow that."

"Defiant to the end, huh?" Amusement rang in Martin's voice.

"The very thing the priests hated." Stakel climbed out of the pool and dried off. He grabbed another towel, gestured for Martin to leave the water and tossed the towel to him. "Go back to your room. I'm sending Antioc with some food. Don't block him out, Martin. That man loves you more than everything except Rathian. Take his love and revel in it."

Martin hugged him tight and pressed a kiss to his cheek. He watched the younger man run from the chamber. Walking to the doorway, he spotted Darius resting against the wall.

"Go find Sub-commander Antioc. Tell him to bring some food to his suite and Lancer Martin will be waiting for him."

"Yes, sir." Darius gave him a bright smile and raced away.

Stakel made his way to his suite. He poured a glass of wine and carried it over to the chairs in front of the fireplace. Martin would still have nightmares and some bad days, but now that he was willing to let Antioc help him, those days would get fewer and further between. He sipped on the wine and stared into the fire.

What he'd said to Martin was true. He'd chosen to trust Rathian because he wasn't willing to allow the demons to win and there was something about the Imperator that told him Rathian would never hurt him deliberately. He was used to pain but not pleasure.

Warm lips brushed over his hair. Looking up, he saw Rathian standing next to him. He smiled at his lover.

"Is Antioc with Martin now?"

"I assume so. As soon as Darius arrived to inform him that Martin was waiting, Antioc ran from the room as if he were on fire." Rathian knelt down next to him and touched his knee. "Thank you for stepping in."

"I could see how Antioc was starting to take his frustration out on his men. Martin needed to know that things like this happen, but he couldn't allow it to mar his life forever. Especially since he had Antioc willing to stand with him." Stakel ran his hand over the prince's short curls. "It was the same decision I had to make."

"I'm glad you chose to open yourself to me." Rathian nipped at his naked thigh. "Not just your body, but your heart as well."

"I think we were meant for each other, Rathian. The High God had a reason for me being brought to you.

It's amazing that Xasel used Excelsie that way, considering the man doesn't believe in him." Stakel shifted, spreading his legs wider.

Rathian trailed fingers up over Stakel's warm skin to where his cock nestled in the bed of curls. He moaned as Rathian's rough fingers teased his balls.

"I love how you touch me," he groaned.

"Good, since I love touching you." Rathian caressed the small piece of skin behind Stakel's balls and moved down to rub against his hole.

Stakel rocked his hips, trying to encourage Rathian to ease inside him. Rathian moved to kneel in between his legs and licked a line from the base to the tip of his cock. Rathian swirled his tongue around the bulbous purple head, pressing the tip of his tongue into the slit and making Stakel hiss.

"Rathian." Stakel cradled Rathian's head in his hands, holding the man tight and thrusting his cock deep into the warm, moist mouth.

Rathian took advantage of Stakel's movement to impale him with his finger. Stakel couldn't believe how good it felt, fucking Rathian's mouth and getting fucked by his finger. One finger became two, then three. His lover sucked harder, drawing his seed from him in a quick rush of pleasure.

"Wasis." He threw his head back and buried his cock deep in Rathian's throat.

Rathian swallowed his seed down, throat muscles milking Stakel dry. When Stakel finished moving, Rathian cleaned him then settled back on his heels.

"I want you," Rathian growled.

Stakel stood, offering his hand to his lover. "Then you can have me."

\* \* \* \*

Later that night

Afterwards, Stakel never could say what had woken him up. Whether it was the soft grunt, the cool breeze or the dull thud of the blade hitting the mattress next to him, something had disturbed him. He opened his eyes to find a knife buried deep in the furs beside him.

Rolling over, he looked up to see Excelsie standing next to the bed. Stakel glanced back to the knife. Who was the general trying to kill? Rathian wasn't in the bed with him. He didn't know where his lover had gone, but it didn't matter. He leapt to his feet on the other side, facing Excelsie.

"What are you doing?" he demanded.

"You won't be his Custos. That is my position." After speaking, the general snarled and stalked around the end of the bed.

"I don't think either of us can change it, General." Stakel searched the room, searching for the blade he'd taken from the training arena.

"Yes, we can. If I kill you, Rathian will choose me. I've put up with this disgusting country for years to get my chance." Excelsie lunged.

Stakel dodged, diving for the dresser where he'd laid the blade. "Why?" He needed to keep the general talking.

"After I become his Custos, I'll arrange for an accident. There isn't anyone to take over as Imperator. With Rathian dead, they'll turn to me and then the ducenti will take the Launioc throne. As my father planned all those years ago when he sent me here."

Excelsie swung the knife he'd pulled from the furs. Stakel jumped out of the way but not far enough. The tip of the blade sliced through his stomach. The shock of the wound made Stakel gasp. He hesitated. Unfortunately it was long enough for Excelsie to swing again and he jerked as the blade bit into his thigh.

He snatched the short blade up and moved into the middle of the room. There was less furniture for them to run into as they circled each other. The blood was pouring from his wound, causing him to slip on the wet pool forming under him. Weakness ate away at his strength. Where the hell was Rathian?

"They wouldn't allow you to become the Imperator. The Vanguard wouldn't fight against the Launioc army." Stakel studied his opponent's movements, waiting to find the opening he could use.

The door to the bathing chamber eased open and Stakel could see Rathian standing there. Fury twisted the prince's face, yet there was a hint of hurt and Stakel knew his lover had heard Excelsie's words.

"The Vanguard ducenti would fight for me if I was their Imperator. They are loyal to their leader, not their king. It is perfect. There is no force as well trained or as tight knitted as these men. I can use their own loyalty against them and their stupid king." Excelsie must not have realised Rathian had entered the room.

Stakel manoeuvred so Excelsie stood between him and his lover, facing Stakel. Blood coated his body, but Stakel paid no attention to it. He'd spent so many years covered in blood that it didn't bother him anymore. Taking a step forward, he slowly encouraged Excelsie back towards Rathian.

His lover crept up behind Excelsie. Something must have given Rathian away because the general swung around, driving his blade deep into Rathian's chest.

"No," Stakel yelled, rushing across the floor before he tore Excelsie from Rathian's body.

Wild laughter broke from Rathian's attacker. He cradled Rathian in his arms, their blood mingling together. Excelsie raced to the door and yanked it open.

"Guards to the Imperator's room. There's been an attack," Excelsie yelled, strolling back to where Stakel knelt with Rathian.

Stakel didn't take his attention off his lover. Rathian raised a hand and cupped his cheek. Placing a kiss to Rathian's palm, he smiled shakily.

"It'll be all right. I can heal you." He pressed a hand to the wound in Rathian's chest. His power surged, but it was weak and he knew the loss of so much blood would make it difficult for the magic to work.

"Get away from him," Excelsie ordered, pointing the same blade that had just been buried in Rathian's chest.

Rathian's bodyguards streamed into the room, surrounding them. Stakel glanced around but didn't move away. There wasn't a chance they could part him from his lover before he closed the wound.

"When I got here, he'd already attacked Rathian. We fought and I injured him. When I had a chance to call for you, he returned to the Imperator to finish the job." Excelsie's eyes gleamed with mad triumph.

Antioc slid into the room, followed by Martin and Darius. Stakel eased the power from him into Rathian. He knew there wasn't enough strength in him to heal both Rathian and himself. So he made a decision. It was really the only one he could make. Ignoring the commotion around him, he sank into himself and let his power go.

All Rathian could think was that the bastard had stabbed him. Excelsie had certainly shown a crazy sort of courage. He had never thought the general had it in him to try assassination. It didn't matter now. The blood was pooling on the floor under him. He could feel the cooling sensation of the liquid.

Glancing up, he saw Stakel kneeling beside him. He reached up and cupped his lover's cheek. He couldn't speak. It felt like a hot poker had been driven through his chest. Damn that hurt. He shot a look down to see Stakel pressing his hand into the wound. There was a lot of blood. More than just his mingled on his skin. He remembered seeing the wounds on Stakel's thigh and stomach before Excelsie had turned.

Warmth seeped into him. He frowned. He'd been told by the medicus that when death was upon a man, he would feel cold because his life force was draining from him. Heat washed over him. He'd felt this warmth before. A golden glow began to blur his vision. Stakel's face was disappearing into the light. What was happening?

Was Xasel honouring him by making his death less painful? He thanked the High God, but he wanted to say he didn't want to die. He wanted to live. To enjoy Stakel's body. To give his own body to his lover. Yet how did one turn down his god's gift?

Blinking, he cleared his vision and saw Stakel still holding him, but there was something different about his Custos. It looked like Stakel was fading. Not just in strength, though Rathian knew the man's wounds were serious. They could even be fatal if he didn't get help. The loss of blood wasn't what he noticed. As he got warmer, Stakel seemed to become less substantial. Almost transparent.

"Take him," Excelsie ordered.

Rathian raised his head to see his bodyguards moving in to reach out and grab Stakel. They were going to pull his lover away from him. With a shove, Martin and Antioc pushed into the middle, standing over them with swords drawn.

"Your Highness, what is your wish?" Antioc's eyes met his.

"Arrest General Excelsie. He attacked the Custos and me," Rathian managed to grate out. His breathing eased.

"Get that mad man away from the Imperator. He's confusing his mind. I found the prince with the sword wound. I fought with the Villious. That's how he was wounded." Excelsie's gaze darted from one man to the other.

Rathian knew the traitor wasn't finding sympathy in any of their eyes. His bodyguards were loyal only to him and no one else. Also, Antioc would never believe that Stakel had attacked him.

He touched Antioc's ankle. The sub-commander glanced down at him. "Sub-commander Antioc, I give you a direct order to arrest former General Excelsie and hold him as a traitor and would-be assassin of the Imperator and his Custos."

Each word came out stronger. By the end of his order, he climbed to his feet as Stakel's arms fell away from him. He met Excelsie's eyes and glared.

"How dare you? You accepted my hospitality and my friendship. You lied and put my men in danger with your arrogance." He held out a hand and Martin gave him a sword.

Rathian stalked towards the general. Excelsie's eyes widened with fear. The man swung wildly, missing Rathian by several inches. The prince wasn't worried about his old friend. Excelsie never had never been a good soldier. He relied on others to fight his battles while he stood in back and claimed the glory. Another wild swing and he blocked it with ease. He made a quick hard circle with his own sword, jerking Excelsie's weapon from his hand.

The general dropped to his knees, holding his arms out to his sides. "Please, Your Highness. I was only trying to protect you from the enemy."

"The only enemy here is you, Excelsie. I heard all your poison and no matter how much you beg me, you will never convince me that you had my best interests in mind. Or even the interests of Launioc."

Reaching out, he gripped Excelsie's hair and yanked the man's head back, baring his throat to the tip of his blade. "It's my right as Imperator to execute you now." The tip cut into the general's skin. A drop of blood trickled down.

Excelsie whimpered.

"Your Highness, the Custos."

Rathian turned, tossing his sword to Martin and gesturing for his bodyguards to take Excelsie away. Stakel lay on his side, breathing shallowly. Darius knelt next to him, his hand hovering over Stakel's shoulder. Crouching, Rathian slid his arms under Stakel's body and lifted him.

"Get out, everyone," he snapped.

Antioc nodded to all the guards. "If you need us, Your Highness, we'll be outside."

Rathian nodded but didn't say anything. Excelsie kept screaming as the guards dragged him from the room. The prince waited until it was clear before laying Stakel down on the bed. He pushed the dark curls away from Stakel's pale face. His lover gave him a weak smile and opened his eyes. The dark brown colour was leeching from his eyes.

"You're all right." Stakel's voice was low and rough.

"Yes. Thank you, my love." He placed his hand on Stakel's chest where a slow heartbeat pulsed.

The stomach and thigh wounds had stopped bleeding, but they weren't healing like Rathian remembered happening the first time he'd seen Stakel.

"Why aren't you healing?"

Stakel sighed. "Not enough energy to heal both of us. You're more important than me."

"No. You're the most important person in the world. You're my Custos. Without you, I'm nothing more than a shell of myself." Rathian wrapped his arms around Stakel, pulling him on to his lap. "You can't die."

"Don't have much of a choice. There's nothing inside me to help me heal." Stakel's eyes drifted close and he snuggled closer to Rathian. "Hold on to me."

"I will."

Tears welled in the prince's eyes. *How could Xasel do this to me?*

He dropped his head, resting his chin on the top of his love's head.

*"Xasel, High God, please don't take him."*

*"For every life given, something must be taken. It is the law. Not even gods can break those."*

"I love him." There was nothing else he could say. *"I'd give you everything I own, even my life for him."*

*"That isn't right. He gave his life for yours and now you want to waste his sacrifice."*

*"What can I do? I don't want him to die. I don't want to lose him."* He yawned, exhaustion setting in.

*"Sleep, my loyal prince. When you wake, your wish just might be answered."*

Rathian didn't want to rest. He was afraid that Stakel would die while he was sleeping, but a heaviness drew his eyelids shut. Taking a deep breath, he tightened his grip on Stakel.

* * * *

Rathian sat up with a jerk. His bed and arms were empty. Climbing out of bed, he stared around. Had it all been a dream? He looked down at his chest where the wound had been and saw a pink, newly healed scar. So it wasn't a dream, but where was Stakel? How long had he slept?

Scrambling around, he grabbed his clothes and pulled them on as he made his way to the door. It swung open just as he got to it. Darius stood in the doorway, panting like he'd been running around the house.

"Your Highness...General Excelsie..." Darius gasped out.

"What about Excelsie?" He grasped the boy by the arms and shook him. "Where is Stakel? Is he still alive?"

Darius' head whipped back and forth. The page couldn't get breath to speak.

"Sir, stop before you break the boy's neck." Antioc's voice preceded his hand, wrestling Darius away from Rathian.

"Where is he?" He rounded on the sub-commander.

A puzzled frown appeared on Antioc's face. "Where is who?"

"Stakel. He isn't dead, is he?"

Antioc's puzzlement disappeared. "No, sir. Your Custos is examining General Excelsie's body."

"Take me to him," he ordered.

"Certainly, sir." Antioc saluted and started to head down the hallway.

Rathian gave Darius a quick hug. "I'm sorry, boy. I shouldn't have treated you like that."

"It's all right, Your Highness. You were worried." Darius grinned. "He's fine. It's a miracle."

"I'll burn a special offering to Xasel tonight."

"We all will."

Rathian rushed down the hall to where Antioc stood waiting for him. They continued along the next corridor.

"We weren't sure what to do with the general, so I had him confined to his room. The guards took out everything he could have used to escape or kill himself." Antioc scowled. "We didn't want to give him an honourable death."

Rathian grunted, but his mind wasn't on Excelsie. He needed to see Stakel and touch him. He wanted reassurance that his lover was alive and well. He didn't care what had happened to his second-in-command. The man had destroyed any emotion Rathian might have had for him when he had attacked Stakel.

Antioc stopped in front of an open door where three men were gathered. "He's in here, sir."

The group parted to let him through. He focused his gaze on Stakel, who was bent over something on the bed. He didn't pay any attention to the others in the room. He stalked up, whirled Stakel around and crushed his lover to his chest. Burying his face in Stakel's dark curls, he breathed in the man's scent and absorbed the heat of his body.

He shuddered, relief filling him with weakness. Stakel's arms wrapped around his waist and held him up when his knees threatened to buckle. A sob tore from his throat.

"Hush, love," Stakel murmured. "I'm fine. You're fine. It's all right."

He drew in another deep breath, trying to calm down. His men gathered around and he didn't want them to see how close he was to losing his control. Stakel's hands traced up and down his back, soothing him.

"How did this happen?" he asked as he stepped back, letting his hands drop from Stakel's shoulders. "I felt you dying."

Stakel shrugged. "I'm not sure. I don't remember anything but trying to heal you. When I opened my eyes an hour ago, you were healed and I was fine, except for a few more scars." He gestured to his stomach and thigh.

Rathian reached out a shaking hand to trail a finger over the scars. "Why didn't you wake me?"

"You needed to sleep. I managed to heal you, but you still lost a lot of blood." Stakel nodded towards Darius. "I was on my way to the chapel when Darius ran into me, stuttering something about Excelsie. I sent him to get you and came here to check for myself."

Under control and reassured that Stakel was fine, Rathian looked down at the body on the bed. Excelsie's eyes had been closed, but there was a permanent grimace of pain and fear on the man's face. He didn't see any wounds.

"How did he die?" Rathian searched the faces of the men surrounding him.

They all shook their heads. Stakel rubbed a hand over his face.

"No one knows. The medicus is on his way, but I doubt he'll be able to find an explanation either. Strange things happened while we slept."

"You're alive after I felt you die. I prayed to Xasel to heal you." Rathian cupped Stakel's cheek and rubbed his thumb over Stakel's bottom lip.

"For every life given, something must be taken. It is law. Not even the High God can break it." The voice ringing through the room caused everyone to jump.

Rathian noticed Stakel didn't seem surprised to hear this particular voice.

"But no one said what or who had to be taken."

They looked down at the dead body of Stakel's attacker. Punishment had been delivered by the highest judge and the most implacable jury. It did seem that the High God took care of his own.

# Chapter Twenty-Nine

Having ordered the removal of Excelsie's body, Rathian and Stakel returned to their rooms. Stakel talked quietly to Darius as Rathian stared out of the window at the dark mountains in the distance.

He'd told his men to bury the general in a simple grave. No funeral pyre or grand mourning for the would-be assassin. Rathian's heart was sore. How had he missed the disgust and contempt Excelsie had had for them?

"Come." Stakel took his hand and led him to their small bathing chamber.

Rathian felt the heat rising from the water, but he didn't see the room. He was remembering all the fun times he and Excelsie had had while they had grown up. Excelsie had come to live with them when Rathian had been six and Excelsie had been five. They'd become close friends.

"How did I miss it?" he murmured.

"Miss what, love?" Stakel stripped him quickly.

"The hate and disgust he had for me." He stared into Stakel's sad brown eyes.

"I think he loved you and he couldn't handle that." His protector eased him into the water and helped him sit down.

"He loved me so much that he tried to kill you, and would have killed me." Rathian shook his head. "That doesn't sound like love to me."

"When he came to live here, did your father make him cut all his ties with his family?" Stakel soaped up his hands and ran them over Rathian's body.

"No." He frowned. "It would be cruel to cut a boy off from his family."

"There was your mistake." Stakel rinsed off the soap, making sure he touched every inch of Rathian's body.

The prince had a feeling that Stakel was trying to keep him from sinking into depression. He slipped under the water, getting his hair wet. When he broke the surface, he asked, "Why was that a mistake?"

"I don't know what country Excelsie came from, but I'm guessing they don't believe that men fucking other men is proper. They might even believe it's evil. Excelsie probably heard about that in every communication he had with his father. Then to find that he'd fallen in love with you when he knew it to be wrong pushed him over the edge." Stakel grimaced. "No matter how much he loved you, you were the enemy. He wasn't strong enough to turn his back on what he'd been taught. So he convinced himself the only way to save his soul was to kill you and conquer Launioc."

He leant back, resting his head on the side of the pool. Closing his eyes, he let the warmth of the water and Stakel's touch seep into his soul. The hurt and disappointment slowly dissolved. He sighed as Stakel's hand lay on his chest, over his heart.

"Here, love. Drink."

He opened his eyes to see Stakel holding out a cup of wine to him. He took it and drank. The slightly bitter aftertaste made him scowl at his lover. Stakel smiled, climbing from the pool and helping him step out.

"Did you drug the wine?"

"Yes."

Stakel dried both of them off and they made their way to their bed. The sheets were clean and the curtains drawn against the rising sun. He flopped down, before closing his eyes.

"Rest, my prince. When you wake up, I'll be here and I'll be eager to show you how much I enjoy the way the ducenti Vanguard does things."

Rathian felt Stakel's lips brush his cheek then he fell asleep, secure in the knowledge that Stakel would still be around when he woke up.

* * * *

A few hours later, Stakel looked down at the sleeping prince. Rathian's face had become more familiar to him than his own. He traced a finger over the man's nose, down to his slack lips. The tension of the war and the fear of Stakel's death were eased and he could see what Rathian must have looked like when he was younger and not worried about his men.

He let his hand wander farther, pushing the blanket out of the way and revealing Rathian's broad chest. Stakel leaned over and licked one flat nipple, before blowing a puff of air over the wet flesh. The small nub hardened and Rathian shifted on the bed. Smiling, Stakel slid down to rest his chin on Rathian's hip, breathing in the warm, musky scent of Rathian. He had the perfect way to wake Rathian up.

A swipe of his tongue along the length of Rathian's cock caused him to groan. Rathian's ass lifted off the blankets, following Stakel's tongue. He chuckled, enjoying the thought of teasing Rathian awake. He eased his way between Rathian's legs and spread his thighs wider. Grasping Rathian's cock, he stroked once and the flesh in his hand lengthened.

He gave Rathian's balls a kiss before sucking one into his mouth. Rathian patted his head. Letting the first one go, he took the other in, pressing his tongue to it.

Rathian murmured something that sounded like Stakel's name. He let go of the ball and moved back up Rathian's cock. Hard and already leaking liquid, Rathian's dick called to Stakel. He swirled his tongue around the flesh, gathering the salty liquid, and sucked just the tip into his mouth. Holding it lightly between his teeth, he pushed the tip of his tongue into the slit and Rathian jerked.

"Stakel." Rathian's voice held lust and sleep.

"Hmm…" He wasn't interested in talking.

Wrapping one of his hands around the thick base of Rathian's shaft, he took Rathian in with one long suck. When his lips met his hand, he stopped. Rathian's cockhead hit the back of his throat and he swallowed.

"Wasis. Are you trying to kill me?" Rathian asked, his back arching as he tried to plunge deeper into Stakel's mouth.

Stakel wiggled his head slightly. He slipped his other fingers into his mouth, getting them wet. He pulled them out, and then reached down behind Rathian's balls to tease his hole. As he thrust one finger inside, he started moving his head and hand.

"I think you are trying to kill me." Rathian rocked between Stakel's mouth and finger. "If this is the way I have to die, I'm not going to complain."

Two fingers in and Stakel picked up the pace. His own cock ached and he rubbed against the furs. He was becoming overwhelmed with scents, sounds and tastes. The salty bitterness of Rathian's seed. The hot tight passage of his lover's ass and the pleas falling from Rathian's mouth. Stakel wanted to impale Rathian, fucking him hard and fast, but he held on to his ragged threads of control. He'd bring Rathian to climax first, then he'd take Rathian.

Stakel used three fingers to stretch Rathian's hole, pegging the spot inside that was guaranteed to make Rathian cry out.

"Stakel, I'm going to…" Rathian warned.

Stakel took Rathian as deep as he could and swallowed. The first shot of seed flooded his mouth and he drank it down along with the second one. Before the third came, he pulled off. He stroked the third and fourth bursts out to cover his hand. Stakel removed his fingers from Rathian's clenching inner passage.

Rearing up on his knees, he coated his cock with Rathian's seed. Rathian hooked his hands behind his thighs, pulling his legs back and farther apart. Stakel grasped Rathian's ass, tilting his hips up so he could position his cock at Rathian's puckered entrance.

"Gods," he hissed, sinking into the tight channel.

Rathian's head fell back and his eyes narrowed. "Fuck me now, love. I want to feel you."

"Brace your hands on the headboard," Stakel ordered Rathian.

Rathian stretched out beneath him, large hands pushing against the top of the bed and his legs wrapping around Stakel's waist. Stakel gripped Rathian's hips and slammed their bodies together. The sound of skin hitting skin filled the air. Rathian's muscles flexed, massaging Stakel's cock with each thrust in and out. Stakel angled Rathian's hips.

"Right there," Rathian shouted as his body flushed and jerked.

Stakel grimaced. His balls drew closer to his body and he knew it wouldn't be long. Rathian was hard again, his seed painting wet tracks over his stomach. More ropes of pearly liquid spilled from Rathian's cock and Stakel grunted as Rathian's ass clenched down so tight on his cock it was painful.

"Now, Stakel. Please. I want to feel your seed fill me. Come with me." Rathian's eyes burned into his.

One last thrust and he came, exploding deep into Rathian's body. He froze and stared down at Rathian, seeing love and happiness in the Imperator's green eyes. Rathian milked every drop out of Stakel's cock. When the lust had left him, he cuddled with Rathian.

Their harsh breathing eased and Stakel could feel his heart beat slow down. Rathian outlined the scars on Stakel's back while soft kisses were placed along his temple. His soft cock slid from Rathian and they moaned. Rolling over onto his back, he sighed.

Rathian planted another kiss on his chest and stood. "I'll take care of us and then we'll see if Darius can bring us some food."

He grunted. He didn't have enough energy to form words. Rathian returned from the bathing chamber with a wet cloth and Stakel lay there, letting his lover take care of him. When they were clean, Rathian took the cloth to the other room. Stopping next to a bell pull, he tugged on it once.

Within seconds, Darius was knocking.

"Come in, Darius," Rathian called.

The page peeked around the door and grinned at them. "I brought you some food." He backed into the room, carrying a tray of steaming plates.

"Bring it here." Stakel gestured to the bed where he lay covered with blankets and resting back on the pillows.

"Yes, sir." Darius set the tray down and went to pour two glasses of wine for them.

Rathian joined him on the bed, filled two plates and started eating. Stakel glanced at Darius for a second.

"Darius, sit." He pointed to the end of the bed.

"Sir." The boy gave him a curious look.

"Did you or any of your fellow pages see Excelsie talk to anyone out of the ordinary?" Stakel felt Rathian stiffen beside him.

"Out of the ordinary?"

"Yes. Someone who wasn't a member of the Vanguard, or even the regular Launioc army."

"What do you mean?" Rathian stared at him. "Do you think he was working with someone else?"

"Just a feeling I have." Stakel shrugged.

"Two days ago, I was out taking a walk. I always do it at the same time every night before I go to bed." Darius seemed uncertain. "I saw General Excelsie leave the fortress and head towards the Villious line."

Darius' hands were shaking and Stakel reached out, taking them in his. "Don't worry, boy. Nothing is going to happen to you. I just need to know what you saw."

"I followed him. I don't know why. Maybe it was the way he'd never liked you and was always trying to get you in trouble with the Imperator. Whatever my reason, I made sure not to be seen. He met some man in a dark black robe. I couldn't get close enough to see a face or hear anything."

"You did enough, Darius. Though I would suggest taking some kind of weapon with you next time you decide to follow someone. You never know what sort of problem you might face." Stakel patted the page's cheek. "You can go now and thank you."

Darius smiled at them and raced from the room. Rathian sighed.

"So you think he was working with the Villious as well?"

"Besides him, who had the most to gain from your death?" Stakel finished his snack and set the plate aside. "I know he was your friend, but even the most loyal of soldiers can be corrupted. He wasn't all that loyal, so he was easily swayed."

"What do I do now? Who should I promote to be my general?" Rathian frowned.

"Why not Antioc? He's loyal and he's a good leader. Most of the men seem to respect him. We know he won't completely fall apart in a crisis. His bravery is beyond reproach." Stakel took Rathian's plate, setting it and the tray aside as well.

Rathian didn't stop him as he pulled the prince down. He settled his lover at his side, tucking Rathian's head under his chin. He ran his hand over the Imperator's strong back.

"Let's sleep. Tomorrow, you can promote Antioc and then we'll discuss how we should go about killing the queen. We need to end this stupid war soon before winter sets in. I want to spend winter with you at the manor."

Rathian nodded. "Sounds good. I want this war over as well."

Stakel held the prince until his lover's breathing was soft and even. He'd told the truth. The time had come to end the war and make sure the Villious Queen couldn't raise the demons again. He didn't want another boy to suffer like he had.

# Epilogue

Rathian sat on his horse, facing the Villious Queen and her Consorts. There were fifty men surrounding her. Twice as many as Rathian had with him. Stakel's hand brushed his as his Custos came to stand beside him.

A voice cried out and Stakel translated.

"You are outnumbered, silly prince. Lay down your weapons, kneel before me and I'll make you my Head Consort."

"Not much of an offer," he said, loud enough for his men to hear him.

His men laughed and he moved a little farther in front of them. Stakel followed. Staring out over the battlefield, he studied the men he'd be fighting later that day.

"I would rather die than live as your slave, Queen. My men feel the same. Come, the sun is rising and I have no wish to fight during the hottest part of the day. I want to be back at my camp by sundown." He gestured for Antioc to bring the troops up to form behind him. Imperator Rathian turned to look at his men. There would be a few who wouldn't be there by the end of the day and he tried to memorise all of their faces so he could mourn when he had time.

"Remember, the Consorts have no more power than we do. They are mere mortals now. We believe that when the demon priests died, the powers went away. Custos Stakel took care of that for us. We don't believe they know it."

"That's why you chose to bring a small unit of men here to this pass instead of the entire army." Antioc grinned.

"Yes. The Villious army won't continue to fight if the Consorts are destroyed. Capture the queen if you can." Reaching out, Rathian gripped Stakel's hand for a moment.

"The Consorts aren't likely to protect the queen if she chooses to stay and watch. None of them have any love for her." Stakel squeezed his hand. "We can defeat them. They've come to rely too heavily on their power. Once they realise they don't have it, I wouldn't be surprised to see them run."

A scream drifted over the battlefield and Rathian swung his horse back to face the advancing Villious. He shared a quick, warm glance with Stakel. If today was the day he was to die, he had nothing to complain about. Though he would have liked more time to spend with his lover, he was happy. Raising his hand, he signalled for the unit to charge.

\* \* \* \*

The battle was bloody and seemed to be over within minutes, though Rathian knew they must have fought for several hours. He'd been aware of Stakel by his side or at his back the entire time, but he'd become focused on each Villious Consort he'd faced. He hadn't worried about the others. They were trained to take care of themselves.

Cutting a swathe of gore and death through the main body of the Consort unit, he made his way to where the queen stood, confident in her victory. When the last man standing between them died on Stakel's sword, her smile wavered and dimmed. Her crazed eyes skated over the bodies littering the ground. She glared at Stakel.

"Head Consort Stakel, how nice of you to return to me." Her voice sounded like glass breaking.

"I haven't returned to you. I've come to stop you." Stakel held the tip of his bloody sword to her chest.

Rathian wasn't sure if his lover would kill her. He hadn't given a kill order. Figured it would be easier to bring the woman to his father, then maybe the war would end. In the back of his mind, he had an uneasy feeling that even if this war was over, his father would find another enemy to fight.

"I shouldn't have trusted that pathetic general of yours. I should have known you would find him out." She scowled.

"Excelsie?" Rathian felt sick.

"Yes. I had one of my spies contact him. He was to kill you, Imperator, and take over the Vanguard. We were then going to take over the throne." She grinned. "It was a perfect plan. With my Consorts' powers and your men's fighting ability, we would have been invincible."

"Your Consorts aren't so powerful now." Stakel twisted his wrist and a thin trickle of blood eased down the queen's throat.

"It was you, wasn't it?" She gestured to the Consort dying at her feet. "You took their magic away."

Stakel shook his head. "It was the gods. They chose to take away your power because of your madness and that of your priests."

"My madness was their fault." A brief moment of clarity shone in the queen's eyes. "Given to them as a child to raise and train. How could I be anything other than what I am?"

"Yes, my lady." Stakel's face held sadness and pity. "That's why I must do what I was ordered to do."

"What are you going to do, Stakel?" Rathian had a feeling he wasn't going to like what was about to happen.

"She must die or she'll be compelled to find the priests and raise the demons again. The Villious Queen is connected by blood and flesh to the dark gods. She is the key to opening the portal to bring them back. Death is the only way to keep them from returning." Stakel closed his eyes and took a deep breath.

"Do it," the queen commanded.

Rathian placed his hand on Stakel's back. Not to stop him, but to let his Custos know that he was there, standing by him and lending his support. Stakel stabbed once, driving the sword deep into the queen's chest. Rathian saw a flare of happiness ripple over her face. Peace came over him. He didn't want to see the woman die, yet he knew it was the only way—like Stakel had said, the demons, though gone, had left their marks deep in her.

Stakel whispered something in a guttural tone. A death prayer probably. Rathian didn't ask. Wiping his sword on the queen's gown, Stakel turned before kissing Rathian hard.

"Gather the men. This is over." Stakel walked away to kneel.

Rathian didn't object to being ordered around. He knew his lover needed time to himself. He turned and found Antioc standing close by, sword at the ready in case any of the Villious chose to attack.

"Regroup, General Antioc. Collect the dead and help the wounded. We'll be heading back to camp in thirty minutes."

"Yes, Your Highness." Antioc saluted and moved off to issue orders.

Rathian looked over the battlefield. Several of his men were down, injured or dead. This war had cost him so much. Good men and soldiers he'd trained himself. It had cost him the man he had thought was his closest friend, but Excelsie had been a festering wound that had had to be cut out before he infected the rest of the ducenti. He would always mourn his loss.

Antioc's voice drifted over the field and Rathian smiled. He'd gained a more than competent general, though. Stakel had been right in telling him to promote Antioc.

An arm encircled his waist and he leaned against the warm body standing next to him.

"It's over." Stakel stared out at the men.

"For now, and we'll go home to rest and train. There will always be another battle for us and our men." Rathian couldn't feel sad or worried about that prospect. It was what they'd been born and raised to do. None of the ducenti were happy when there wasn't some sort of fighting going on.

"Rest and train sounds perfect to me." A kiss was pressed to his neck. "As long as you're doing it with me."

"There's nowhere else I'd be." He turned, taking Stakel's mouth in a deep crushing kiss.

Yes, he'd lost much in this war, but he'd gained far more than he'd ever expected. His Custos. Lover and friend. Stakel was his forever and there would be no moments of regret for that.

# About the Author

There is beauty in every kind of love, so why not live a life without boundaries? Experiencing everything the world offers fascinates TA and writing about the things that make each of us unique is how she shares those insights. When not writing, TA's watching movies, reading and living life to the fullest.

T.A. Chase loves to hear from readers. You can find her contact information, website details and author profile page at http://www.total-e-bound.com.

# Total-E-Bound Publishing

www.total-e-bound.com

Take a look at our exciting range of literagasmic™
erotic romance titles and discover pure quality
at Total-E-Bound.